GOSPEL

A Novel by
Daryl Rothman

GOSPEL
Copyright © 2024 by Daryl Rothman

FIRST EDITION SOFTCOVER
ISBN: 162253574X
ISBN-13: 978-1-62253-574-3

Editor: Lane Diamond
Cover Artist: Kris Norris
Interior Designer: Lane Diamond

EVOLVED PUBLISHING™

www.EvolvedPub.com
Evolved Publishing LLC
Butler, Wisconsin, USA

Printed in Book Antiqua font.

BOOKS BY DARYL ROTHMAN

The "David Rose" Series

Gospel

DEDICATION

For those most lovable of souls, for whom we stand, undaunted. We can no more possess them than we might hope to hold in our hands the sun and stars, but should remain instead indebted, forever grateful for their light.

And for my children, the best of me, who make me luckier than I deserve, and epitomize why we remain, as the final word of this book intones, onward.

INTRODUCTION

"Death twitches my ear; 'Live,' he says... 'I'm coming.'"
~ Virgil

PROLOGUE

It was always interesting, the lines between things. The Crooked River—belying in this sense its epithet—segmented the town of Petra rather neatly from north to south. Beneath the bridge that connected the two parts of town, the river ran rough, and in rainy seasons vessels had best be mindful. The preponderance of households sat clustered west of the river, the majority of businesses east. The boy's father once told him that if a man followed the sun each day in their town, east to work in the morning, and west home at the end of the day, then he'd done pretty well for himself.

When the boy was eight, his father took him camping for the first time, in the state park about fifty miles outside of town, where tributaries broke off from the river, spawning countless fords and lakes. Every father in town fancied himself something of an outdoorsman, but his own wore the part well. They hiked and fished and rafted, and his father even showed him how to fashion a slingshot from materials found mostly in their surroundings. When it at last came time for the boy to release his inaugural shot, he knew instantly his aim was true, and it felt like he'd been doing it all his life.

The can jumped as if by the hand of some aerial puppeteer. The boy looked at his father, who grinned at him and dug in his pocket for more stones.

Three shots later, after the cans had jumped each time, a knowing look traveled his father's features. He nodded at the boy and said, "You've got the knack."

The boy practiced with the slingshot in the backyard, each day after school, on cans he placed at increasing distances, the ranging plink of his marksmanship luring many a curious kid from the neighborhood. His accomplishment was uncanny, and the other kids delighted in bringing items for him to shoot, and wagering him on targets of ever-expanding breadth. Not once did he have to ante up. One evening after supper, and assuring his mom that his homework was done, he returned to the backyard and resumed his ritual, seeing only by the ambient light of the house and brume of moonlight that seeped through the cloud cover, tallow and faint. Still, he found his mark, the resultant clinking of cans ringing thinly into the evening like uncertain chimes. From a distant yard, a dog retorted.

After a while, his father emerged and stood on the back porch watching him, a cigarette dangling from his lips. He struck a match and raised it to the cigarette, cupping his other hand near his mouth.

"Mom kick you out?" the boy asked, grinning.

His father grinned too. "Go on, then, while you still can make things out a bit. Your mom will be calling you in soon enough."

***

She would have to call him in on countless occasions in the weeks and months ahead. As time went on, he constructed for himself additional slingshots, and on his 9th birthday, he was elated to receive a professional-grade model, ordered by his father from the outdoorsman magazine to which he subscribed. His skill blossomed further yet.

His mother had never fully approved. More than once she stopped him in the doorway and cautioned him of the potential perils of his beloved pastime. "Those things worry me sick," she often said.

He assured her he always took precautions and never missed.

She usually sighed and told him to never, ever shoot at a living soul, not even a bird or animal.

He'd never harbored such intentions, but once he shot back, "Hunters shoot at animals."

She promptly rejoined, "Are you planning to catch, clean, and cook us a feast from those critters that pass in our yard? If so, then I might well make an exception. But that aside, they are all God's creation and you ought never for sport take the life of some innocent creature. What we do when the life of another rests in our hands says much about who we are, and ever will be."

One afternoon in his tenth year, a jackrabbit loped into view just as he was loading his first shot at the line of cans he'd assembled at the far periphery of their yard. He paused and stared at the animal, which, after inspecting and nibbling at a patch of grass near the tree line, paused and looked up, and stared back at him with yellow eyes. Rabbits were not uncommon in their yard, but jackrabbits were, and he knew from his father that they were really hares, not rabbits, anyway. The torso tufted squirrel-grey, the underbelly, whiskers, and tail white. Its hind legs looked to extend at least twice as high as a rabbit's, and same with its ears, which had perked to attention upon noticing him, and which dimpled toward him now, twitching almost imperceptibly. It was a beautiful creature, beautiful and, he knew, possessing of astounding speed and spring.

He crooked his head toward the house, then back again. He'd grown weary of shooting cans.

The hare studied him a bit longer and then lowered its head and began to step haltingly about the swath of yard it had begun grazing.

The boy reached into his pocket for a stone, then paused, remembering his mother's caution. He probably wouldn't hit it anyway—too attentive, too agile. He angled himself left foot forward, centered the stone, crimped the pouch slightly, and sighted his quarry between the two sides of the fork. His left hand gripped the middle of the handle firmly but easily. He never used a wrist-hold. He extended his left arm fully and straightly before him and cupped the exterior of the pouch with the thumb, middle, and index fingers of his right hand, securely but relaxed.

A twig snapped from somewhere beyond the tree line, and the hare froze, crouched. When at last it lowered its head, the boy silently drew the pouch back, poised to execute a locomotion as he'd done countless times previously. This was no different.

No different.

Except, now, as he pulled the payload back taut, close to his cheek, the tubing perpendicular to the handle, all sound seemed to drain away from the yard and the space around it. The late-afternoon sun, typically ebbing and spliced by the foliage, fell over the yard unmitigated, the space between him and the hare laid out unequivocally, like a road.

The hare looked up at him, then sprang with disarming suddenness, coursing for the tree line. He corrected for the movement, not knowing how he did so, and released the shot. The stone whistled through the expanse of the yard in a blink, and whether the crash of the hare into the brush attributed to his accuracy or merely the animal's panicked flight, he could not yet know.

He took a few giddy steps forward, then stopped. A butterfly, violet-hued save for its black outline, fluttered leisurely across the funnel of light. Maybe he should just go inside. Maybe he had missed, and the animal was long gone. Probably, he had missed. There was no need to check.

Did I hit it?

He glanced again toward the house. It was crucial that he made it look like he was checking on the cans, per usual, but by then, he knew. He knew before the rustling, but the rustling confirmed things, and something knotted in his stomach. He meandered into the brush and when he looked down, the thing in his stomach twisted. It took quite a bit for him to keep from turning away.

He'd shot it though the eye, and what bits of it remained dangled from the gaping socket. Blood had matted the fur on the left cheek, and still oozed in thin rivulets. Its head spasmed every few seconds. Each time it would fall still, and then spasm again. Its hind legs articulated in the grass and air, seeking such purchase that would never come.

His mind bubbled with desperate notions. He could sneak a blanket from the house and stealthily take the animal to Dr. Redmond's just across the bridge. He'd say he found the poor thing in his yard. No... no... the doctor's son went to school with him and had watched him shoot, and so the doc would put two and two together, sure enough. Maybe he could tend to it—stop the bleeding, cleanse the wounds, bring it food and water. He glanced back down at the writhing creature, then turned his head quickly so that it sat just out of his line of sight. This was not a wound that could be mended.

In the tackle box in the shed was the large fishing knife. The boy glanced edgewise once more at the squirming animal, and then went to the shed, brushed cobwebs off the tackle box, and retrieved the knife. It was not a thought he'd ever had in all his ten years — to hope that someone, or something, had died — but when he edged back over to the hare, shielding the knife from view with his frame, he saw clearly it hadn't, that his task still beckoned.

He gritted his teeth and regarded the animal full on. The blood was clotting, slowing, and he could see along with the mangled pieces of the eye what appeared to be small bits of brain matter lodged in the yawning socket. He scooped the creature into his lap, careful not to get blood on himself. He thought it might feel cold, but it was warm and soft, and though he saw in the dying pinprick of light within its iris that it was beyond the realm of knowing, he held it because he thought nothing should have to die alone and untouched. He cradled it in the crook of his left arm and elbow and readied the knife in his right hand. Just then its legs spasmed again and the boy started, but it was just the throes of reflex and ebbing life. Adjusting the animal to ensure he wouldn't run his own hand through with the blade, he brought the tip of the knife over the hare's temple and paused, the weapon poised and quivering.

He thrust the blade through with considerable force, for he'd no interest in maiming it any further.

The hare's eyes, glazed and fluttering the moment previous, flew open as though beholding something wondrous. The boy cringed as the body of the creature tensed and spasmed and blood oozed from where the knife still lodged, but he held the animal until all movement ceased. Its chest heaved a final time and froze, and its still-rapt eyes froze as well, lifeless pools regarding vacantly all before it.

He lowered the animal gently to the ground, covered it loosely with brush, then rose. To the east ran the river, and though two miles off, he felt sure he could hear it now. Its dark waters would be tinting gold in the fading afternoon light, reflecting perhaps the stealthy orbit of hungry kingfishers. He ran. He ran for the river, avoiding as he could all signs of people, for whether they be souls known to him or not, he felt wholly incapable of meeting their gaze. He would go to where the river ran and would run with it, following it perhaps all the way to its termination, that in so doing he might leave behind all reckoning of this day.

When he arrived where the river flowed under the bridge, the sky had already shifted, bruised clouds massing dolefully over the town, and the first spits of rain began to fall. He'd been right about the kingfishers though. Perhaps a dozen rolled and dived in the low sky above the bridge, galvanized, it seemed, by the gathering pall. When he reached the banks, he bent forward, hands on his hips and catching his breath. Then, rising up with a great cry, he flung the slingshot as far away into the river as he could.

It disappeared momentarily before bobbing back up and skirting downriver atop the bustling current.

He rolled his eyes at the silliness of his own notions. He would not be following the river. He would not be running away. The sky rumbled and the rain fell harder, and he realized the only place he would run for now was for cover under the bridge. He made it just ahead of the deluge. The river roiled in a mad vortex beneath the bridge. The dark sky, along with the underside of the bridge, had made it pitch as night. The rain thrummed and the wind gusted in periodic bursts that contorted the downpour every which way, even sideways, lashing at him. He stepped back a few more steps, until he stumbled upon something in the dark.

He looked down at the misshapen bundle of tattered blankets and clothes and, as his eyes adjusted somewhat, he peered about and saw that the place was well-strewn with all manner of debris. But the debris at his feet was moving now, shifting. He scrambled back, stopping just shy of the downpour. Fear exhorted flight but curiosity stayed him for the moment, and he stared as the tattered rags undulated and gradually alighted from the fetid floor of the place.

His father had told him about homeless folk before, how some of them sometimes lived under the bridge and other such places, and how he should have sympathy for them but caution too. The vagrant shuffled forward and the boy took another step back, but in so doing breached a frigid curtain of rain that jolted him like voltage, and he stepped back under the protection of the bridge.

The face of the vagrant hunched slight and inconspicuous beneath the wrapping of rags, sooty and wan. His jaw was thin and angular, and the teeth within it, the boy could just discern, were discolored and few. But the eyes... the eyes gleamed, sky-blue, crystal, yet not quite these colors or any color at all—diaphanous, less color than light. The vagrant extended his arms, the layered rags which sheathed them sweeping upward, like a forsaken pair of once dazzling wings. The boy was cold, but that was not the cause of his trembling at present. The skeletal hands protruding from beneath the tags were upturned, plaintive.

The boy remembered the change in his pocket and dug for it while the vagrant watched. He stepped forward, haltingly, and dropped what he had into the crimped, outreached palm.

The vagrant raised his hand to his eyes for inspection. After a moment, he withdrew it back into the folds of his rags and conferred through his eyes his gratitude. The vagrant then shuffled toward the river. The rain had ebbed a bit, sporadic prisms of light splicing through the lingering cloud cover.

The boy followed the vagrant's eyes to one such swath, within which sat a cluster of elephant rocks. He narrowed his eyes and saw that his sling had washed over and lodged in the crook between two of the rocks.

The vagrant muttered vaguely as he went. "Cucariva," or some such gibberish.

The boy did not mean to linger long enough to find out.

It was just a drizzle now and he decided to make a run for it. He watched the vagrant a moment longer, tottering toward the river in the slowly dissipating gloom, belonging to this place as much as any other, if he belonged anyplace at all. Then the boy ran.

When he arrived home, he spent a minute catching his breath on the side of their house, then slunk quietly around to the backyard. He meandered to the shed, emerged a moment later with a garden spade, and eased his way over to the tree line. Though nearly dark, an early moon had risen, and by its light he buried the hare and said the best words he could think of, and after standing there quite a spell, he returned the spade to the shed.

He went into his house and slipped up to his room unnoticed, changed into dry clothing, and lay in his bed, where smells of supper cooking wafted up to him.

He would tell nary a soul about the hare, or about what happened at the Crooked River. And he meant never to hold a slingshot for the rest of his years.

Chapter 1 – Reason One

As a beginning writer, Jacob Fallon had been exhorted with, endeavored to embrace, and ultimately disavowed the well-meant, but surely apocryphal, write-what-you-know adage. He didn't know anything.

Well, maybe a little.

He loved Anabel, and a more abiding truth he'd never reckoned. He didn't believe in love at first sight, for love to him was a verb, an action, a doing, but he'd been captivated, instantly and eternally, by the spirit and gentility brimming in those eyes—wide and amber and inquiring. They flickered like wondrous constellations drawn somehow and suddenly near, as though he, a novice astronomer, stumbled upon a one-in-a-million happenstance with a most fortuitous twist of his lens. It raised the possibility of who and what he might still yet be, the possibility of with whom, of partnership and promise, forgiveness and hope. She was otherworldly beautiful: shoulder-length sienna hair that rose and fell upon the breeze; the softest lips in all creation; and a simultaneous air of assurance and humility, which disarmed him utterly.

When they'd met, despite their mutual feelings, Anabel had been hesitant. They were at different places in life, and both in the throes of failed relationships. They fell in love, but still, she demurred, once even telling him that though she loved him more than she'd ever loved another, for every reason that it might work, she could think of a hundred why it wouldn't.

We need but one, he'd thought, and gone home and, in the space of an evening, written out a hundred and one reasons why she was the most lovable person on earth.

They'd later gone for a walk along the river, draped in the sun's last light, and when he handed her the list, she'd cried, and they wrapped each other in an embrace which said this, right here, is home.

"I love you," she'd said, their lips pressed together. "For all my doubts, and all my fears, I cannot deny this bond. It's like our hearts are connected with ropes of steel."

"Hang on," he'd begged her, "please. Until we get our chance."

The road to that day was rocky, but it finally came, and he'd kept a pocket-size journal, carried it with him always, and added to those 101 reasons each day. And when a few years later Gabriel was born, that love burgeoned to proportions beyond all telling, like the birth of a star that would, even should all the universe one day fall to darkness, illuminate the world for all time.

Jacob's thoughts returned to the moment as he fumbled for his key, his head hung beneath an albatross of guilt. He'd stopped at the neighborhood bar on the way home, and he was a bit drunk. He'd been rejected again, by the publisher he'd really wanted, and the letters from his creditors kept piling up. Anabel had never pressured him about money, about his career, but things were tight. She was an attorney — a public defender — and they'd been living on her salary all these years, while he hunkered down with his dream of the next great American novel. She never made him feel badly about that—she'd done nothing but support him—but with their mortgage in jeopardy, things were approaching critical mass.

He thought about the jasper on that sun-dappled afternoon, the first day he took Gabriel to the Crooked River. Gabe ran barefoot alongside the coursing waters, feet splashing in the shallows, scaring up waterfowl as he went, thrusting his arms out as though, if he ran fast enough and caught just the right breeze, he might ascend with them. He'd stop and sink to his knees in the sand, engrossed with rocks or driftwood or other bits of discovery. At one point, his eyes lit up, and he scooped something from the sand and came sprinting back to his father.

"Look at this one, Daddy."

Jacob had nodded, impressed, at the mottled, dark green stone.

"It's a jasper," he'd told his son. "Gemstone."

Gabriel's eyes grew wide, and he pocketed the stone and went sprinting off again in the sunlight, as if he'd found Heaven.

Jacob watched him through squinting eyes, knowing full well he'd found it too. That for all his frailties, he remained tethered to an unshakeable covenant, and would always. That he lived for the boy, would die for him, would do anything. Yes, his writerly dreams were floundering, but one thought of his family buoyed him instantly, for what greater dream could there be? As long as he had them, he had everything.

Those thoughts drifted off again as he considered the moment. Strange, how you could feel something missing, more palpably than something there. The house sat dark save for a living room lamp near the coffee table. He wanted to call to them, but could not bear the silence that would answer. A folded letter lay on the coffee table, small but inescapable in the modest arc of light. A terrible knowing at once subsumed him, and he unfolded the paper as one might an obituary.

Jacob,

There is no easy way here, so I will just cut to it. Gabriel and I are moving in for now with my parents. This will no doubt shock you and that's frankly part of the problem.

When we met all those years ago, it did not take long for me to fall in love with you. Your kindness and heart, imagination and humor and wit. Your writing, the stories you'd tell. Yes, I knew there were pieces you carried, painful, perhaps broken pieces, but I loved who you were, every piece of you. Most of all, I loved how you loved me, and from the first time I felt it I knew I wanted to make a family with you.

When Gabriel came along it was obvious I was right, that you loved him more than life itself, would sacrifice anything for him. But as time went on, your demons began to get the better of you. We all have them, and I know the relationship with your father has always haunted you, even if you never admit it. You wouldn't go see him, wouldn't take Gabe to see him. And so much more. You retreated into your pages, became boxed in by your fears. The world became boxed out, even us. Your writing spiraled into obsession, and one day I woke up and realized that you'd come to engage life more for how it might be written, than for how it might be lived. Life requires action sometimes. Your writing became your fortress, your words and pages your walls. I tried to break through, and when I could not, I tried to prod you to get help, but you would not. Yes, money has been a strain, but I never minded being the breadwinner while you pursued your dream. You are good, but it's tough to break through, and I never got discouraged, but your own discouragement pushed us farther away.

We fought a little, but it was when the fighting stopped that my hopes faded. It was never good for Gabe to see us fight, but it was even worse when he saw us stop. When he saw the last remnants ebb away from us. It was like a light gone out. I don't want him to be without his father, or you without your son – and so I've no intention of keeping him from you – but I do not want him to grow up thinking this is how a marriage is. A family. It's like you're lost in shadow, and part of me will always feel I failed by not being able to pull you out. But in the end, I think this is something only we can do for ourselves. I'll be praying you can, but in the meantime, I don't want Gabriel to be lost in shadow. He's young. He needs a bit more light.

Give us a day to get settled, please. Then come see us. It's Halloween, and Gabe will want you to take him trick-or-treating. Jacob, I don't know what's going to happen, only that we must for the sake of our son work out the best way to move forward. I know this is extraordinarily painful, and my faith in things – in us – is shaken, but I remain certain you will do whatever you must do for our boy. Thank you for that.

Anabel

His arm fell limply to his side, and he looked straight ahead, into the wall, on which perched countless photos of them all—them, a family, a unit. There was no him. He peered into the wall, past it, seeing through it, seeing nothing. He felt himself become unsteady, and he tottered over to the nearest wall, felt for it, braced against it. He felt like he had when his dad had left, like he had when his mom had died. Felt he must do something, that this was an emergency, that he was an adult, and that something was required of him now, if he could only remember what. He felt his right hand move to his heart and fall upon the journal, secured, as always, in his shirt pocket. He thought of withdrawing it, feeling for whatever reason compelled to harken back to the very first listing, but there was no need. It was emblazoned in his mind's eye, indelibly.

Reason One.
You are the love of my life, the most lovable person on the face of the Earth. You rescued this dormant heart and it is yours, now and for always, and beyond all reclaiming. Come what may.

CHAPTER 2 – THE ANGEL'S SHARE

Jacob fell.

He wasn't sure how long he'd leaned against the wall at home, but at length he'd stumbled back out of the house and shuffled back to the bar, where he tumbled down the modest stairwell, just five or six stone steps leading down to the entry of the establishment. Never in his life had he felt more unsteady. He was glad Gabriel hadn't seen it—so difficult to build a parent back up in the eyes of a child. When he scrambled back to his feet, the door swung open, and a short man with wild eyes lurched out.

"Watch it, pal," the man muttered, before pushing past Jacob and stumbling up the stairs. A raft of smoke billowed out, curling into the night like errant wraiths.

Jacob stepped inside, where the emancipated smoke had scarcely diminished the choking layer which remained. He went to the bar and ordered a whiskey, rocks.

The barkeep, an older man whose twirled moustache conjured notions of a bygone era, clinked a glass tumbler onto the table, poured, and held up six fingers.

"How much for the bottle?" Jacob asked, quietly, as if the inquiry might be cause for offense. The barkeep mumbled some figure, to which Jacob nodded, and the barkeep sidled toward the far end of the bar. When he returned with the whisky, Jacob paid him, grabbed the bottle and his glass, and turned around.

He wound his way past some occupied tables until arriving at a small, empty one toward the back of the bar, and sat. He wanted to go to her, to them, but her request for time to get settled hovered in his mind's eye. He removed his phone from his trouser pocket and started to dial hers, but he paused before finishing.

He pocketed the phone, lifted his glass, paused. The hall undulated through the lolling cubes. He drank, and swept his gaze over the establishment.

The barkeep conversed with a gaunt, bloodshot woman, polishing the same tumbler all the while. A stout man with thick glasses sat hunched a few seats over, grasping his beer with two hands. There were perhaps a dozen tables and booths, most occupied, and from a far corner of the place came the knocking of billiards.

But it was the man at a table roughly halfway between Jacob and the bar who apprehended his attention. He was attired in a maroon vest, crisp white shirt, trousers, and a thin, brown tie. He had dark, neatly combed hair, wore fitted black gloves, and smoked what looked to be a fine cigar. When he drew upon it, his eyes glowed crimson behind the flare.

Jacob fumbled for a proper way to write him in his mind, for at once he was macabre, lurid, even funereal, yet as unequivocal as anything he'd ever seen. When the cigar dipped away from his face, his eyes blazed cobalt and cold and seared into Jacob through the space between them.

Jacob downed a shot. He would rest a few moments more before throwing himself back into the evening, that which remained of it anyway, for what was time but the pretense of man? Days rose and died under an aegis not their own, and when all calibration fell away, there was only darkness and only light.

And from the darkness now approached the man with the gloves. "Forgive me," the man said, "but you look like you could use some company."

"Forgive me," Jacob said, "but looks can be deceiving."

The man smiled. "They can indeed."

They observed one another with a calm that belied the pregnant feel of the moment, the kind of moment that had a way of soldering inexorably a sliver of time to all those to come.

The man nodded toward the chair opposite Jacob. "May I?"

Jacob shrugged.

The man smiled his thanks, pulled back the chair, sat. "I am Justus," he said.

"Jacob. Sorry if I was curt. Just thinking about my family."

"As a man should," said Justus. "And yet, we find you here."

"Needed a drink," Jacob explained, irritated at himself for feeling somehow compelled to do so. "Don't want my boy to see me like this."

"Sins of the father," Justus said.

Jacob ignored the comment. He took a drink, set it back down, and nodded at Justus's hands. "Why the gloves?"

"A frailty of mine, I fear. Humans are something of an infectious lot, wouldn't you say? Diseased. Part of their inherent condition, really. Illness, pestilence, plague. All at first festered by a single germ. And so, I am careful, though I dare say our prints reside upon more things than we may suspect."

Jacob swished his whiskey, as might a sommelier. The cubes spun and clinked, the dingy barroom light prisming through them like wisps of lightning. "I don't suspect anything."

"And, why would you?"

Jacob finished his shot and set down his glass.

Justus nodded at the bottle. "You know why they call them spirits? Distillation involves the release of vapors, not unlike a spirit departing the body. There are those who cast the first shot away as the angel's share — something of a sacrifice, if you will. Do you believe in sacrifice?"

Jacob did not answer.

Justus leaned forward, eyes glinting. "Well," he said. "We're soon to find out."

Jacob groaned. Perhaps this stranger was, however inexplicably, the first manifestation of his penance: enduring this odd interlude, when all he wished was to be left to that purgatory he'd authored by his own hand. But in those eyes that remained fixed upon his own, Jacob registered unmistakably the intention that he endure far greater.

Justus reached into the folds of his vest, withdrew a large, manila envelope, and extended it across the table. His hand's shadow preceded it, sepulchral and claw-like. Jacob eyed the envelope as Justus leaned closer toward him. "You are in this moment contemplating the most expedient way to culminate this matter — refuse the envelope and brave whatever reaction, or indulge me in hopes that may bring matters to the quickest resolution. I strongly recommend the latter."

Reason meandered somewhere distant and ethereal in the vast sea of Jacob's infirmity, but seemed to be suggesting the path of least resistance. He snatched up the envelope, dropped it, snatched it up again. An unnerving smile formed upon the stranger's features as Jacob withdrew four photographs: an older, graying man; a younger, but somewhat disheveled man; an attractive, brunette woman; and a coquettish, young girl. Jacob studied them momentarily before glancing back up.

"Am I supposed to know them?"

Justus furrowed his brow. "An uncertain thing, the question of that which we should know." His eyes burned. "It is arguable that you should, but what truly matters is that you will."

Jacob narrowed his eyes. "Is that so?"

"Oh, yes," Justus said, reaching across the table to refill Jacob's glass. "Because I'm going to kill them if you don't."

Jacob lowered his glass. "What did you say?"

Justus sat back. "You heard me correctly."

Jacob glanced at the photographs, then at Justus, then at the photographs. When he looked back up, the establishment tilted and swam with unsustainable imbalance.

"I have to go," Jacob said.

"You surely do. So, I must now know if we are agreed."

Jacob braced himself on the arms of his chair, attempted to push himself up, but the place was spinning and things tried to rise from his stomach, and he slipped back down with a grunt.

"You will seek them out," Justus continued. "Find them, come to know them. Each of them. Know them, and then, write them."

"What?"

"Write them," Justus said. "I present you now with the opportunity to elevate your craft. I shall cover all expenses. Your first flight departs tomorrow evening. You have two weeks. Write them. Make the case for their lives."

Jacob's gaze broke back to Justus like a shot. It was dark, he was drunk, but he focused in on the eyes — he'd always heard you could read a man from his eyes — and went cold from what he saw.

"Be mindful just now," Justus said. "Do not think I fail to observe you in this moment, searching me out, scrambling frantically within the pool of your despair to decipher this abhorrent turn of events. Do not make the mistake of adjudicating this moment through your writerly lens. Illusion plays well in your tales, but it does not become you here, so let us waste no time enduring it. Had you decided some things differently along the road to this day, you would not find yourself here upon the breach. But the breach, as it were, has found you."

"What," said Jacob, "do you know of my despair?"

Justus grinned and said, "I know that it exists. Would you have me believe otherwise?"

"Just leave me alone. I've had a bad day."

"Ah, but not merely a bad day now?" Justus folded his arms upon the table, and addressed Jacob in a serpentine whisper. "Let us put aside these games." His eyes seared into Jacob, marking him.

"How...."

Justus flourished a hand in agitation. "How I know doesn't matter. All that matters is that I do. And I offer you a reprieve." Justus plucked a thick wad of cash from his vest. "Should you accept and succeed, not only shall you preserve their lives — " He gestured at the photographs. " — but I shall become the benefactor you have for so long sought." He held up the money. "A quarter million advance," he said. "The money you've never made from your dream, but which could allow you to continue, renewed, in its pursuit."

Jacob stared. He was tipsy, but surely not to the point of hallucination. No, this man was real, this terrible man, and Jacob shifted in his chair, ashamed of the way the money made his heart accelerate. Bullshit, probably, but on the small chance it was legit, there was no way he could entertain such a dastardly bargain. Not even if it would save their house, maybe his marriage. He clenched his eyes shut. When he opened them, he bent forward, and Justus did likewise, the shadows of each man enjoining like alien beings seeking to assemble the wayward pieces of these proceedings.

"I don't know who or what you are," Jacob said. "Maybe you have mental issues. Maybe I should just call the police."

"I am a man," said Justus. "Like you. And you should do what you must. Report me, curse me, strike me down. I would hardly begrudge this. An honest act it would be. Honesty is all we have in this world. You of all people know that. You're a writer. You know—even with fiction—when your prose rings true and when it does not. That is all I ask of people—that all that they author, by pen or by sword and in all manner of their lives, they do so with honesty."

"How can you speak of honesty, or anything moral?"

Justus straightened in his chair. "I've no use for morality," he said. "I live honestly, free of the oppressive cloak of pretense borne by so many. Truth is truth, and knows not between good or evil."

Their eyes locked. Jacob gripped the base of the whiskey bottle. He imagined plucking it up and in one deft motion shattering it atop the skull of this man poised before him like some conjured, craven being.

"Your answer, then?"

Jacob's hand slid from the bottle, and Justus grinned. Jacob pushed off from the chair one more time and this time gained his footing, tenuous though it was. He squinted for the door and made his way there, but his hand slipped off the handle at first attempt. He tried again and pulled the door open, and slipped back out into an evening whose hour he could not reckon.

CHAPTER 3 – CALAMITY

He clambered up the stairwell to the street, which tilted crazily, forcing him to steady himself on the railing. When something brushed his ankle, he looked down oafishly and stared as a bevy of rats scampered past. He would cut through the park.

It loomed pitch and silent beyond the pale glow of the streetlights, but soon his eyes adjusted and the park's architecture budded into resolution — the benches, the walking path, the oaks looming tall and imprinted like midnight sentries.

It was a perfect night, really, almost enough to persuade him that this ordeal now was as ethereal as the stars dropping away along the slope of the blue-black firmament, as the city slept. He crossed through the park, which fell out before him, flat and dark and promising ahead only darkness still, a great promontory at the edge of the Earth. Things were still spinning, and so he stumbled to a bench in hopes of regaining a semblance of stability. He closed his eyes and savored the fleeting reprieve permitted by things unseen, by the desperate hope that out of sight meant out of mind, and maybe better still, that it had never happened. But the knotted dread in his soul wrenched him from such folly. And, as if to ensure no misunderstanding, now sounded the steady clip of footsteps.

"I have traveled countless lands, and endless miles," said Justus, "and I shall traverse countless more.

But as for you, I might question your flight, which only delays the inevitable."

Jacob groaned and staggered to his feet. The world spun madly, a wretched carnival. "Can't you just leave me be?"

"In fact, yes. But be sure of that choice, for as I promised, there are others who shall not be spared."

Jacob spat dryly. "You're crazy."

Justus grinned again. "Maybe. And so, it becomes a matter of what you are willing to chance."

"What's going on here?"

Jacob shielded his eyes and squinted at an officer sweeping the beam of his flashlight over the opposed figures. Jacob felt his lips moving. Here was his chance.

The officer sidled up to them, lowered the beam slightly, his other hand poised near his holster. "I said, what's going on?"

"Nothing," said Jacob, hoping the alcohol wasn't too stark upon his breath. "Just walking home."

The officer frowned. "Not sure I buy that." He nodded at Justus. "What's your story?"

Justus grinned. "Same as any man," he said. "Proceeding where the tides may bear me."

"See that they bear you somewhere else. Both of you. We don't like loiterers." The officer regarded them expectantly.

"Understood," said Jacob, and turned to go.

"One thing more, officer, if you please. This man and I are at something of a crossroads, I fear. I've tried to convince him I am in fact a killer, but he hasn't quite come around."

Jacob froze, then turned slowly back.

The officer narrowed his eyes, and his hand gripped his revolver. "What did you just say?"

In one blinding moment, Justus reached with his black-gloved hand into the folds of his coat, withdrew a dagger, and plunged the blade into the officer's chest.

The officer gasped, and his eyes fixed with a look more curious than dismayed. One hand flew up to the blade handle, which protruded flush from his chest, while the other shot out and gripped his assailant's shoulder.

Justus exclaimed in disgust, yanked the blade from the officer's chest, and stepped back.

Jacob rushed forward, but was too late, and the officer crumbled to the stone path, one hand still clutched to his chest. Breath seeped out in slow intervals beneath his body.

When Jacob rolled him over, the officer wheezed — like air going out of a balloon. His arm lolled from his chest and flopped to the ground. A thin rivulet of blood trickled from a corner of his mouth, and he looked past Jacob into the depthless night. A dark blossom spread across his chest, and for several moments Jacob sought frantically to staunch it with the pressure of his own hands.

"Stay with me," he said.

The officer's eyes had gone all rolling and aslant, but they fixed for the briefest of moments upon Jacob's. "Be sober," he rasped. "Be vigilant...."

"Hang on," Jacob said. He pressed more forcefully upon the fomenting wound but the slow rise and fall of the officer's chest ceased, and when Jacob looked into his eyes, he saw only that celestial light which they reflected — all that had ever burned within them had flickered out.

Jacob looked up at Justus, who was dusting the spot on his shoulder the officer had grasped. Jacob turned his palms upward: warm, sticky, imprinted so darkly crimson as to be hedging black. A faint banter of voices and laughter sounded from somewhere in the distance. Other bar patrons, surely.

"I suggest," said Justus, "you not tarry. Being apprehended would not behoove your cause."

"What?" Jacob narrowed his eyes. "You killed him. You killed him with your own hands!"

Justus looked down at Jacob, almost paternally. "But whose prints will they find upon him?" He cinched up his gloves as the voices drew closer. "Remember: refuse the task, they die. Go the police, now or at any time, they die. I ask you a final time: are we agreed?"

"I don't know those people," Jacob spat. "How do I know they exist? That any of this is real? *Why me?*"

"Essential questions," Justus said, "the answers to which should improve your chances the greater. And now—" He stepped closer. "—I'm afraid I must insist. Succeed, and their lives are spared. Succeed, and the money is yours. Your answer, please."

Jacob knelt before this unfathomable figure, everything he'd loved and known torn asunder, teetering uncertainly, yet something inside him told him he must believe Justus. He told himself it was only their lives he was thinking about—these strangers—but in the pit of his stomach, he knew. Anabel may have said it wasn't the money, but a quarter million dollars....

What have you become?

"Give it to me," Jacob seethed.

Justus extended the envelope to his kneeling subjugate.

Jacob hesitated, then grasped it. He watched the envelope blot crimson beneath his grip, a blood oath.

"There is ample cash there," Justus said. "More than you'll need. The quarter million will be on top of it, should you succeed. We are men of honor, and I take your word as your bond, as our contract. A man is nothing, but for his word."

"How in God's name can you speak of honor?"

"For one whose faith is lacking," said Justus, "you invoke Him frequently. But you should know I do nothing in His name. His word has failed us for time immemorial, eloquent though it can be." He withdrew a cigar from the folds of his vest, stepped back a few paces, out from the pale light of the lampposts, and into shadow. "I have my favorites." The slash of a striking match preceded an orange flare within the blackness. "Isaiah, 11:6."

A strong wind rose from the north, off the river, and Justus's words drowned out upon it. When it subsided, there were no more words and he was gone, borne away in much the same manner, it seemed to Jacob, in which he'd come.

"Hey! What's going on?"

Jacob looked up at the group who'd entered the park, now paused perhaps thirty feet away, their faces materializing palely into view. He ducked his head beneath an arm, behind the envelope, then turned, rose, stumbled, rose again, and lit off into the darkness toward the far reaches of the park.

"Hey! You!"

"Stop!"

"Call 9-1-1!"

"Did you get a look at him?"

"I think so!"

"I'm going after him!"

"No, he may be armed!"

"I'm going!"

Incredulity pounded through his brain as his feet pounded over the pavement. *What the hell is this? A fugitive fleeing in cover of dark.* His head throbbed and his heart hammered against the *rat-a-tat* of racing feet. He ran faster, and it grew louder. His own footfalls, or his pursuers'?

Don't stop to look. Faster. Bench, veer left; hanging tree limb, duck.

He flew through the first subdivision, and then the next. He zipped between houses and emerged onto the street that would lead to his own. A police cruiser cornered into view and Jacob froze, panting desperately. He glanced behind him, and was grateful to neither see nor hear anyone.

But, would that be all bad? To be set upon by those who saw me, and have the police summoned? I could explain things and they would find and apprehend the guilty party.

But nothing set upon him beyond the calamity of his own thoughts. When the cruiser disappeared, he continued on, walking this time, glancing back every few moments.

When he reached his dwelling, he approached head down — the windows, its eyes, no doubt falling reproachfully upon him; the door, its mouth, no doubt conjuring salvos of rebuke. 'You bought me,' it would say as he slunk past. 'You bought me fourteen years ago and built and repaired parts of me with your own hands. You did these things, and yet this is not your house, for by those same hands have you imperiled the only things which ever made it yours.'

He tried the door and found it locked — of course it was locked — and fumbled for the key in his trouser pockets, then shirt, to no avail, and cursed. He lumbered around back and went to the kitchen window, which they sometimes left unlocked, but it was not unlocked, so he unbuttoned his shirt and removed it, and stood in his undershirt and trousers wrapping the shirt around his hand. After glancing furtively about, he levered his swaddled fist into the window. It shattered in a shrill jangle, and he cursed again. He'd sliced his hand at the base of the thumb, near the wrist. He pressed a section of the garment hard onto the wound, held it there a moment, then rewound the shirt tighter. Large shards of glass protruded from the window frame, pocking the hole he'd created like monstrous teeth. He nudged each remnant with his reinforced fist, until they clattered away, leaving a more feasible space through which he might slip.

He cast one last look around, a lost man, before contorting himself through the broken window of his own home. His house a box. His study. Within these spaces more boxes still, and even the windows imposed upon him this same effect, framing the world in manageable portions and perspectives. He suffered no illusion that a light would flicker on and his wife's voice, alarmed and admonishing, yet angel-sweet, would echo down the hallway. That their son, unable to sleep, would emerge from his room, shyly at first but then whisking down the hallway in his pajamas and bare feet. Only silence.

In his study, in a mahogany cabinet, resided a dozen or so cigar boxes, inside which lay volumes of his observations of the world, accumulated through the last dozen or so years. His way of journaling, really, which they said every writer should do. He'd journaled volumes on literature, on love and life and people and psychology, on religion — the faithful and faithless — on good and evil, and many other things. He was an observer of life, and what he observed he pondered, and what he pondered he wrote. Once, when Gabriel was a toddler, the boy found his way into the cabinet and left the boxes in disarray. Jacob gently admonished him, explaining that certain things were not to be touched, and that now Daddy had to put everything back in its rightful place.

What a job you've done.

He staggered to the bathroom and fumbled in the medicine cabinet for antiseptic and some bandages, and dressed his wound. He moved to the darkened living room and sank into the easy chair. Sometimes when he wrote, commotion rose within and without the dwelling—a blaring television, a honking horn—and he'd lament these intrusions. Oh, how he longed now for any such portents of normalcy. Through the far window, the world loomed silent and pitch and his own breathing, though slowed by intoxication and weariness, sounded to him horribly loud, as if he'd awakened alone in some dead and ruinous land. Silent wires of lightning materialized in the distance, casting the room in fleeting illumination, like entreating gods sweeping the expanse of this wasteland for survivors. He closed his eyes and unconsciousness rushed like a river to meet him, attended by tributaries of guilt. How dare he sleep!

His head in a vise.... He didn't have enough experience with hangovers to recall whether eggs were thought to offer any relief, and if they did, he'd no idea whether to eat them or drink them or quite what, exactly, but he needed to try something. He pushed off from the chair and wobbled to the kitchen. The refrigerator hummed in the moonlight as he pulled open the door and squinted against the dingy light, and spotted and retrieved the egg carton. When he nudged the door shut, something fluttered from the cluster of items affixed to it, and when it settled on the ground, he saw it was the picture Gabriel had drawn of the family — sketchy and cartoonish and exaggerated and perfect — but then the carton fell from his hands and one egg rolled out, fissured and leaking.

Jacob dropped to his knees and snatched the picture before it could be stained by the mess he'd made, and as he clutched it to his chest, an involuntary sound rose within him, resonant and primordial.

He lit the stove, fried the eggs, and ate them, then gulped a large glass of water. He returned to the bathroom and, as he stood over the toilet with hands pressed on the wall, his gut seized, and he doubled over and vomited. He remained for some time, panting, feeling the sweat on his face and body, and shaking strands of regurgitation from his lips. He moved to the sink, flipped open the cabinet and snatched the mouthwash, knocking a toothbrush into the sink. He fumbled with the cap, and when he'd finally twirled it open, it spun off the plastic neck and ricocheted somewhere behind the toilet. Jacob lifted the bottle to his lips, titled his head back, and gulped a mouthful of the minty liquid, cringed, sloshed it about, spat.

He returned to the living room and sank back into the chair. At one point he heard sirens, and he leapt to his feet, scampered over to the window and peered out from behind the curtains. When no one came and the sirens faded, he crept back to the chair and collapsed into it once more. He faded quickly, desperately reaching for evaporating strands of lucidity. He would rest. He must. Tomorrow — or was it today? — he would go see his family — his loves, his life, those pieces of him more him than he was. He would go to them, and he would lie.

He closed his eyes. Darkness came with boundless arms, entreating him.

He is a boy again and there are other kids around his age and they are gathered near the river where his father and another man are preparing the raft for their adventure. The kids are jittery with anticipation, chasing each other to and fro and playing tricks. Every so often one of the adults exhorts them to settle down, or asks them to help load up this item or that onto their vessel. It is warm, sunny, a high and cloudless sky. The river is running calmly, glimmering in the morning light. A stack of orange lifejackets rests in one corner of the raft. It is difficult to imagine they will be needed. The children continue to play, eager to set off. It is shaping up to be a perfect day.

CHAPTER 4 – COVENANT

His son Gabriel had once heard Jacob lamenting the dreaded write-what-you-know adage, and it became something of a joke between them. Whenever he confronted a bad case of writer's block, Gabe would tell him, "Just write what you know, Dad."

How can you think about writing? A man is dead.

Jacob rapped on his in-laws' door. Muffled voices and pattering footfalls sounded from the house, and as the door swung open, he could feel his spine stiffening against the miasma of his own duplicity.

His father 'n law stood in the doorway, regarding him with a look calibrated somewhere between forced cordiality and measured reproach. Anabel's mother materialized briefly over Henry's shoulder, spied Jacob, and disappeared. He'd never felt welcome there. It wasn't outright hostility — more so unmitigated disapproval. It was the writer thing. Their daughter was beautiful, brilliant, and accomplished, and to their way of thinking, these traits corresponded more precisely to doctor, lawyer, investment banker. Writer may as well have been actor, inventor, or circus clown.

"Jacob," said Henry, still guarding the doorway.

"Henry," said Jacob. "May I come in?"

Henry grunted and stepped back, and Jacob stepped into the house. An aroma of coffee wafted over him. Anabel was sitting on the couch in the living room. She stood and regarded Jacob and what he read in her eyes pierced him like a blade—the sort you dared not pull out, lest all the life run out of you.

"Hi," Jacob said.

"Hello," replied Anabel, her arms folded across her chest. It sounded like a condolence.

Jacob turned back around, saw Henry eying him like a court-ordered chaperone, and scanned the premises for Gabriel.

"He's playing," Anabel said. "He'll come down in a bit." She looked at her father. "Dad, do you mind?"

Henry frowned slightly but nodded. "I'll be in the kitchen with Mom."

Jacob turned back to his wife. "It's just me, Anabel."

She inhaled deeply. "I know." She sank back into the couch and patted the space adjacent her.

Jacob came forward and sat.

"I know. But I'll always be their baby girl."

"And to me?"

"Jacob... you read my letter."

"Yeah, I did. You're my wife, and after all this time, that's what it comes to? Leaving me a letter?"

Anabel nodded, swept her shirtsleeve across her eyes. "I have been trying to tell you for a very long time."

Jacob tensed, a cauldron of discordant emotions. He wanted to be angry, but couldn't. Wanted to pull her to him, but wouldn't. In his mind's eye, he could see Justus, cradling an hourglass, from which disgorged torrents of sand, bearing away precious grains of time. And so, he must look into Anabel's eyes, for which he'd fallen from the first, and to which he figured always to return, and lie.

"I am going to see my father," he said. "I know it's something you've felt I should do, and I've done some soul-searching these last twenty-four hours, and decided you're right. I need to see him, try to help him, try to figure things out. You asked for some time, and so I figured this is a good time to do it. And honestly, it might be good for me to get away for a bit."

Anabel looked surprised, but nodded. "After all this time?"

"Better late, huh?"

His wife smiled wistfully. "Your mother would have been happy."

Jacob swallowed. "Yeah."

"When are you leaving?"

"Tonight," he answered. "Soon. I only have a few minutes. That's why I swung by."

Anabel frowned. "Can't you wait a day?" she said. "Even a few hours? Gabe wanted so bad for you to take him trick-or-treating."

"I am so sorry," Jacob said. "I got a really inexpensive offer, and you know how those go. You have to book right then. You know things are tight. I'm sorry. That's why I came, to see Gabe first."

Anabel nodded dispassionately, his words seeming to have confirmed something for her. "How long will you be gone?"

"Could be a while," Jacob said. "A few weeks. I have to talk to a lot of specialists, figure out lots of things, and after all this time, I mean, I should spend some good time with him."

"It'll be hard on Gabe," said Anabel. "You being gone that long. He's going to need both of us to help him through this."

Jacob simmered briefly. *I'm not the one who left.* But once again, he couldn't be angry. He could never do anything but love her.

"You can be angry," Anabel said.

His heart rushed and melancholy swept over him, for here again she'd read him flawlessly, and in so doing tendered a poignant reminder of one of the many reasons he'd considered her his soulmate, a reminder of precisely what now was lost.

"Part of me wishes you would be."

"Would it," Jacob inquired, "change your mind?"

She answered unhappily with her eyes, but before Jacob could say anything else, he felt a different set upon him, and turned to see Gabriel standing at the edge of the living room. If in the eyes of his wife resided the depths of his heart's profession, in those of their son flickered any remnants of his soul. Gabriel regarded his father with imploring eyes. When the boy's lip quivered, Jacob's eyes welled, and he held out his arms and Gabriel ran to him. Jacob could feel his son's thumping heart against his own.

"I heard you," Gabe said. "You're going away?"

"Yes." Jacob held his grip. "To see Grandpa. A few weeks. But I'll be back."

Gabriel stood back, then scampered onto the couch between his parents. He spoke to his father in rapid fashion about a great many things — how he was excited about trick-or-treating but wished he could take him and how the pet snake at school was fed a rat but didn't eat the rat and there was a TV that was in his room here — and Jacob listened and nodded and tendered related questions, which Gabriel answered enthusiastically, and then Jacob told his son and his wife that unfortunately it was time for him to go. He inclined instinctively toward Anabel but then demurred, and turned to Gabe for a final embrace.

"Wait!" The boy pulled away suddenly. "I want to give you something."

Jacob looked on as Gabriel darted from the room, and his in-laws shifted in the foyer. When Gabe returned, he pressed a folded note, inside which was something solid and small, into his father's hand, and instantly, Jacob knew.

Jacob knelt back down and pulled Gabe to him, feeling wetness on his cheek. "It's yours, Gabriel," he whispered. "Yours to keep."

"Take it, Dad. Please. You might need it." The boy's voice seized, and his father held him more tightly than he ever had before.

"Okay," he said. He thrust the note and the jasper deep into his pocket. "Thank you. I'll be back before you know it, and you can put it back where it belongs."

"Promise?"

"I promise."

Releasing his son tore at every remaining fiber of his soul. He stood and nodded at Anabel and her parents, then leaned down a final time. He dabbed Gabe's tears with the back of his hand, kissed him on the forehead, and gripped his shoulders.

"I love you," he said, then turned and stepped back out into the gathering night.

***

A low sky hung this night, mottled catawampus with clouds of haphazard arrangement, as though from different skies entirely, piled one atop the other like discarded watercolors, a logjam of days since past. Billowing cumulous rafts, twisting cirrus ridges, and rising now against this white and berry canvass, a flight of swallows flared this way then that, south at first, then back north, as out of sorts, it seemed, as that jumbled sky beneath which they wheeled.

Darkness fell quickly, and all manner of creatures set about. Jacob stood festooned at the end of his driveway, another ornament on this night of wayward souls. A ninja and robot sidled past saying nothing, but their vampire friend mumbled, "Hi Mr. Fallon," through bulging fangs. Jacob complimented their costumes and pointed them toward the bowl of candy on his porch. He felt badly not being with Gabriel tonight, and even worse for the lie he'd told to explain it, but he could not spare a day, and would not dare expose his child to the insidious truth.

The cab pulled up, and a pirate got out and took Jacob's bags and put them in the trunk of the vehicle.

"Argh," said Jacob.

"I'm not a pirate," the cabbie said. "I'm a ferryman, of the River Styx. But no one knows what that looks like, so I figured pirate was next best thing."

"A cloak," Jacob said.

"Huh?"

"Do you have a cloak?"

"Who has a cloak?"

"They sell them. You could buy a cloak and carry a staff or something."

The non-pirate fidgeted with some things on his console, then shifted into gear. On either side of them passed painted faces and billowing ensembles. Above them, a paper moon, yellow and egg-like, roosted just beyond a stenciled patchwork of violet clouds.

"To the Netherworld," said the ferryman.

"The airport, please."

The driver pawed at the console, and a flurry of red digits flickered.

Jacob sat back and inhaled deeply. His meter was begun.

CHAPTER 5 – OF EYES, AND SUCH

His heart raced when going through security.

They couldn't have heard, not yet, right? A cop-killer at large. A description couldn't have been tendered and circulated so quickly.

But, maybe it could. All things being equal, he would hope that it could. Cop-killers should be caught, and he was no killer. But things were not equal, and he was the one they'd seen.

He passed through without incident, and sank into a chair at his gate, waiting to board. A torrent of considerations coursed through his mind, each less comprehensible than the previous. A man was dead, a police officer. Other lives, if he were to believe Justus — and he did — rested squarely in Jacob's hands. His soiled hands, not only from blood, but blood money. He wanted to vomit. He was for a moment glad his mother was dead, and his father incapacitated, for at least they would not know the shame. Through it all, and it piqued his own shame all the greater, all he could think about was Anabel. The love of his life. He must win her back, for what life would it be without her?

"...police officer late last evening, and though the killer has not been apprehended, witnesses did see a man, described as...."

Jacob's eyes widened as he glanced slowly up at the TV monitor hanging nearby. No sketch was presented on-screen, but a description was articulated: Caucasian male, brown hair, 5-10, 5-11, thirty-five to forty-five years of age. He glanced furtively about; a few others were watching the screen, but no one was looking at him. He tried to relax—that description fit countless people, anywhere—but his insides roiled. Justus had killed a man—wantonly, brazenly--and disappeared like the wind, yet here Jacob was having to worry, on top of everything else, that he'd be fingered as the culprit.

When at last they boarded, an old woman took the seat beside him, as a mother and her young son filed into the aisle across from theirs.

"They're like eyes," the boy said, pretzeling his body toward the window as far as his seatbelt would permit.

His mother had already begun reading a magazine. "What are, sweetie?"

"The windows." The boy surveyed his surroundings. "They're like eyes looking out of the plane."

The old woman seated beside Jacob smiled. "Children are precious," she said. "Don't you think?"

Jacob nodded.

"Precious about the eyes," the woman said. "What's that they say—the eyes are the window to your soul? I think that's what they say—whoever they are." She chortled.

Jacob smiled, then turned and peered out his window as the plane took off. Truth be told, he didn't care much for the quote. It was airy, quixotic, ultimately hollow, as were most airy and quixotic things. He had no issue about the eyes—they were as good a conduit as any. But to what? Did a glimpse inside truly reveal this rarefied thing with which folks were so frequently preoccupied?

If he'd hoped by virtue of their lofty vantage for some epiphany, or even the slightest perspective, he was disappointed. The earth some 30,000 feet below set out flat and homogenous, neatly segmented, no manner of life distinguishable, even the most prominent structures mere specks, and to one peering up from below, their plane but a speck as well.

And was he, when all was said and done, something markedly greater? The likes of Whitman might exhort but he'd contributed verses—countless— which came from within, but once expelled became something without, pieces of him which were not him, and which at any rate had failed him utterly when it mattered most. His family gone, an officer dead, and here he was, off on a mad crusade, having lied about seeing his father, on top of it. His father, whom he'd scarcely seen the last thirty years. Who had been his hero for his first ten.

A wave of incredulity suddenly beset him. Why was he doing this? Engaging this inanity on behalf of four strangers, when he ought to be devoting each ounce of energy to reclaiming his family? If he'd lost his faith, why place it in this most contemptible of men? He saw the woman looking at him, the one who'd spoken of eyes, and he looked down, nervously, remembering the policeman. As if she might be conscious, somehow, of his complicity in that abominable act.

He thought of Anabel, and felt remorseful about this too, under the circumstances, but he couldn't help it. Amidst the shock, the trauma he was well-aware afflicted him, within the bewilderment of this inexplicable commission, he couldn't help thinking of her. What little industry he might be capable in this moment of summoning, ought rightly be devoted to his task, but in his heart, all that mattered was winning her back. He could do it, too—had to do it, for him, and for their son. He'd won her heart before. He could do it again.

He bent and retrieved his backpack, unzipped it, and withdrew the book. Anabel's book. He flipped to a random page.

> *Reason 47. Your touch. Brings me to a standstill, every time, exhilarates and calms me, all at once. And not just your physical touch, and not just with me. You touch everyone, even a stranger in passing, and they're all the better for it, every time. The way you perceive, and convey, their humanity. The way you smile at them, bring them a little more light than they had before.*

He was flying into Billings, Montana and renting a car for what he'd been told was roughly an hour drive to his lodgings at the foot of the Beartooth Mountains. From there, he would commence his search for his first charge: one Danny Marcus. He hadn't had much time before packing, but naturally he'd looked him up. Danny Marcus, Billings, Montana. Nothing. Daniel Marcus. No. Danny Marcus, Beartooth. Nada. Danny and Daniel Marcus, period. Too many to know where to begin, and no pictures. Maybe if he dug deeper, went down some rabbit holes.... He'd also called information, for Billings, and proximate cities, but to no avail. He paid for the in-flight Wi-Fi and searched some more, but got no closer.

A handful of threadbare towns marked the way along Highway 212, the Beartooth Highway, and he'd elected one not far from Silver Gate, near the northeast entrance to Yellowstone. He'd packed light, despite the potential duration of his journey—a week's clothing, which he'd wash as necessary, his passport and money, his laptop and phone and chargers, and of course, Anabel's book.

The mountains hove first into view, behemoths so indented into shadow as to appear at first but phantom mesas. But soon they were flying low, and the peaks and slopes sharpened into contrast, vast and gray and jagged, and beyond them a twinkling of lights.

When they landed, Jacob retrieved his luggage and rental car, programmed his coordinates into the GPS, and set out beneath a cold and dimming sky. Few other cars appeared, and so for long stretches little materialized before him save for that illuminated by the twin beams funneled forth by his vehicle. He glanced skyward as an array of stars flickered against a sky rending otherwise pitch. He spied the Big Dipper and traced down from it with his gaze along its handle, through Polaris and dropping farther still to the M-shaped constellation he knew to be Cassiopeia. He detected the hallmark square torso of Pegasus, that great winged steed of lore, bestowed unrivaled powers of poetry and dispatch. Oh, to be graced with but a fraction of such.

He had no reason to doubt the GPS, but a wave of misgiving flooded over him, and he guided the vehicle slowly onto the shoulder, where he sat with pounding heart and stared up at that expanding vault of night. At length, he remembered the folded slip in his pocket, from Gabriel.

He withdrew and opened it. The boy had been rushed and distracted and could be forgiven the homophone:

Right What You Know.

CHAPTER 6 – GOD'S COUNTRY

He got in late, and knew he should sleep, but also knew it was likely to elude him, especially if he went to bed clueless about the story and whereabouts of Danny Marcus. He had two weeks, and now he'd already expended one day. He set up his laptop and dug back into the elusive catalogue of Danny Marcuses, navigating by geography, approximate age, and the like. Nothing. Nothing he would know to be something, anyway, for he had nothing to go on. His mind faltered and veered, plagued by exhaustion and the bewilderment of his predicament. After a few more futile hours, he crawled to bed, where slumber called quickly.

He'd not cinched the curtains fully shut, and when the day's first light carved into his consciousness, waking him before his early alarm, he basked ever-briefly in that delicious wisp of a moment before memory returns. But it did, of course, and he groaned upon its arrival. He made coffee in his room—it was terrible, but he didn't care—and stepped out into the frigid morning. Holy hell, it was cold. He couldn't imagine what winter was like here. He wanted to slip back inside to the comfort of a heated room and hot, awful beverages, but this was not an option. A diner across the street seemed to beckon, and he eyed it wistfully a moment. A blue twist of smoke exuded from the chimney, scarcely moving, painted, it seemed, against the frozen sky. A decadent aroma of grease and better coffee suffused the air. He licked his lips, gulped, and headed for his car.

Jacob wondered how many such towns were left, but this one was small and quaint enough that it had a town square, and he felt at least a twinkle of luck upon discerning a city hall and post office, adjunct to one another. He parked and strolled up the sidewalk, aware he was being watched. The handful of locals out and about—and some inside shop windows—were not shy about surveying this stranger in their midst. It didn't matter.

He swept into the post office, hopeful. There was a man being helped, by apparently the lone worker present, and a woman waited in line. All three eyed Jacob briefly. When it was his turn, the employee, a middle-aged woman with a rather severe countenance, asked him for his number.

"Sorry," Jacob said. "I didn't grab one."

"They're over there," the woman said, gesturing with her head.

Jacob turned around, then back. "There's no one else here."

"You have to have a number," the worker said.

Jacob took a breath and retrieved a number.

"How may I help you?" the woman said.

"I'm looking for someone."

"We're not a lost and found."

"I understand," said Jacob. "But you know your town. You deliver mail, have addresses. I need to find someone."

"We're not a detective agency," the woman said. "Now, do you have a parcel to send?"

"I do not."

"Then I'm sorry, but—"

"Wait," Jacob interjected. "I do. But I don't have it on me."

"Sir—"

"Wait, please. I don't have it on me, but this is a post office, right? You can sell me an envelope, sell me a stamp?"

The woman sighed. "Yes."

"Okay," Jacob said. "I am going to buy a stamp and envelope and mail something to a friend who moved. I need you to write the correct address, please, and send it to him."

"If the person left a forwarding address with the post office, we can place the correct address on the envelope and mail it back to you." She plucked up a pen. "To what address shall I mail it to you?"

Jacob frowned. "Mail it to me? Look, please, if you're going to do all that, can't you just tell me the address?"

"We cannot sir. Privacy and safety. Now what is the person's name, sir?"

"Danny Marcus."

The woman looked up from her scribbling. "Danny Marcus?"

Jacob's eyes widened. "Yes. You know him?"

The woman started to reply, stopped. "Yes," she finally acknowledged. "Everyone here does, but I still can't tell you his address."

"Please. I need to find him. It's for his own good."

"I cannot, sir. And in this case, literally. Danny Marcus does not list an address with us. He has a post office box, nothing more. Comes down once a week to empty it. And that's a good bit more than I ought to have told you."

"Comes down?" Jacob eyed her. "From where?"

The door swung open and a woman bustled in with a large package. She came to a stop behind Jacob, bumping him slightly with her parcel.

"Sir," said the worker, more sharply. "Do you have anything to mail? Is there anything else you need?"

No," said Jacob, offering a smile. "I appreciate your help."

***

He'd gone straight over to City Hall, but they were every bit as reticent. Yes, they had records of most everyone, concerning all manner of things, but nary a one permitted them to disclose personal information to someone else, much less a stranger to their town.

He made the short drive back to his hotel, the jaunt to town a mixed bag. He was no closer to a precise bearing on Marcus, but had confirmed he was here. He'd held out hope of finding him today, but that had been optimistic. He needed to eat, and get more rest, then, come hell or high water, do whatever it took to find Marcus tomorrow.

When he entered late that evening through the frost-stamped doors of the diner, there were five other individuals within, three patrons and two workers. Each stopped — mid-conversation, mid-pour, and mid-chew — to regard him, eyes brimming with neither acrimony nor welcome, but something else that conveyed unmistakably Jacob's outlander status.

He checked his watch.

"Open all night," said the man behind the counter, behind his thicket of a beard. Manager, read his nametag.

Jacob nodded, though his concern hadn't been their hours. He blew into his hands.

"You ain't seen nothin' yet," advised the waitress. She finished pouring coffee for two men whose unkempt appearances rivaled the manager's.

Farther down the counter sat a woman, still in her coat, muttering quietly to the mug around which her gaunt hands remained clasped.

"Order up!" The gravelly voice sounded from a window behind the manager, preceding the appearance of a meaty paw, which clubbed down upon a shrill bell.

The manager, who'd been watching Jacob, spun to the window, and upon turning back, clutched a skillet in either hand, atop both of which sizzled a dark and silvery fish, lightly dressed and smelling of oil and lemon, fixed upon a crisped pile of potatoes. Jacob's nose twitched as the manager pushed the plates across the counter to the men. The one closest to the woman dug in, wielding his utensils as might a young child, the handles wedged tightly in the balled fists of either hand. The man closer to Jacob did not yet eat, but rather had swiveled toward him, and was eying his boots.

"Mountain trout," said the waitress, sopping a light spill of coffee from the counter with a towel. "Fresh cut. Fancy some?"

"Please," Jacob said.

The waitress nodded, placed her hands on her hips, and gestured with a crook of her head. "Well come on in, then. I ain't gonna bring it to ya standing over there."

Jacob moved a few feet toward the dining area, then paused. There were three booths, and a few empty stools at the counter. While he must not overstep his welcome, more pressing still was his need for information. He made his way over to the stool between the muttering lady and the man who'd gotten the head start on his trout. He unzipped his coat, left it on, and sat.

"Evening," he said quietly, to anyone who might care to hear it.

The man to his right gurgled in possible response, but did not pause in his consumption.

To his left, the woman continued muttering, pausing occasionally for a sip of her coffee.

The waitress filled Jacob's mug, and he nodded his thanks and wrapped his still-thawing hands around it.

He made small talk while his food was being cooked, asking his counter mates if they lived and worked around there, if they had families, and the like. The woman to his left lifted her head and half-smiled, but after what appeared a moment of contemplation, she returned her focus to her mug. The men were less reticent, though hardly forthcoming. They both lived within walking distance, born and raised here, and both worked at the feed store about a mile yonder in town. Neither had families.

"Them's prisons, man," the man closest Jacob muttered through a forkful of potatoes. "I'm not the type to be tied down."

The waitress set a steaming plate in front of Jacob and rolled her eyes. "You ain't nobody's type, Flint," she said. "No wonder you ain't never found a woman."

"You hush," said Flint, "and just keep the coffee coming."

The waitress dismissed him with a wave and returned her attention to Jacob. "What about you, stranger. You got a family? What brings you to our cheery corner of the world?"

Jacob finished chewing his first bite — it was hot, savory, good — and lifted his mug. Here was his chance.

"I have a family," he said. "Wife and son. I'm a writer. That's why I'm here, doing a little research. I'm trying to find someone who may be able to help me with some of it. Danny Marcus. Do you know him?"

The diner fell silent, save for the sizzling of oil-soaked skillets.

Jacob took a sip of coffee, and set it back down. "A story there, huh?" He smiled nervously and glanced at each of them, even the meaty-pawed cook who'd leaned his frame into the kitchen window. Jacob settled his gaze upon the waitress, whom he'd determined in these fleeting moments to constitute his best bet.

She returned his smile, though her own demeanor seemed in this moment slightly less assured. "There's a story," she said. "But no one really knows what it is. Danny Marcus came here many years ago. Had to be a reason why he came, but he wasn't telling. He comes down to town every now and again, but otherwise, he's off the grid, as they say."

"Francine." The manager glared at her.

"Oh relax, Harold," she said. "I ain't telling what anyone 'round here don't already know. It's the truth." She turned back to Jacob. "Danny Marcus lives in the hills," she said. "High up in the mountain. God's country. Whatever he was leaving, he left it far behind. He's kinda become an urban legend with the townsfolk, especially the young-uns. You know, the crazy old mountain man, place is haunted, stuff like that."

"Francine!"

She topped off Jacob's mug. "Now I've told you something," she said. "It's your turn to tell me. What do you need him for? What kind of story? He may be a crackpot, but he's *our* crackpot, you know? We get protective of our own."

Jacob gripped the steaming mug. He could feel eyes upon him. "I'm writing about that very thing," he said. "People who have gone off the grid, as you say. I don't recall who pointed me to him — we're kind of like moles, writers are — digging this way and that after a million leads, before we finally end up somewhere."

He sipped his coffee, clinked it back down. "I think they may get a bad rap. Mountain men. Folks who might be running from something, maybe with good reason. I want to know their story. I want to make the case for them, cast a better light on them. Fairer, anyway."

Francine, who'd folded her arms on the counter and leaned forward with attention, nodded and straightened back up. "I think that's pretty nice," she said. "And I wish you good luck. But you best remember not all lost folks want to be found. Danny Marcus might not want a better light cast on him, or any light at all."

Jacob lifted his mug. "Thanks," he said. "I'll remember that." He sipped his coffee, grateful for the progress despite the knot of guilt for his lies. Well, part lies, anyway; there'd been some truth laced in, much as he could spare. Far too much lately of that sort of thing, of half-truths. For weren't they then but half-lies, and once any measure of dishonesty were attached to a thing, did that not sully the whole affair? But the touchstones he'd always carried were evaporating as quickly as the steam spiraling from the rim of his mug.

They ate silently for a bit, and what occasional conversation did arise was of casual, non-Danny Marcus things — the trout, the cold, the need for good boots in weather like this. When they finished eating, Francine brought the bills.

"Please," said Jacob. "I want to take care of it, for everyone." He pulled his wallet from his back pocket, withdrew a C-note, and sheepishly pushed it across the counter.

The woman to his left kept muttering, but looked up and smiled briefly.

"Obliged," said Flint, returning his own wallet to his pocket.

The man who'd eyed Jacob's boots nodded his appreciation.

Francine snatched up the bill, seemingly impressed, then went to the register for change.

"Please," Jacob said, "keep it. You've been most helpful."

Francine paused, and glanced at her boss.

Harold nodded, shrugged.

"Well, thank you so much," said Francine. "Please let us know if we may be of any help during your stay."

"You have been," said Jacob. "I would only ask if you could point me a little more clearly on my way. Where exactly is Marcus on that mountain? Is there a road, a path?"

"Just one," said boot man. "And it ain't much." He extended a hand, which Jacob shook. "I'm Parsons. Not wise to try it, unless you know your way." He nudged Flint. "We do."

"Great," Jacob said. He turned and peered through the frosted windows. "Can you tell me?"

Parsons glanced at Flint, then regarded Jacob with glinting eyes. "We can do better than that."

Chapter 7 – Ascending

Jacob was beyond exhausted, but if he'd slept, it wasn't much, more a fitful purgatory from which he emerged more drained. He dressed in tallow lamplight before stepping out into the cold and dark of a day yet come, and walked back to the diner as Parsons and Flint had instructed. They already sat inside drinking coffee, and a steaming mug awaited him. He sat and warmed his hands, and drank. They ate steak and eggs, and Francine refilled their coffee, complaining all the while about having to return so damn early.

After they'd eaten, Francine brought the bill, and after a glance from Parsons, laid it before Jacob. He took no umbrage: they were giving up their Saturday to shepherd him up the mountain, and had declined his offer of compensation. He paid the bill, and when they ventured back out into graying dawn, Flint pointed toward the mountain range that seemed to be materializing about a mile off.

"We'll head there," he said, then gestured toward a nearby pickup truck. "We can drive a ways, then it's on foot." They threw their gear into the bed of the truck and climbed into the cab, then Jacob squeezed in between his two chaperones.

When they reached the base of the mountain, Flint pulled over in a lot and motioned them out. They stood by the hood, Flint and Parsons cupping their hands to their mouths to light their smokes. The wind lashed them as the peaks loomed disdainfully, gray and white and cold, unmoved by the trials of all things below.

"Last chance, mate," Parsons said, expelling a vortex of smoke into the brume of breath and fog. "Are you sure?"

Jacob nodded. "Yeah," he said, his mouth so dry he was unsure he'd made a sound. He turned his head and spat, but nothing would come.

A great howl echoed down now from the unseen peaks. Whether raging wind or some life hunkered within it, Jacob couldn't be sure. They could see their crystal breath, and already his feet burned cold in his boots.

His guides stamped their feet like pack animals.

"Okay," said Parsons, casting Jacob a sideways glance.

They stood a few minutes more, and then Flint and Parsons crushed out their smokes beneath their boots, and all three returned to the truck.

Jacob understood his guides were dubious at best. Engaging them in this matter was risky, but every hour that ticked away appropriated with it layers of comfort and consideration. That they meant to rob him was entirely possible, but if they offered even a sliver of a chance to find his man, he must cling to that sliver.

They wound their way up the west-facing range on what seemed to be some sort of service road. The mountain shrouded them in shadow at first, so much so that it was like night again, but soon day broke, and its first light spilled over the summit like a molten waterfall. Jacob squinted, then shut his eyes. The engine was strong—had to be, out here—but Jacob could feel it fighting the pull of the increasing gradient. The morning coffee had not vanquished his exhaustion, so he tried to rest, but peace would not come. The sunlight seared through his eyelids, transforming in his mind's eye into the flashlight of the dead cop. *What's going on here, fellas?* A gleaming blur. A gasp. Blood.

Jacob's eyes flew open, and he glanced at his hands.

"You okay there, bud?" Flint regarded him.

"I'm okay."

Thirty minutes later, they leveled off and pulled into the modest parking lot of a scenic overlook.

"Hoof it from here," Parsons said.

They grabbed their packs from the bed, and Jacob glanced up at the towering peaks. They'd snaked their way up a good ways, but he was taken aback by the prodigious portion that remained.

Flint nodded toward the tree line.

"No trail?" Jacob inquired.

"No trail," said Flint.

"How does he get to his house?"

Flint and Parsons exchanged glances.

"He keeps to himself," Parsons said. "We don't ask questions. We just told you we could get you there. Coming, or not?"

The vast congress of pines filtered the winds valiantly, but every so often as they climbed, a great blast of frigid air funneled down over them. They proceeded in this manner for an hour, until finally the forest thinned and hazy shafts of light slotted through the gaps among the remaining alpines. Soon, the ground leveled and they stepped out upon a sizable plateau.

Parsons leaned and spat dryly.

Flint turned and took a step back into the forest and, with his back to the them, began to urinate. "Anyone else?" he called back behind him. "Plenty available!" He guffawed, shaking his head in self-appreciation.

When they resumed, the plateau ranged out farther than Jacob had guessed, sprawling for miles, until the horizon of the next crag, so removed from the first as to appear another range entirely. Wildflowers had apparently carpeted the plateau in the summer months, but now, save for the random cluster of violet, they'd been reduced to crystal skeletons of their former selves. They crunched underfoot, compelling Jacob to step gingerly at first.

Parsons had enjoined a brisk pace, straight on for the ridge, it appeared, with Flint close behind.

Jacob hunkered down within his parka and hurried after them. The wind marauded with impunity, causing him to maintain a bead on his convoy through tearing eyes. The terrain rutted in spots, and he stumbled here and there, but remained fixed upon his guides and the towering promontory toward which they strode. At length, he perceived a peculiar black line etched into the land a distance away, cutting across the whole of the plateau, it appeared.

They walked silently a half hour more, their progress slowed incalculably by what felt at times like gale-force winds. They were not small men, but on several occasions, each took to thrusting their arms out sideways to steady themselves, like high-wire acrobats. In between gusts, Jacob glanced up at the crags looming thousands of feet overhead — the "teeth" of the range. White-capped and slate-gray, they tapered down into a sweeping expanse of tundra.

Where the hell is Marcus in all this, Jacob thought. *If he's here at all.*

The strange cuts in the terrain seemed to be expanding, and in the fleeting moments of clarity, Jacob saw that they weren't cuts, but rather the fall-away into a deep-slotted canyon, yet another world, within this world apart.

His knees throbbed, yet he'd little choice but to descend the slope bent-kneed, lest he go cartwheeling down the rest of the way. The canyon fell out into a ripple of considerable alpine slopes laden with spruce and fir. Boulders furred green in spots, slicked cold obsidian in others. The canyon floor appeared a carpet of rusty green and gray, and some white from the dusting of snow off the treetops. A tributary of light wound its way through the tree-shadowed floor of the canyon.

The canyon walls offered welcome windbreaks, but Jacob reckoned cold mountain air pooled in the basin, and as they drew nearer, his suspicions were confirmed. Upon reaching the base, they ambled forth from the shadows like strange forest dwellers and made for the slat of light, for the warmth of it. The hazy shaft seemed to carve the canyon down the middle, its resultant halves like dark, canted walls set aslant.

They walked a while before angling back up into the brush, and then climbed again, the trees inclined at them like bowing minions. The forest crimped in upon them, largely obscuring the daylight.

When, perhaps an hour later, they reached the top of the ridge and stepped wearily out onto the plateau, Flint raised a hand and said, "We can rest a bit."

Jacob nodded, grateful for the reprieve. Part of him bristled, as time was everything now, but he knew there would have to be what would surely prove an elusive compromise in this unhappy odyssey. He must proceed urgently, but if he compelled himself to the point of collapse, all would be lost.

They eased down onto some large, rounded rocks. Jacob's feet ached despite his rugged boots. They drank some water, and Parsons handed Jacob and Flint a beer, and opened one for himself. Hot coffee would have been preferable, but Jacob nodded his thanks and drank. They spoke casually, mostly about beer and girls and some guy at the mill who'd insulted Parsons and would soon have his reckoning. Parsons passed them a second round, and Jacob thought of making more inquiries after Marcus, but refrained. They clearly were disinclined to divulge more, and besides, here they were on the mountain now, and they would either lead him to Marcus, or they wouldn't.

When they resumed their trek, the sun was already angling down toward the west. They hiked alternately across plateaus and up forested slopes, and when perhaps two hours later they came to yet another expanse, evening had fallen. Flickering constellations laced across the blue-back sky.

"Here," said Parsons, stopping.

Jacob eyed him and frowned. "Here, what?"

"We'll make camp here," Parsons replied. "As good a spot as any."

Jacob's eyes widened. "Make camp? We can't reach him tonight?"

Flint and Parsons glanced at one another once more.

"No," Parsons said. "We can't."

They pitched the tent, set out a griddle and some tin pots, and Jacob offered to collect the firewood, but his guides amicably stayed him, insisting one of them would do it, and that he should sit and take a load off. Within twenty minutes, they all sat before a crackling fire.

Jacob held his chilled hands out toward its warmth, more leery of his companions than ever, but in this moment grateful for the light and warmth they had by their hands provided.

CHAPTER 8 – PROVINCE

Jacob's eyes drew hypnotically to the crackling flames that rose and cowered with each lick of wind. It moved in one moment as a single, blazing entity, the next as a medley of smaller flames which would elongate briefly, conflagrant phantoms seeking an embodiment that would never come. Every now and then, a constellation of errant sparks alighted from the flame, setting off like fireflies into the uncertain darkness, before burning quickly away.

"I appreciate all you're doing," Jacob said, his voice tremulous for the chill. "Is everyone around these parts this generous?"

"There ain't a whole lot of everyone around these parts," said Parsons, glancing briefly at Flint. "But we're a pretty friendly lot."

They'd finished dinner and were seated around the fire at three points through which a triangle might be traced, each of them inclined toward the flames, a beer clasped between both hands.

"Most of us, anyway." Flint put down his beer, removed his gloves and extended his bare hands toward the fire. "There's good and bad in any lot, you know?" He regarded Jacob through the scissoring flames.

Jacob met his gaze. "I know."

They sat silently a while, drinking their beers and warming their hands and listening to the crackling flames. Above the fire, the aspens loomed black and ornate, ink-wrought upon this slate of night. At one point, Parsons rose and fed more branches into the fire, which fleetingly caved in around them, before cracking loudly and rising back up, renewed. Through the sparse gaps in the treetops, a trace of stars glimmered against their blue-black canvas, clearer here than in most places.

Jacob gestured with his head into the blackness, toward the unseen ridge. "Marcus lives up there?"

Flint eyed Parsons. "Yeah," he said. "Each to his own, huh?"

Parsons leaned forward and held his hands closer to the fire. "We've all got our demons. Maybe he just wanted to find himself out here."

"Well," said Jacob. "There doesn't seem a whole lot else to find."

They drank more beer, and fed the fire, and listened to it crackling in a night gone silent save for the wind, and the doleful cries that rode down from fathomless peaks. At one point through a haze of curling smoke, Jacob was sure he saw the face of the officer materialize and stare at him in petition, and his heart jumped, but then an updraft whisked away the smoke, and with it the dead man, and Jacob inclined back toward the fire and exhaled.

Parsons finished another beer, then cast the can into the fire. The flames jumped a moment before falling back upon it, and the can quickly began to blacken and cave.

Jacob stared into the fire. Should he consider that his guides might in fact be good Samaritans after all? He shifted on the log, and grunted as something gouged into his backside. He relocated a few inches over, but when he sat the log bit at him again, and he reached into his pocket and realized it was the jasper. Gabe's jasper. All notions of allowance ran from him like a river of solemnity, in which there coursed no other notion, save one. He would need to choose his next words carefully.

"I need to go to the bathroom," he said.

The men eyed him through the quivering flames.

"Then go," said Parsons. He motioned with his head into the darkness. "Plenty of good spots."

Jacob rose from the log, his body aching. "Toilet paper?"

Were he writing the moment, he'd been loath for his protagonist to specify what bodily function beckoned, but articulating the matter to Parsons and Flint—casually, perhaps even crudely—was paramount. The longer the occupation meant the longer before they'd think to go looking for him. There were other details, none less vital than the next, and his mind raced in silent adjudication. He would not return and double back the way they'd come, if he even could—they'd figure his flight to take him back to the car, to the road, and then the hotel, where he would surely alert authorities.

"Sorry, fella," said Parsons. "Plenty of good leaves."

Flint snorted.

Jacob tread a modest distance from the camp and stopped behind a stand of spruce, his back pressed against the trunk of one, a terrible game of hide-and-seek. Gabe had liked to play this game as a young child, even so young as to have once believed covering his face with his own hands shielded him from view of the world.

Were it only that simple.

There were no such reprieves, of course, a lesson all children learned in due course. Life regarded you whether you were ready or not, with favor or rebuke, and just when you finally began to figure this part out, you realized that you were forever the seeker, that neither life, nor fate, nor gods reserved for you any plans, that you and you alone sojourned through this world. The notion of his mortality swept over him, carrying with it thoughts of his wife and son, and he was glad in that moment for the bracing of the spruce. The whole of the distance between them seemed to well up with impossible density and close around his heart like a frozen fist. He dreaded not what might become of him, but what he had become. He gritted his chattering teeth, but they rattled so badly that they slid apart and caused him to bite his tongue, and he winced. He must not succumb to the madness of his task, and each task within it, but rather embrace them, for in each resided critical distraction from his despair, an opportunity to focus on tangible, incremental steps.

He switched on his phone's flashlight, but its illumination seemed drowned in the plumbless dark. He conjured in his mind's eye an image of the plateau and valley and steep escarpment that beckoned, in hopes of forging some semblance of navigation. Traversing such country in peak visibility was treacherous, but he was flying blind. It had been perhaps five minutes. He inhaled deeply, the chilled air burning his lungs, invigorating him. He felt for the jasper in his pocket, squeezed it, then pushed off from the trunk, the void seeming to rise up against him, like the first step upward on a badly listing ship.

He took an immediate starboard turn, and proceeded in a manner he'd estimated roughly parallel to the valley floor. Pace was vital: one brisk enough to put as much distance between them as quickly as possible, yet not so fleet as to divert him from his course, or perhaps headlong into a tree.

Traveling the canyon floor would have been preferable, but those things that cast in its favor—

comparatively unobstructed and bathed in moonlight—might also betray him. He floundered through this sightless, canting gulf, extending his arms before him like a blind man. The jutting trees threw him immediately from his intended, parallel course, and he undertook in his mind the painstaking effort to correct for, to the best of his ability, each such deviation.

It was a helluva thing to think about, so he tried like hell not to—here he was, fleeing in a wilderness he'd never been in, following a path he knew not where, adhering to a province he could not know. He wondered if they'd gotten up to look for him yet. He hadn't been gone long, but if they meant him harm, then they were men of a type who didn't wait long, men who trusted no one, least of all one they knew didn't trust them. Time and space pulsed now in wily and indeterminate ways. Jacob knew what happened to folks in situations such as these. He'd heard things, read things, and researched things for his tales. Disorientation and miscalculation prevailed, wild over- and under-estimations of distance traveled or time elapsed. He suspected that in his caution he'd progressed rather less than what it felt, but what if not? What if he'd overshot and would soon find himself plunging into the darkness? His plan—unfixed though it was—called for him to travel most, but not all, of the forest, before finally chancing a segue across the far end of the canyon floor.

He was going forward, not back. As the knife-edged branches assailed him, it was not lost upon him—it gnawed deeper, in fact, the farther he went—that fleeing might have been a grave mistake. The mountain seemed to be swallowing him—the sort of thing that killed you. The sort of thing where his frozen body would be discovered months later, if at all. But he pressed on, for what choice did he have now? Find his way back to camp and offer some implausible excuse? No, he would go forward. The mountain might kill him, but Flint and Parsons might too, and hell if he was going to sit around awaiting it.

A few minutes later, he stopped, caught his breath, then trailed down toward the tree line. He paused upon reaching it, an odd reticence curdling within him. The canyon floor sat aglow in moonlight, and were his guides eyeing this swath, he'd be illuminated as though by search light. But he'd no choice, and when he stepped from the tree line, the cold, pale light suffused him, and he strode briskly toward the far end of the canyon. Leaves crunched and the occasional twig snapped underfoot, frightfully loud.

When he reached the opposite end of the clearing, the bowing trees welcomed him like an army of shadowed scarecrows—back into darkness, a new comfort. He was sweating, and this was not good. Sweating from stress and exertion, but it was freezing, and more so with every upward step. It occurred to him that the goal of eluding his guides and finding his way back down the mountain was quickly reshaping into one of locating shelter and surviving the night. Then, as the slope leveled off into a clearing, he spied a clutch of shadows. It seemed an illusion at first, this illumination of dark within dark, but as he stared, heart hammering and brain churning, it registered that nothing could throw its own shadow without some presence of light.

Now, as he fought to catch his breath against the cold burning in his chest, he found it, faint at first, flickering, but there it was: a small but certain glow, and forming darkly around it the unmistakable silhouette of a window. The Marcus place—it had to be. Jacob shook his head, amazed by both his fortune and the idea that anyone had managed to build a home up here, much less wanted to. But then, who was he to say? God's country, Francine had said. Maybe a man went up a mountain less on account of what might be found, than be forgotten.

He edged across the clearing toward the light. Perhaps Marcus had heard him. Perhaps one who lived on the mountain became as one with it, attuned to its sounds and rhythms and those that did not belong. Perhaps he'd detected Jacob and quietly registered him within the sights of a firearm. Whether Marcus was the type to own one, he couldn't know, but it would hardly be surprising, given the requirements of a life up here. He was wide-open in the clearing, and though he could perhaps veer wide and angle back through the periphery of timber encircling the home, he pressed straight on.

He exhaled upon making it to the front of the cabin, and took a quick look around. A worn-looking jeep sat upon a dirt driveway that led out to a road. Of course, there was a road. Flint and Parsons had lied.

He knocked sharply upon the door, his heart kicking into a gallop, then took a step to the side. He wanted something to happen, and quickly — not a gunshot, certainly, but something. For Marcus to call out or pull open the door, but now he imagined himself in the shoes of this man who'd fled to this inhospitable peak, imagined the surprise and anxiety he might feel upon this perhaps unprecedented rapping upon his door. One didn't live in such a place to be called upon.

Noises now sounded from behind the door; someone was coming. The knob began to turn, then paused. Jacob swallowed, and took one more step to the side.

Chapter 9 – Lost

"Who's out there?" The voice sounded suspicious, guttural.

"My name is Jacob Fallon. I—" He stopped, lost as for what should come next.

"What do you want?" the voice growled.

"I'm lost," Jacob called back.

The knob twisted again, paused again, and then the door swung open. A rectangle of yellow light spilled out across the porch and Jacob braced, more than a little expecting the barrel of a shotgun to breach the doorway next. It did not. Instead, framed there in the tallow light of the doorway stood a man he knew from the photo to be Danny Marcus. About Jacob's size, and, from the looks of it, about his age, though with features greatly weathered by the elements into which he'd immersed himself, so that at first glance he might be mistaken for a much older man.

Marcus peered out at Jacob with narrowed eyes, and motioned with a crook of his head. "Come into the light," he said.

Jacob did, extending his hands from his side, in unmistakable view. "I'm sorry to disturb you," he said. "But I am glad I found you."

Marcus eyed him silently a moment before furrowing his brow. "How the in the name of all things holy did you stumble your way up here?" He craned his neck and peered about into the darkness from which Jacob had materialized.

"I don't know," Jacob said. "Like I said, I got lost. I was hiking, the weather worsened, I panicked a bit. Guess I should have tried to retrace my steps back down the mountain, but I got disoriented."

Marcus eyed him for several uncomfortable moments. "Well, that can happen easy enough. Hiking by yourself? That's not always a great idea, especially if you don't know the mountain." He nodded at Jacob's hand, the one with his ring. "Where's your family?"

"Back home," Jacob said. "I'm a writer. Wanted to get away from things, maybe get some inspiration."

Marcus nodded languidly. "Well, I can relate to that. The getting away part, anyway." His eyes fixed momentarily upon some indeterminate point in the darkness. "Come on in, then," he finally said.

Jacob nodded his thanks and stepped into the cabin. He felt badly, but he hadn't lied, not exactly. More a case of notable omissions.

Bloody hell. What have I become, plying myself with such dissembling? A lie is a lie, no matter how dressed, and into what peril have I now placed this welcoming stranger?

A lone bulb hung from the ceiling in the living room, but its pale glow seemed garish.

"I already ate," said Marcus. "But I got leftovers, if you're hungry." He stood at the edge of the kitchen.

"Very kind, but no thank you."

"I can put some coffee on."

"If it's no trouble," Jacob said. He didn't much fancy the idea of more caffeine, but craved the warmth, and an opportunity to talk.

"How much trouble could it be?" Marcus flicked on the kitchen light and disappeared.

Jacob removed his coat. Gingerly, for he ached all over. He waited a few moments but then edged over to the front window, through which the faint, yellow glow had just minutes previous proven his salvation. A simple couch abutted the lower portion of the pane. He glanced out—toward what end, he couldn't be sure. Distinguishing anything in the pitch of night from his palely lit vantage was impossible, and besides, did he expect Parsons and Flint to be standing there waving in plain sight? Still, he looked, guilt welling within him. Running water and more clinking came from the kitchen. Perhaps they'd assume his flight to have been back down the mountain, but who could say? This world into which he'd stumbled, and this burden that compelled him, were nothing if not lawless. Justus might have set this infernal plot in motion, but Jacob had borne it to the doorstep of an innocent.

"Won't be long."

Jacob snapped around, eyes widening for the briefest of moments in his initial misapprehension.

Marcus stood at the edge of the kitchen, a soothing fragrance suffusing the cabin, and nodded to the table in the living room.

Jacob moved from the window and slid his coat over one of the chairs, and they sat.

Marcus looked him over. "Writer, huh?"

"Yeah." They studied each other. Jacob wondered if he were the first save Marcus to sit there. The coffee burbled in the kitchen. "What about you?"

Marcus cocked his head. "I survive," he said. "Used to do remote computer stuff for a company, but not anymore. Connection up here is spotty as hell, as you might reckon. Anyway, saved my money from that and my younger days, and I just live now. My expenses are low. What do you write?"

"Novels," Jacob said. "Fiction. Out here seeking inspiration." He nodded at Marcus. "What brought you up here?"

A low whine sounded from the kitchen and Marcus pushed back from his chair. "How do you like it?" he called back.

Jacob managed a faint grin. It was nice to consider such things. "A little milk, if you've got it."

Marcus returned with two steaming mugs. "What's your book about?"

Jacob took a sip. He owed this man answers; more than answers, really. He owed him truth, and though he'd adorned things thus far with as much of it as possible, full disclosure was out of the question. But at the very least he must endure and engage this serve and volley, if he'd any hope of gleaning what was needed to fulfill this leg of the task. "Redemption." He took another sip. "Or so I thought. But lately, I've been thinking there may be more to it."

Marcus eyed him. "More to what?"

"Everything. Redemption. Loss. I'm thinking my protagonist must learn that, about what really matters in this world. The depth of anguish when they're lost."

Marcus seemed to be considering this. "Does he find it again?" he asked. "Redemption? Of the kind you mean?"

Jacob stared into his beverage. "I really don't know."

Marcus nodded, accepting this implicitly. "We may be writing very similar stories," he said.

Jacob looked up from his coffee. "You're writing one too?"

"Aren't we all?"

GOSPEL

Their mugs had drawn low, and Marcus went to the kitchen to retrieve the pot.

Jacob rose too and went to the window and peered into the darkness. The moonlight sifting down through the treetops hung about like smoke. Beyond the clearing loomed the shadowed imprints of the highest peaks of the range—the Beartooth portion.

"You keep looking out there." Marcus stood with the coffeepot.

Jacob returned to the table and sat. He pressed his hands around the piping vessel and nodded his thanks as both men sipped and lowered their mugs. "Just wanted to get away from it all—you know, being with nature and such—or something else?" Jacob lifted his mug again and regarded Marcus from across the rim.

Marcus appeared unaffronted but in no hurry to respond. His eyes seemed distant, tracing the slow twist of steam curling up from his mug. "Well, that's a story too," he finally said. "What sends a man up a mountain can be as long as the mountain itself."

Jacob nodded. "I'm glad to listen," he said, and took another sip.

Marcus cupped both hands around his mug. "I don't know," he said. "I don't get down to town too often, and when I do, folks seem to know better than to ask me things." He eyed Jacob. "And it never really struck me I might have visitors up here."

"Fair enough," said Jacob.

He should let it be for the moment. That Marcus was even considering confiding, that he'd even welcomed him inside, boded more favorably than he might have expected. Despite the urgency—an urgency of which Marcus must remain unaware—Jacob must not in this moment overreach. Whatever compelled a man to an existence of such remove, that existence was, unavoidably, an honest one. The mountain and its inhabitants, the darkness and the bone-chilling winds, the solitude—each of these things singular and raw. It struck Jacob that one did not finesse an existence on the mountain so much as carve it out, for to make it up here required a person to be every bit as singular and raw as each element around him.

They sipped their coffee and did not speak. At length their mugs drew low, but when Marcus gestured with the coffeepot, Jacob demurred, and Marcus nodded and did not refill his own mug either. They sat listening to the rise and fall of the wind, and to the lupine calls which rose upon it, setting forth down the mountain in haunting, beautiful refrain. Jacob felt himself relaxing—incongruous a notion though it was— but it made a bit of sense, too. He was spent, mentally and physically, reposing quietly in the warm, soft light, out of the squalling elements. He could see why Marcus had chosen this place, and perhaps that was something to build on. Perhaps he could take that and run with it, cull and shape from it a likely story, a compelling one, bringing to bear every ounce of legerdemain at his disposal.

But, no. In his mind's eye, he saw Justus, back at Sub Rosa, and he could almost hear his voice rising upon the winds along with the forlorn baying. "*Do not make the mistake,*" Justus had said, "*of adjudicating this moment through your writerly lens.*"

Marcus was regarding him intently, as if he'd heard it too.

"Tough childhood?" Jacob asked, not entirely certain why.

"Not at first. Not always." Marcus grabbed the handle of the coffeepot but did not lift it. He stared into the pot, past it, eyes glassy and distant.

Jacob watched him. "Something happen?"

"It's hard for a kid," Marcus said, softly, his gaze still fixed upon the pot. "Childhood ends for everyone, but it's a tough thing when you can say exactly when."

"When was it, for you?"

Marcus narrowed his gaze, and for a moment, Jacob feared he'd crossed the line, but his host's features softened now.

"Thirty years or so," he said.

Jacob nodded, waited, but Marcus seemed in no hurry to offer more. This was, Jacob understood, his prerogative. He cupped his mug, and as he did, his wedding ring glinted in the lamplight.

Marcus gestured with a nod of his head. "Married man."

A knot twisted in Jacob's gut. He touched his ring. "Yeah, and we have a son."

"Very nice," said Marcus. "You two close?"

Jacob felt for the jasper in his pocket. "Yeah, we are."

"That's good," said Marcus. "That's good. A father and son should be close."

Jacob wanted to reply, but his throat caught, so he took a sip of coffee instead.

"Your folks still alive?" Marcus asked.

"Only Dad," Jacob replied. "Mom's been gone awhile."

"What about him," Marcus said. "Your father. You guys close?"

Jacob had started to raise his mug again, but he set it back down. "We used to be," he said, quietly. "When

I was a kid. He left when I was ten or eleven. I can't remember much at all about that time. Maybe been blocking it out."

Marcus sipped his coffee, set it back down. "I'm sorry," he said.

"It's okay," Jacob said. "What about you? I know you're up here alone, but do you... did you...."

"Never married," Marcus said. "I think I could have. I wasn't that Unabomber type whack job you think of when you hear about a guy living alone up on a mountain. I wasn't some tragedy. I hung in there a while. I could talk to people. Had relationships. Got close." He lifted his eyes to Jacob. "But that's the thing, ain't it? Getting close to someone. The closer you get the more it weighs on ya. The more you fear losing them, and then fear becomes paralysis, and then you're done, and you don't want to damage someone else, for the damage been done to you. You know?"

"Yeah," said Jacob. "I think I do."

"I'd offer you something stronger to drink," said Marcus, "but I never touch the stuff. Sorry."

Jacob waved his hand. "No apology needed." He pondered all Marcus had said. "Did you have a problem?"

"Nope." Marcus cast his glance to the window, to the rounding darkness beyond. "Was just leery of the stuff. Seen too many folks get lost looking for answers there. I wasn't looking for anything. Had seen enough to know I didn't want to see no more."

Jacob fidgeted with his ring and regarded his host. He'd worried greatly about striking a plausible — and agreeable — demeanor, but it was a needless worry just now. He perceived in Marcus a great reservoir of despair, despair borne of loss, and the man before him in many ways a construction of walls around this void. Strong walls, tough, but enduring within them that endless hollowing that besets the most grief-stricken souls. And sitting there in the faint dome of lamplight, listening to the howling wind and baying wolves, there was no demeanor to be conjured, for in Jacob's own soul, a self-same hollowing had begun.

"May I ask," he said to Marcus, "what it was you saw?"

Marcus studied him. "You may," he said. "But I ain't likely to answer." He leaned forward in his chair. "It ain't you, hear. It's me, whole way 'round. I plum can't do it. What it was, set my path to right here, right now. Where we sit. I can't do it, see? From fear it may set me tumbling back down that very road." He fixed his eyes upon Jacob's. "We've all seen things in this world, huh? You've the look of someone who's seen his share."

"So, what's the secret?" Jacob leaned forward, entreating. "You go up your mountain, leave the world behind. But it leaves holes, right? Inside. Those you take with you, can't ever outrun 'em. So, then what?"

Marcus grinned unhappily. "Well, you're right as hellfire about that. Can't outrun 'em." He folded his arms behind his head and rocked back in his chair. "I think right about now I'm regrettin' not keeping something stronger here to drink."

Jacob smiled weakly.

"Well, maybe that's it," said Marcus. "Maybe that's the whole thing right there. You can't outrun things. Oh, maybe for a spell, but they catch up to you, sure enough. They catch up and, more often than not, you see they been there all along." He shrugged. "And so maybe it ain't about escaping your demons. Maybe it's escaping everything else. Then it's just you and them, anyway. Maybe there's some peace in that."

Jacob nodded, leaned back in his chair. *Peace.* The word hung in the air, some apocryphal notion. Peace might have brought Marcus here, but his own arrival presaged anything but. *And it's not just that, is it,* he exhorted himself. *Not only do you sit here in this tangle of your own deceit, trespassing upon the refuge this man has made for himself, but you have failed to come to peace with your own truth. You kindle hope, where no hope remains. And whatsoever ignites there will only burn you all the deeper.*

"Well," said Marcus. He'd squared to the table again, and his features had squared too, like someone returned from a journey. "I reckon you're plum tired. I am, sure enough." He nodded at the couch behind Jacob. "You're welcome to it."

"Obliged," said Jacob. "Truly." He wanted more, felt at the precipice of getting more, but Marcus was clearly done.

They pushed back from the table, and Marcus returned the coffee pot to the kitchen while Jacob brought the mugs and placed them in the sink. He waited while Marcus used the bathroom, and then he used it, and when he came out, Marcus was in his bedroom with the door closed. Jacob went to the couch, removed his boots, and sprawled out. It felt heavenly, but then, just about any berth would have seemed the most comfortable in the world about now. His eyes grew quickly heavy, but he willed them back open, and labored into a sitting position. He had work to do.

When the wind kicked up, shadows from the trees twisted upon the ceiling. Shadows, even though the house sat in pitch save for the spectral glow of filtered moonlight that seeped languidly through the curtains.

Would his guides look for him here? If they found him, they couldn't just kill him, right? They'd have to kill Marcus too, and they wouldn't do that, kill one man just to kill the other, all for a wad of cash and pair of boots. Would they?

Jacob rolled his eyes. God help him if he ever wrote something so guileless. Men who killed adhered no such edict. They moved in shadow, like those writhing upon the ceiling, and were themselves as dark. He could afford to assume nothing but the worst, and to assume its most imminent arrival. He opened the notepad on his phone and contemplated the most unusual literary challenge of his life. The silence pressed in upon him with an accusatory burden. Into the chasm swam all manner of calamitous scenarios: that back home his prints had been discovered upon the officer; that Flint and Parsons would find him here; and that this, along with any number of other factors, would prohibit him from successfully completing his task. From saving the life of Danny Marcus, and the others. And just how, exactly, was one to write a life? Any life, much less that of a stranger? Jacob was accustomed to making the case for a protagonist, but to editors, the paramount considerations were of story and character, description and theme. This was different, the pleading out of a man's life before a capricious and uncompromising court.

Then there was the sheer ignominy. Literary supplicant to Justus, who awaited his entreaty with what manner of pen and gavel in hand, Jacob could only wonder.

He waited until it seemed Marcus must be asleep, then began pecking away upon the keypad. He'd intended to use his computer, naturally, but it was back in the hotel room, and every minute was precious. More precious than rest, which at this moment pulled at him achingly. He began to outline the narrative as he would any project, then saw he had no signal. Of course he didn't. He nudged apart the curtains with his fingers and peered out into the darkness.

He'd considered going to the authorities with the drop box provided him, but Justus would have thought of that, of course, and had made clear to Jacob the consequences of any such attempt. And where was Justus? Lounging in the same hotel, perhaps, or poised somewhere outside the cabin of an oblivious man? Perhaps nowhere close at all. He could be anywhere, but had come to feel very much like everywhere.

Guilt flayed at Jacob's insides, knowing the man who'd sheltered him on this desperate evening might not live to see another. Needing to conserve battery, he powered down the phone, slipped it into his pocket, and nudged apart the curtains to watch for movements. Only darkness stared back, seeming to swallow him up, as had this mountain. He should really stay awake, to keep watch, but the exertions of this day—of the last several days—overtook him, carrying him away on dulcet, if uncertain, tides.

His dreams were fleeting, but at one point he thought he saw his own face hovering outside the window amid a covey of others, each ghost-like and inquiring of the slumbering figure inside. Sometime later, he startled awake to a ghastly wailing, and it took a good few moments to remember where he was and realize it was only the wind, gale-force and bitter, sucking down the face of the mountain and barreling through the aspens, which bent and moaned in protest. He'd felt bitter winds before, wicked straight-line winds that had nearly toppled him and blown off siding and wrested fragile tree limbs, but this was something different. This was wind with an exponent, a downhill tempest squalling and untamed, and the cabin moaned now too, moaned and creaked and contracted, and lying there in the cold, gray spill of moonlight, Jacob shuddered, and pulled the thin blanket over his rapt and unblinking eyes.

***

He feels immediately the pull of the river. The children are clustered shoulder to shoulder along either side of the raft, fidgeting this way and that, craning their necks to catch every view.

"See that!" calls one boy. "Trout. Big 'un."

One man is propped at the back of the raft, oar in hand, watching the river. The boy's father leans at the bow, every so often jabbing his oar into the river, rowing first port side, then starboard. He does so again, before pulling his oar back and looking ahead as the river pulls them forth.

The children laugh and nudge each other over various observations. Not a care in the world.

The boy cavorts along with them, likewise unperturbed, though he remains attuned to the power of the current. He can't help but feel how small and at its mercy they are. Exhilarating, more than anything. They veer slightly toward some reeds, scaring up a squawking flock of gulls. The kids point and laugh. It is a wonderful morning.

CHAPTER 10 – MERCY

He woke stiff, slowly unfolded himself from the couch, and stood blinking in the predawn gray.

The smell of coffee and bacon wafted in the air, and from the kitchen sounded the drip and sizzle of both. Jacob peered from where he stood and did not see Marcus, but clearly he was about. He nudged the curtains apart again, and swept his gaze over that portion of land distinguishable in the nascent haze, not quite morning, no longer night—a cold and uncertain hour belonging to no order save its own. No sign of them, but that didn't mean anything. They could be out there, and he shouldn't tarry longer than he had to, in consideration of his host as well as himself.

Marcus treaded into the room, coffee pot in one hand, two clinking mugs in the other, and nodded. "Mornin'."

"Good morning."

"Sleep well?"

"Yes, thank you." A harmless embellishment. Truth was, the fitfulness of his slumber was hardly the fault of his unwitting host, and fitful or not, reclining on a couch inside a warm cabin beat the hell out of fleeing through dark and inhospitable terrain.

They ate silently. The mountain seemed scarcely awakened. When they finished, they carried the dishes to the kitchen, and Marcus offered to escort him back down the mountain, whenever he was ready. Jacob froze. A ride would save him incalculable time, as well as better his chances at a safe return—a warm, safe ride, as opposed to another frigid, uncertain trek.

But, no. What if they were intercepted on the way down? Marcus would be imperiled, in addition to himself. He could not chance it.

"That is extraordinarily kind," said Jacob, "but no thanks. I've imposed far too severely as is."

"People help each other," Marcus said, flatly. "If they got any decency to 'em, anyway."

"True enough." The sun had at last breached the summit, and Jacob shifted in its light, as if Marcus might deduce something which, until now, had remained obscured. "And I am grateful. But I want to hike around a bit more, I think. Connect with the mountain, and all, you know? For my writing. I can manage. But I do appreciate it."

Marcus shrugged. "Suit yourself, friend. Stick to the road, when you do head down, you hear?"

They shook hands.

"Thank you," Jacob said. "For everything."

He started down the canted road. The fire of breaking day broke over the mountain and spilled down the slope, bursting through the aspens in brilliant, golden shafts. Jacob raised a hand to his eyes as he went. He thought of the officer, saw his face, wide-eyed with horror, substantiating upon this cold and distant reach. He stiffened, breathed in the frigid mountain air with freezing lungs and pounding heart. The sun was blinding, and he veered into the woods a short ways for the filtering the foliage would provide. He would keep the road in sight.

He thought of his family, always there with him, whether front of mind or just beneath the surface, even as he was distracted by the enormity of his present burden. He grimaced, angry. The distraction incensed him as much as the task itself. He wanted to call them. He checked his phone: still no signal. He would call from the hotel. Another grimace, in contemplation of the lies he must tell, about where he was, about his father.

A twig snapped somewhere nearby and he flinched, and looked about. A small bird stepped about in the leaflitter. It paused and met his gaze. Jacob moved on, but now a loud snap sounded beneath him, and he glanced down and saw he'd trodden upon a fallen branch, and when he looked back up a moment later, Flint stood in front of him pointing a revolver at his head.

"I thought you was a dodgy bastard," said Flint. He chuckled and spat, then cupped his free hand to the side of his mouth. "Found him!" His call rang out and echoed before drowning out upon the gusts.

"I thought you were too," Jacob said.

Flint chuckled again and waggled the revolver. "Yeah, well, you were right about that, sure enough. But I'm the dodgy sum-bitch with the gun."

They stared at one another. Jacob watched Flint's eyes shifting this way and that, watched his feet shuffling beneath him, saw his finger twitching on the trigger, and understood implicitly that Flint was not a steady or calculating man. He was a shifting, shuffling, twitching individual who might pull the trigger at any moment and without compunction. Jacob saw and understood all this, but now his mind's eye ranged up and over the aspens so that he was seeing it all — seeing himself — from great remove. But the him on the mountain, with the gun leveled at his head, did nothing at all.

Life requires action sometimes, his wife had said.

Then he saw Marcus.

In the sliver of time his brain had processed the initial movement, he'd presumed it Parsons, but it was Marcus, and he was wielding a log and bursting through a cluster of aspens and swinging it at Flint, who had only just himself registered the disturbance and begun to whirl about.

Flint was too late, and the log crashed into his head with a sickening thud. Flint screamed, and the gun fired wildly before falling from his hand. As he collapsed to the ground, the shot echoed down the mountain.

Marcus stood over Flint's crumpled frame, wide-eyed and panting and wielding the log, as if Flint at any moment might spring back to his feet.

This was not to be. Flint lay before them, spasming slightly, a rivulet of blood tracing away from his head.

"The gun," gasped Marcus. "Get the gun."

Jacob did so, and as he bent for the revolver, he looked at Flint and froze. The right side of Flint's head, and part of his face, was cloved into a yawning, crimson cavity. Jacob picked up the gun and held it, dangling.

Marcus stepped closer and looked down at Flint.

"We have to help him," Jacob said softly.

Marcus looked up. "Past the point of no return," he said. He dropped the log. "I didn't mean to kill him, but he sure enough was even money to do you the same."

"Thank you," Jacob said.

A resounding pop. Jacob dropped the revolver but knew he hadn't fired it, and when his mind snapped back to coherence, he looked past Marcus and saw Parsons stumbling out from the tree line, leveling his weapon for another shot. Jacob's first thought was not to retrieve the gun but to hit the ground, yet when he did so, he saw the gun right there, grabbed it, and kept rolling until he reached the next flight of trees. He crouched behind an aspen and sighted the weapon.

Parsons, in turn, had sighted his upon Marcus, who had in this moment neither weapon nor shelter at his disposal. Parsons moved haltingly to where Flint's body lay unmoving, keeping his gun leveled at Marcus all the way.

"Yous sons of bitches," he said.

"For defending ourselves?" Marcus said.

"Shut the fuck up!" Parsons looked past Marcus. "You better come outta there, or I'll kill him!"

"Don't mind him," Marcus called back behind him. "He's gonna do it anyway."

Parsons sneered. "Look at him," he said, wagging the gun and grinning toothily. "Cowering. You and me both know he ain't never fired no gun." He stepped closer to Marcus and pointed the gun at his head.

"You may be right," said Marcus. "But how does it feel knowing you're gonna be his first?"

Parsons' face drained and his lips bunched sideways in a snarl. "He'll miss," he spat. "Hell, he probably won't even shoot."

Jacob sprang from his haunches, strode forward, and leveled the revolver. "I'm out of time," he told Parsons, almost apologetically. "And so are you."

Parsons sneered, but Jacob read in his eyes the first seeds of doubt. He saw him start to step closer to Marcus, and understood in a heartbeat what Parsons intended—he would make Marcus a shield, and dare the first-time shooter not to miss. His brain began to process from its accustomed place of remove, but something within him interceded, and his body roused into action. His arm rose in tandem with his stride, fluid, certain, and he felt the tension rippling through his forearm and into the gun itself, and when a fraction of a second later the weapon was head-level with Parsons, he fired, and Parsons—not even having finished his second step toward Marcus—flew back and lay twitching upon the hardened earth.

The shot echoed over the mountain. Jacob felt it ring inside of him and knew instantly that it would do so for the rest of his days.

Marcus stepped over to Parsons—who was no longer twitching—and after regarding him a moment, looked back at Jacob. "Holy hell," he said.

Jacob eyed the revolver, which sat smoking at the edge of his still outreached arm. He lowered it slowly, wanted to cast it away, but wary of an accidental discharge, he placed it down delicately, then stood back up and swept his gaze over the bodies of the two men who'd led him up the mountain.

"Both dead?"

Marcus looked only at Jacob. "Dead as it gets," he said. "And I think it's my turn to thank you."

Jacob shook his head. "No," he said. "No. This is my fault. They were up here because of me."

He looked at Marcus, not knowing how he could meet his gaze, only that he must. When he did, he saw in it no measure of the reproach he unquestionably deserved. Only the acceptance of one who'd long ago learned life, in its immutable path, had a way of casting us wayward from our own. Marcus held up a hand, and Jacob understood explanation was neither required nor preferred. There was only the matter of what must now be done.

"Do you think anyone heard it?" Jacob said. "Think anyone will come?"

"I've shot bears away before," Marcus said, calmly. "I don't think anyone would think much of it. If anyone even heard."

Jacob nodded.

"But still," Marcus said, "we can't just leave 'em."

"You're in this because of me," Jacob said quietly. "We'll handle it however you say."

Marcus looked like he wanted a cigarette, or a drink. He looked at Jacob. "It seems to me you're in something of a hurry to be on your way. You must have good reason. And I think you'll not be surprised to hear I'd as soon dispose of this matter as quickly as possible."

The ground was too hard in which to bury them, so they dragged the bodies a quarter mile to one of the deep crevasses. Snaking crimson traces marked the path they'd come.

Jacob peered down into the precipitous chasm, then turned to Marcus. "Shouldn't we say something?"

Marcus, panting from the exertion, studied him. "You a man of faith?" he asked.

Jacob didn't answer.

"Well," said Marcus. "We should say something anyway."

The dead men stared up at the rising sun, as if astonished to find it there, or to have in turn been found. They seemed to Jacob in this repose strangely more knowing than at any time previous.

"Kill anyone before?" Marcus asked, with an unnerving dispatch, as if there was a fair chance of it. When Jacob didn't answer, Marcus said, "Me neither. Guess neither of us is the killing type, until today."

"What are you saying?"

Marcus regarded the bodies. "Ain't saying nothing but that we've done."

"Something I never thought I'd do," said Jacob.

"Well, that's the thing, right?" Marcus looked back up at him, hopeful. "We didn't neither of us have time for thought. It was kill or be killed, and we did what we had to do to both still be standing here discussin' it." He regarded the bodies. "Right? That's the difference there, between us and other men who done it. Men who think about it first, and still go and do it."

Jacob pondered the gawking eyes of the deceased. "I reckon so."

Marcus glanced slantways at him. "They have families?"

"They told me no."

Marcus nodded. "Let's hope that's true. Still, they're each of them somebody's son. Brother maybe. Uncle."

"Yeah."

Marcus folded his arms and bowed his head, so Jacob did likewise.

"Lord, you work in mysterious ways," Marcus said. "I know that sure enough. I'll never know when and why you call home one of your children, but as for these two men, we ask you show them mercy, such as that they lacked themselves to show us." Marcus blinked up at Jacob a moment, to see if he'd anything to add.

Jacob shook his head.

"Amen," said Marcus.

Marcus straightened, and they nodded to one another and rolled the bodies into the breach, and listened to them drop like whispers into the fathomless depths below. They dropped in the revolvers too, and went back for the log Marcus had used, and dropped it in. Then they gathered brush and other logs, and a few large stones, and dropped them in as well. When it was done, they looked to one another, and into the land around them for answers that could not come.

Jacob felt for the jasper in his pocket. "I have to go," he said.

"I'll take you," said Marcus.

"Not sure how I can ever thank you."

"How about next time you need some inspiration, don't come looking for it here."

"Fair enough."

They hiked back up to the cabin and cleaned themselves up, used the bathroom, drank water and coffee. When they climbed into the old jeep and set off, Jacob saw things once more from that celestial remove: three men gone up a mountain, two men coming down. Including one who would return up it, to that home and life he'd forged beneath its peaks.

When he entered his hotel room, he powered up his laptop and set immediately to writing.

> *There's no pretty writing here, and I don't right now care if you like it or not. Two men tried to kill me today, and I killed one of them. Killed him. Something that will haunt me for the rest of my days. All on account of this sick game of yours. Danny Marcus killed the other. I've scarcely slept in days and I don't even know what day it is now, but that's what I can tell you. I killed a man and Danny Marcus killed the other, to keep him from killing me. Danny Marcus, who lives on a mountain, because of something that happened very long ago. He doesn't trust anyone, just wants to be left alone, and he had no reason to help me, but he did. That's what I've got to say about Danny Marcus, and you can make of it what you will.*

GOSPEL

He'd fallen asleep within moments of his dispatch, but his slumber was fitful, visited throughout by dead men who shouldn't be. In the cheap hotel with its flimsy curtain, the morning light filtered through easily the next morning and bathed him in its glow, and he allowed himself a moment to savor it before lifting his phone to his eyes to receive the next installment of his fate.

Sure enough, Justus's response materialized and he clicked it open.

> *Your message is received. Hope you got a spot of rest. Eat something, and meet me at the Black Iron Ranch, off Highway K, no later than noon.*

He cursed, and resisted an urge to cast the device hard as he could into the wall. Who was this man, to compel him into such allegiance? Just a man, like him, and like any man, mortal, fallible. Yes, he'd wantonly murdered the cop, but this only made him an evil man, insidious, but hardly unconquerable. He would call the authorities, then would call Anabel and Gabe. He'd tell them he was coming home to see them.

He lifted the phone and dialed. Anabel answered and Jacob seemed to watch from afar, threaded by invisible bonds to a woman two thousand miles away, and to whom he would remain so, even should she relinquish her end. Even if she already had.

"Jacob?" Her voice disarmed him, as always, even if in this moment freighted with things not each of them pleasant.

Not ever had he encountered a soul who with one word or one look could evoke so much. With one gesture. With no gesture at all. Could set the fault lines of his own soul so easily to spasm. He told her things were going decently all in all and though he was prepared for her to inquire of him many things, she did not, and before he could say much of anything else at all, told him Gabriel wanted to say hi.

"Daddy?" Sheepish. Inquiring. Perhaps uncertain his father was really there.

"Gabriel," he said, trying to sound as much like himself as possible.

He thought to tell him that he would be coming home soon, but the boy had launched already into an animated accounting of his last few days: of getting to stay up late with Grandpa; of a dream he had about a cowboy on a horse; of playing outside the previous afternoon at school. His voice sang with an earnestness known only in the hearts of children. A flawless and unfettered grounding in the moment. In its living, and now, in its telling. Jacob listened and was overcome, not just for that which his son told, but that he was telling it, for the heavenly simplicity of it, of a father hearing his son—a few gilded, unspoiled moments. And in a few moments more, he would tell his son he'd be coming home, and hear about all of these things and any such things as the boy so wished, face to face.

"...and a few days ago, we played kickball and there was this strange man watching us, but then it started raining and Miss Tuttle came over and made us go in."

Jacob felt his face drop. "What strange man?" he rasped, doubling over, for he felt he might be sick, but nothing came up, and he straightened.

"Just some man standing outside the fence at recess," Gabe said. "I had to go get the ball and he smiled at me and he was kinda creepy but also cool, like a cowboy or something. He had black gloves."

Jacob tried to speak but no words came, only those of Justus, metered out upon the unwilling canvas of recent memory.

The wolf shall dwell with the lamb....

"Daddy?"

"I'm here, Gabriel."

"Is everything okay?"

"Yeah." Jacob cleared his throat. "It is."

"Okay. I love you, Daddy."

The boy's words, and the undeserved faith that compelled them, pierced Jacob through.

"I love you too, Gabriel. Always."

***

The irony was not lost upon Jacob: that a better place might not exist to escape everything, than that chosen by the one he so desperately wished to elude — dreamlike in its remoteness, this unbroken range, carpeted far as he could see in tall and golden grasses, and wildflowers still purple save for silvery clusters, where they leaned glistening in their frosty sheaths like sculpted blossoms. The sky high and deep-set and blue, except where unfurled here and there billowing, alabaster scrolls. Nothing else between heaven and earth, but quiet uncertainty.

Along the periphery of this range jutted a protracted expanse of fence-line, dark-hued and tall and extending well beyond Jacob's vision. Directly ahead of him, perhaps a hundred yards, Justus leaned upon this latticework with his back to Jacob and arms outstretched to either side so that, given his own dark attire, he might have been part of the fence itself. Jacob stared out where small plumes of dust alighted from a spot a hundred yards farther still, and traced his sight along Justus's own, and made out a bucking mustang, and a cowboy, lasso in hand, endeavoring mightily to wrangle the huge and vaulting equine.

"It's great theatre," Justus called behind him, when Jacob had neared to maybe twenty feet. "Join me."

He did. "Stay the fuck away from my son," Jacob said.

"You do appreciate you are not in the best of positions to be making demands," Justus said. "Well look at that!" He nodded out toward horse and rider, where the latter had for the moment ensnared the beast and was easing gently toward it.

"I don't care," said Jacob. He turned to Justus.

Justus did not turn but nodded once more. "And you are prepared, if necessary, to face the consequences of that conviction? To die for it, perhaps?"

"Try me," Jacob said.

Another nod, and now Justus withdrew a cigar from his vest, and a matchbook. "Good," he said. "That is living. That is good." He clenched the stogie between his teeth and slashed at the fencepost, and the match popped and flared into effulgence. Justus raised it, bent his head, and cupped his hand for the light. He raised back up a moment later, snuffed and ditched the flame, and expelled a tight coil of rings. "Freud spoke of horse and rider, do you know?" His eyes remained fixed, almost wistfully, upon the range. The hand had steadied the great horse, which snuffled and stamped, raising little vortexes of dust, but looked to be otherwise calming. "No matter how skilled, no matter the prowess—" Here Justus paused once more in his exhalation. "—and clearly this man possesses it—he can only so well and for so long suppress the raw nature of the beast. He is the ego, fighting valiantly, but in the end vainly, to control the id."

Jacob gritted his teeth, in no mood for parable. But perhaps there was a clue there, something in this man's discourse suggesting even faintly his identity and motivations. At any rate, he'd little choice but to endure it.

"Your submission," Justus said now, "is approved. Mr. Marcus, I might add, is indebted to you that it is. I am granting my dispensation not because he has demonstrated the requisite appreciation for his life, but because of your appreciation of his role in preserving yours." He angled toward Jacob, the tip of the cigar burning hellishly at his draw.

Jacob exhaled, deeply, despising the obeisance suffused within this moment.

"How did it feel?" Justus asked, eying him intently. "Killing a man?"

"I didn't feel anything," Jacob said, quietly, as if his words might, like fallen leaves, rise upon a sudden wind, borne off across this vast and fathomless place, to that judgment which might await. "Not when I did it. He was gonna kill us. All I could think of was Gabriel. All I could think of was making it back to my son. I just pulled the trigger, and now a man is dead."

Justus's eyes burned for a moment like the glowing rim of his cigar. "And at no other moment have you ever been more alive."

Jacob shook his head. "No," he said. "No."

Justus smiled, shrugged, and turned back toward the range. The cowboy had eased a saddle onto the mustang and was still stroking the animal, talking to it.

"You prevailed in that moment," Justus said between draws, "because you surrendered to nature.

Put ego aside. Oh, we can carry on all we'd like, most times even get by with it. The world expects as much." Another plume of rings rose as, out on the range, the cowboy prepared to mount. Justus glanced edgewise at Jacob. "The world is wrong."

"I don't know," said Jacob, observing the uneasy detente between man and beast. "I think it's worth the effort. He seems to be doing pretty well."

Justus nodded. "He does indeed. This time. Maybe the next thousand times. But eventually, the horse will throw him, or worse. And even if it never does, the fury of that spirit broken will plague him for the rest of his days."

"So, what would you have then? Everyone just indulge their every impulse, their basest nature? What you propose is chaos."

"To the contrary," said Justus. He checked the cigar, which had drawn down perhaps a third of the way. "I propose the kind of order only achievable when that nature is obeyed. We can continue the charade only so long. Easy when the road is smooth. Only in our darkest times are all things tested, when all pretense and luxury are stripped away and we stand bare, with only our truest nature to guide us. Only then is the curtain pulled back. Only then are we finally and truly free."

Jacob shook his head and watched the rider break into a slow trot.

"At any rate," said Justus, pulling his timepiece from another pocket of his vest. "I hope you managed some rest." He snapped the timepiece shut. "Your flight to Kolkata departs today."

CHAPTER 11 – THE DRUID STONE

Though leaving the place, Jacob bore the burden of things done there. He watched the airport and town and even the mountains shrinking away. He'd saved a life and taken one, and had his own preserved—the verdict of this equation yet determined but promised, he was sure, to be gaveled out upon his soul. But for now, no time. He would change planes in New York, then make the trans-Atlantic voyage to Kolkata, where they were scheduled to land at dawn—not one day from now, but two. Kolkata was twelve hours ahead. Five days. One quarter elapsed already of his allotment. He would call on one Reginald Morse, sixty-eight years old, there the last dozen years performing missionary work, from what Jacob had been able to gather from his online searches. That was about all he'd found, only that he'd moved there, not from where—nothing about a family, or any other details.

Something had always unsettled Jacob about missionaries. They did good, and doing good was surely better than doing bad. That they were motivated by faith was itself a harmless, even beautiful thing, but there seemed invariably another side of the coin, one that struck Jacob as the mother of all catches. Water, food, shelter, and all we ask is your soul. For you are either faithless, or of a misguided faith, and while we're here we'll tend to that too. There a difference between doing good for someone, and doing it to them.

He'd managed a few hours of sleep on the plane, but was still exhausted when they landed. Outside the airport roiled a sea of taxis. Scores of passengers crowded nearby, gesturing and whistling and otherwise semaphoring for one of countless bright yellow cabs, knotted and sidling curbside like a giant, chromatic caterpillar—old cabs, like something out of 1950's Cuba.

"First time?" An American, perhaps a few years Jacob's senior, looked friendly enough. "In Kolkata," the man clarified, smiling. "Not hailing a cab. Though I would recommend not doing so here."

"Oh?"

"Can get a little dicey." He extended his hand. "Philip."

"Jacob."

Philip shook out his hand. "Don't mind me. Circulation problems, I fear. Happens dozens of times a day."

"Ah."

"Where you headed, Jacob?"

"Blessed Heart Mission."

"Well, I'll be damned," said Philip.

"You know it?"

"Know of it," Philip said. "I know where it is. I just didn't have you pegged for a missionary, is all. No offense meant."

"None taken," said Jacob. "I'm not a missionary, I'm a writer."

"Well then," said Philip, "I don't feel so bad."

"What do you do?"

Philip withdrew his phone from his pocket and his fingers flew quickly over the screen. "I'm in salvage," he said. "Where are you staying?"

"Not really sure," Jacob said. "Was gonna get a ride to the mission, and take things from there."

"Blessed Heart's not far from where I stay," Philip said. "Walking distance, really, if you can bear the heat."

"I can bear it."

"Well, I've got a car coming," Philip said. "It's a pretty decent hotel. Hop in with me if you'd like."

"Thanks," said Jacob. "I really appreciate that."

"No worries. Gotta look out for one another, huh?"

A sleek sedan pulled up a few moments later, and the driver stepped out from the right side of the vehicle, nodded at them, retrieved their bags and put them in the trunk. He opened the back passenger door and stood grinning as the men clamored inside.

"Shubho shokal," said the driver, turning toward his passengers, touching his fingers to the brim of his cap. The slight man had dark skin and black hair close-cropped beneath a broad flat-cap.

"Good morning," said Philip, and the driver nodded and turned around.

Jacob sat back and stared out his window as they navigated into the day's traffic—vehicular, human, bovine. Yes, cows, and lots of them, some being led, others wandering, all gaunt and sad-looking, and most adorned with necklaces, makeup, or other strange embellishments. At least as many stray dogs about. And monkeys, darting about and chittering with bared teeth, screaming their urgencies to anyone who might listen. No one did. Inured to this roving zoo. A large, colorful bus pulled by, Sanskrit and some English emblazoned on its hull, and everywhere above them rose a cavalry of billboards: beauty products, housing, schools. Concrete, lots of concrete. Rickshaws--motorized and not--trundled through the morass, and stranger yet the numerous mopeds and small motorbikes that weaved in and out, honking, some bearing upon them more passengers than seemed sustainable. Jacob watched all of it go by, peering suspect and alien from behind the glass of his conveyance. Stranger in a strange land. Ferried onward upon this course that ought never have been commenced.

Philip, apparently having seen it all before, smiled and withdrew a book from his satchel.

Jacob titled his head to catch the title. "Sorry," he said. "Writers can be nosy."

Philip turned the cover of the book to Jacob: *Moments of Vision and Miscellaneous Verses*, by Thomas Hardy. "I'm reading one of his poems: Shadows on a Stone. Know it?"

Jacob said he didn't.

"I went by the Druid stone," read Philip. "That broods in the garden white and lone, And I stopped and looked at the shifting shadows That at some moments fall thereon. From the tree hard by with a rhythmic swing, and they shaped in my imagining to the shade that a well-known head and shoulders threw there when she was gardening."

As the vehicle cornered and listed slightly, Philip paused and both men braced themselves. When the vehicle straightened, Philip resumed.

Jacob closed his eyes and took in the warmth of the sun through the windows, the soothing tenor of his cab mate's voice, the elegance of those words he read.

"I thought her behind my back, Yea, her I long had learned to lack. And I said: 'I am sure you are standing behind me, Though how do you get into this old track?' And there was no sound but the fall of a leaf as a sad response; and to keep down grief I would not turn my head to discover that there was nothing in my belief.... You all right, my friend?"

Jacob opened his eyes. "Yes, sorry, just a touch dizzy, but enjoying the poem. Go ahead, please."

"Yet I wanted to look and see that nobody stood at the back of me; but I thought once more: 'nay, I'll not unvision a shape which, somehow, thee may be.' So I went softly from the glade, and I left her behind me throwing her shade, as she were indeed an apparition—my head unturned lest my dream should fade."

Philip closed the book. "What do you think?"

"The poem, or Kolkata?"

"Either."

"Time will tell, as far as this place," said Jacob. "But I did like that poem."

"Do you write poetry?"

"No. I wish I did. I wish I could, but it's hard for me. I admire those who can do it, can distill things down like that, get to the heart of things so concisely and so well. Guess it takes me a novel to say anything."

"Don't be hard on yourself," said Philip. "The world needs both, wouldn't you say? I admire the poets too, but sometimes life warrants a deeper exposition."

Jacob smiled. Beyond the fields alongside which they now rode, a long, mud-colored river snaked past.

"The Hooghly," said Philip. "Or Ganges. Kipling wrote of it. Short story: An Unqualified Pilot." Cliffs rose up beyond the far shore in vast maroon shelves, fissured layer upon layer, millennia upon millennia, indelible. "Impressive, those things which endure."

Their route tracked closer to the river now and Jacob regarded the varied manner of commerce and transport set out upon it. A large trawler was passing, the unfettered sun casting its profile in vivid relief upon the water, like a twin vessel now risen from the river's depths.

When they pulled into the hotel, a doorman hurried over and made to open the back door, but the driver leapt from the vehicle and shooed him away. The doorman protested briefly but returned to his post, where he snickered with a few colleagues and gestured dismissively back toward the driver, who had in the meantime set to retrieving luggage from the trunk.

Jacob reached for his wallet, but Philip raised a hand and said, "Please, let me."

Philip waited until Jacob was checked in, then extended his hand once more. "It's great to meet you," he said. "If you want some company while you're here, give me a holler. Philip Strowman, room fourteen. Or call my cell." He handed Jacob a card.

"All right," said Jacob. "Again, thank you."

He'd meant to drop his things and set out for the mission, but he decided he could lie down for just a few minutes, and checked in to the hotel.

When he opened his eyes, it was night and the room was pitch, for he'd not turned on any lights. The hotel had a café, and he got some food then returned to his room, but idling there proved intolerable, so he decided upon a walk along the road that wound westward behind the inn, through neighborhoods mottled with gray, threadbare dwellings. Most sat darkly along the lampless road, the low hum of fans emanating from each like a loosely arranged hymnal.

Jacob strolled briskly, though nowhere to get to, only time and these sad structures to pass. He mopped his beading forehead with the back of his hand, and paused to regard a bleak house poised some thirty feet from where he stood, dark save for a small, fore room within which Jacob could make out a man seated bedside next to a small, fitfully chattering boy. Jacob cocked his head. Not English. Bengali perhaps. Maybe Hindi. The man was hunched forward upon a wooden chair, jotting frantically by candlelight upon a small writing pad after each utterance from the boy.

Jacob left the road and trod soundlessly across the patch of lawn and stood near the window. The boy muttered again, and the man paused his dictation and bent toward the child, whose eyes, Jacob now discerned, were shut. The man sat back up, features distressed, and resumed his frantic scribbling. Above the bed trundled the uneasy blades of a large, slow fan. The candle above the man bowed with every pass. At the foot of the bed lay a drowsing, tan-colored hound, one eye open, ears set a twitching with each bit of gibbering from the child. This ritual repeated itself, and again, until the guilt rose within Jacob for his voyeurism, and he slunk from the lawn and returned to the road to head back to the hotel.

When he sank into his bed for the evening, he felt himself quickly fading, but he retrieved Anabel's book from the nightstand, flipped through some pages, peered through heavy eyelids at the one upon which he'd settled.

Reason 28. Your light. You always hear about people who light up a room. You are, most assuredly, one, but it's so much more. It's not just that smile, which lights a room, lights the world. It's more than your surpassing beauty. It's more than just being a light in the darkness, and you are every bit that. But you and you alone brighten the light, a notion I had never, before you, conceived. Where there is goodness, you make it better, make others better. Oh, sweet girl, how you do shine.

CHAPTER 12 – WEARY

When the next morning Jacob passed the same house on his way to the mission, the boy he'd seen was playing in the front yard with the dog.

"Hello!" Jacob called, waving.

The boy looked up and half-waved, but then quickly lowered his eyes and did not speak. The canine regarded Jacob tepidly, before nosing the boy's hands in entreaty of the affection so rudely interrupted.

Jacob watched them. He thought he saw in the boy's eyes the same probity which lived in those of his own son, in those of all children, but there was something else.

"What's your name?" Jacob tried.

The boy looked down again.

Just then a woman attired in brightly colored garments swept toward them from behind the small house, a long fall of jet-black hair trailing, a basket of clothes clutched to her ample bosom. She called to the boy, and the boy and the dog went to her, and all stood regarding Jacob.

He smiled and waved again. "Hello!"

"Hello," said the woman with attractive, if wearied, features: skin sunbaked the color of coffee; dark eyes, deep-set.

Jacob slowly approached their yard. "I'm staying in the hotel down the road," he said, motioning with a crook of his thumb. "On my way to the mission."

The woman set down her basket, and the dog sniffed at it, then sat. The boy peeked at Jacob from behind his mother.

"Bhala," the woman said, her voice tinged with mild surprise. "Bhala atmara. Good souls there. But walking? Take good care. Some no-good people out there."

Jacob raised an eyebrow. "Well, thank you, but everyone has been really nice so far."

The woman tendered a dismissive wave of her hand. "Yes, yes. Some very nice people. Same anywhere. Some very not nice people. Same anywhere too."

Jacob smiled and gestured toward the half-moon face peering out behind her. "I was just saying hello to your boy."

The woman looked down at her son pressed into her hip, watching. She tousled his unkempt hair. "Thank you," she said. "But he does not speak."

Jacob tilted his head; the dog, observing this, did likewise. "Forgive me," said Jacob, "but I passed this way last evening, on a walk, and saw him — heard him — through the window. He was speaking then."

The woman raised her eyes to Jacob. "Yes, he speaks at night, in his sleep. Only in his sleep." Her eyes filled now with the same distress as the man Jacob had seen through the window — the boy's father, doubtless.

"It has not always been this way," the woman said. She bent and kissed the top of the boy's head, then straightened and stared wistfully past Jacob, toward days now past. "He used to speak a lot, like any child his age, but then something happened." Her eyes narrowed, returning now. She regarded Jacob. "A few months ago, he was walking back from playing with friends, walking through neighborhoods, through the park. We tell him do not walk back alone, but to wait for us to get him, but he did not listen, and something happened to him, which we do not know, and which he will not tell."

The dog stood now and peered out along the road, sniffing the air. Its tail rose momentarily, then dropped, and the animal sat once more, searching out again the child's hands.

"I am sorry," Jacob said. "I did not mean to pry. Have you gone to the authorities? Taken him to a physician?"

"We have done many things," said the woman. "We love our son. We would give an arm, a leg, gladly take on any amount of pain if only it would relieve his, but nothing has worked."

Jacob frowned. "Your husband... what I saw last night...."

The woman nodded. "Ever since the night terrors," she said. "It is killing him that he cannot help his child. Every night he sits with his paper and transcribes that which he hears. Most nights he does not sleep, and each day he goes off to work, weary of body and of mind. Of heart."

"Have you been able to put anything together?" Jacob nodded toward the peeking boy. "From his words?"

"Words," said the woman. "Some in tandem with the next, most not. Most known only in the dark corners to which he has retreated." Her features draped into an expression most grievous, and she extended her arms before her. "Each with meaning but devoid of their larger truth, mere remnants of a thought which was, a feeling which was. Like trying to gather in the air or the sky and read as one their meaning. One could read or write volumes of this world and still only hazard a guess at its truth. Do you know this?"

Jacob swallowed. "I do," he said.

The boy pulled at his mother's arm, and when she looked down at him, he rubbed his stomach in a circle, and she nodded and spoke to him in their language, and after a quick glance at Jacob, he scampered into the house. The dog looked about his options, rose, then ambled to the door and stared in, until after a few moments a small arm pushed the door open and the dog went inside.

The woman turned, bent, retrieved the basket of clothes. "I must give him his breakfast."

"Of course."

She turned for the house, and Jacob started to turn for the road, but then the woman turned back.

"Everything is bigger to a child," she said. "Every experience. Every hope and every fear. Every word. A hill is a mountain, a pond is a sea."

Jacob moved his hand to the jasper in his pocket, and nodded. "I wish you the best. Might I ask: are there any words he has repeated more than others?"

At this the woman's eyes brimmed with a terrible melancholy. "Manda," she said, and then turned and disappeared into the home, where there was no sound save for the ceaseless drone of toiling fans.

***

A scorched city, its denizens so glazed in perspiration they might have been just out from the rain, but there was no rain, only heat and dust and sweat, and lambent eyes darting behind their sooted masks. The kind of heat you could see. A dog took shape out of the dust and skulked partway across the baking road, then retreated, circling twice before settling back into its former repose. No sanctuary.

At irregular junctures along the side of the road, people behind carts hawked wares. They called to Jacob indignantly, angry sounding, like he was tardy in some compulsory transaction. He walked past, caking in the plumes raised by his tread, compelled by a transaction no one of these souls might possibly requite. He wore sunglasses, but the glare remained infernal. From somewhere came the rumble of a vehicle, and now clattered forth a rust-colored cab, ill-begotten transport borne of the fiendish brume. If its operator spied Jacob, he was unmoved. Jacob executed a hasty sidestep, and felt the hot lash of the auto as it hammered past, raising in its wake a churning plume of baked grime that hove about him like an unbottled genie. A few more unheeding vehicles passed, and a few more hawkers of wares, and soon Jacob strode into an old-world plaza of dust and stone and long-burnt clay. The plaza fell out to the right of the road, an antiquated place rising up in this city both old and new. Bone white structures baked below the fiery eye of that god to whom they seemed reared in supplication.

He was no historian, and no architect, but the construction of the place seemed somewhere between Victorian and Old West, at once ornate and austere. An old church, a post office, a saloon—each had long been abandoned, by the looks. In front of the church stood a baroque and gushing fountain, a small assembly of men, women, and children gathered 'round this unlikely oasis. Two dogs stood on their hind legs with front paws folded upon the wide lip of the fountain, too far from the stream but lapping frantically at the splashing droplets like parched and frothing congregants. Poised in eternal antipathy above the water, a cherub-faced angel, harp in one hand and sword in the other, directly opposed him, clutching his own blade but neck vulnerable at the tapered end of his adversary's, a gargoyle of diabolical expression. Smiling despite his predicament. An inscription etched on the concrete slab of their theatre read: *God is everywhere.*

Jacob peered and squinted as a commotion seemed now to erupt. The dogs darted from their perch and slunk to the refuge of the church façade, where they hunkered and looked on nervously. The women snatched the children's hands and bustled them quickly away, the children's feet scrabbling madly in the dust, their free arms akimbo. At the fountain remained three men, two of whom had bent the third over the lip so that only his floundering lower body remained visible, like a violently protesting baptismal candidate.

Jacob ran toward them and yelled, "Hey!" his voice raspy and choked for the aridness. One of the assailants reached for something, and Jacob's eyes widened as he watched the object in question glint in the fire of the unfettered sun. "Hey!"

The muggers glanced up and squinted against his approach—strange, pale figure materialized out of the scorched and pale haze—but did not free their victim, whose legs flailed in even greater desperation. The object glinted again and the one brandishing it stabbed the victim, whose body seized and arched momentarily, before thrashing about so violently as to compel the second assailant to fling both arms around the madly gesticulating legs.

"Jaldee," cried the one restraining the legs. "Jaldee karo!"

The one with the blade thrust his hands into the pockets of their victim and turned them out. Various effects scattered to the ground, shrouded instantly in the plumes of dust raised by the tumult. The man restraining the victim's legs exclaimed, grabbed at one of the items, showed his accomplice, and scrambled to his feet. The one with the blade pocketed it, released his grip, and along with his ally raced from the scene.

"Hey! Stop!" Jacob, nearly at the fountain, deliberated briefly whether to tend to the reeling victim or pursue his assailants.

The victim, of course, who lurched up out of the fountain presently, choking and spitting and clutching his chest. The dust at his feet molded into crimson rivulets of water and blood.

Jacob resisted a commanding urge to pursue the attackers, so brazen their turpitude, so unjust this scene. And so many like it. He could catch them, if he ran hard enough. Catch them both and bring them down and, fueled by the indignation of a world upended, seize their weapon and run it through their impenitent hearts, the both.

The stricken man drooped over the fountain, coughed violently, and then sank to his knees. Dark prints appeared on the fountain rim where his hands had just been. The women who'd ushered their children from the scene emerged cautiously now, trailing away in the direction opposite, despite Jacob's pleas for help. But now one doubled back, against the protestations of the others, and came and kneeled at the side of the injured man. Jacob knelt with them beneath the unprejudiced eyes of the statuary.

"Here," said Jacob, grasping the victim gently by the arm. "Turn over, sir. Lay down." The injured man flinched at his touch, but Jacob mimed the desired action, and the man groaned and contorted his dripping frame and sat. Jacob placed one hand on the man's back and one on his shoulder, and eased him back until he lay prone, laid out in the blazing sun and bleeding like a horrible sacrifice, hands doubled over his wound, breath rattled and catching. Jacob's hands were slicked with blood. His mind raced: help must be summoned, but so too must the bleeding be staunched. He shoved his hand into his trouser pocket until he found his phone. He withdrew it, shielded the screen from the glare, and dialed 911, groaning as soon as he'd done so; surely that was not applicable here.

"Ek Sau," said the woman, gesturing frantically at his phone. "Ek Sau."

He held out his arms in petition. "I don't—"

"Ek Sau!"

He thought to hand her the phone, but just then the injured man exclaimed loudly in a great spasm of distress. They bent over him. Jacob began to wrest off his own shirt, but the woman held up a hand and Jacob watched as she unwound from her head the colorful pashmina that adorned it. Her hair cascaded like rain. She gently coaxed the man's red-bleached hands from the wound, a crimson outline blossoming across his sternum in their wake. She quickly replaced their pressure with her own, pressing the scarf firmly, and spoke to the man almost imperceptibly. He continued to cough, small bubbles of blood issuing forth with each expectoration, but his body seemed to slowly untense, and he nodded beneath the woman's whispering ministrations.

Jacob stood and peered back out to the road, where the occasional vehicle flew past in the sun- and dust-shrouded obscurity, surreal transports of some beleaguered world. He turned back to the woman and stricken man, and raised an index finger upon addressing them.

"A minute," he said. "I will go for help."

Whether they understood or trusted in his word, Jacob could not discern, but he spun and ran back toward the road. The assailants were long-gone, doubtless, but what mattered now was getting their victim to a hospital. It felt abhorrent to think it, but in truth it was better to not track down the authorities or an emergency vehicle. Better for him. But the man back at the fountain required immediate help, and so when he reached the road, Jacob peered against the sunlight, and when a tortuous minute later another vehicle appeared, he hailed it vehemently, stepping into its path so that its choices were to either stop or run him down. When, much to his relief, it pulled over, he scampered around to the driver's side, where a wide-eyed, middle-aged man stared out at him.

"Help," Jacob cried, pointing back toward the fountain. "We need help!"

The driver's eyes did not follow the direction of his hand but rather the hand itself, which, Jacob now saw, was stained a bright but darkening crimson. The driver looked from Jacob's hand to his face and then his hand again, before permitting his eyes to warily trace beyond him and narrow in consideration of that which he beheld.

"Apakāra?" He regarded Jacob. "Apakāra?"

Jacob could only hope the man had deduced correctly, deduced through what he'd glimpsed by the fountain, and through the universal language that was blood, the nature of this situation.

"Yes," said Jacob. "Apakāra. Help, please."

The man nodded but then waved him away, and Jacob's heart dropped until he saw that the man had just wanted him out of the way so he could pull farther off the road. The man angled his vehicle onto the dusting shoulder, and got out of his car. They walked briskly toward the fountain, and now the man withdrew a cell phone from his pocket, dialed, and after a brief pause spoke urgently into it. When they reached the fountain, the man scanned the scene and spoke rapidly to the woman, who listened, nodded, then replied in turn. The man lowered to his knees and pressed his hands upon the blood-soaked scarf, relieving the woman, who nodded her thanks and flexed her hands. The victim's eyes had closed, but they fluttered at the renewed pressured upon his wound. The new Samaritan spoke to him softly, and the man's eyes eased back shut. He seemed calmer, his breathing slowed, though the laboring hitch still conspicuous within it.

Jacob was trying to determine the best way to inquire, through word or gesture, how he might be of help, but just then sounded the strident wail of sirens. This was good, that help was coming, but he could not stay. Getting embroiled in a criminal inquiry would chance time and discovery. He took a step back.

The man he'd hailed looked up at him sharply. "Aap kahan ja rahe ho?" he said.

Jacob shrugged his arms to his sides. "I don't—"

"Aap kahan ja rahe ho?"

"I'm sorry," Jacob said. "I cannot stay."

The man looked from him to the woman, and the woman spoke, both glancing at Jacob occasionally during their exchange. When Jacob took a few steps farther, the man looked up again, but his features had softened, and he returned his attention to the victim, and he and the woman resumed their dialogue and did not cast Jacob another glance.

The sirens grew louder and Jacob increased his gait. He thrust his hands into his pockets as he went, stained as they were with the evidence of his involvement. Not that he was guilty... of this, anyway.

Only after several minutes, after the sirens faded, did he hazard a look behind him. The plaza was no longer distinguishable, only a depthless volume of sun and stone. A few minutes later, he came upon a public restroom. He scoured his hands in hot water, hot as he could get it, and lathered on copious layers of foaming soap. But the more he scrubbed, the more ingrained seemed to become the impression, washing not off, but in, blood unto blood. *Am I my brother's keeper?*

A shadow fell over him when he exited the restroom.

"Magnanimous," Justus said, cinching his gloves. He appeared devoid of perspiration.

"What are you talking about?"

"Helping that poor fellow, while precious minutes bleed away."

"You saw that?"

"Saw it? I occasioned it."

"What?"

"Come now," said Justus, his eyes burning once more into Jacob's. "We are both authors, in our way, fascinated by the human condition, by choices, behavior. You create your scenarios on the page. I author mine in, shall we say, a more authentic manner."

Jacob shook his head, glared, resisted a welling urge to strike down this most abominable of creatures. "What did you do?"

"I stopped the first people I saw," Justus said, like it should have been obvious. "Offered the first a generous gift of cash, then confided to the next two that I had done so. The rest was up to them. A man chooses to accept the kindness of a stranger, while other men elect to be less kind."

"You are truly sick," said Jacob. He shifted where he stood, wishing he were with his family. Anywhere but here.

"And yet I endure," said Justus.

"I have to go."

"Indeed, you do."

Jacob began to walk away. After maybe a minute, he chanced a look back—no sign of Justus.

A woman was walking toward him, and he inquired if she knew of the Blessed Heart Mission. She nodded, and pointed from the direction she'd come. "You're almost there."

CHAPTER 13 – BROKE THINGS

He was. The mission staff welcomed him heartily, gave him water, assented without question to direct him to Morse. Within the tented enclosure, his back to Jacob, Morse hunched over a table, a diminutive man with gray hair flecked with darker remnants, bent over his labor. A bottle of water rocked gently to his undertaking. He mopped his brow with the back of a sun-withered hand.

Jacob approached warily. He watched his shadow precede him into the tent, long and impertinent, catching the hunched man's eye, who looked up, grunted, and twisted around.

"Forgive me," said Jacob from the entranceway. His shadow drew back into the space beside him. "Reginald Morse?"

The man regarded him with narrowed eyes, otherwise expressionless. The air hung heavy, stale. "I'm Morse," the man said.

Jacob nodded, realizing now that his subject had turned around that he was not so much diminutive as resigned. Reginald, according to the mission director, toiled here solely of his own volition. Both men mopped their brows.

Jacob glanced at the table: a screwdriver, a disassembled clock. "I thought mission work was people work," said Jacob. "Giving folks religion, showing them the light, feeding the indigent."

Reginald nodded and said, "There's that, but there's always other kinds of work needs doing." He nodded over his shoulder. "Repairing broke things."

"Ah," said Jacob. "Kind of the de facto handyman? One of those guys who can fix everything?"

"Not everything," Reginald said

Jacob shifted where he stood. Dust swirled about his ankles like the smoke of a stamped-out fire. "My name is Jacob," he said. "I am a writer." He paused, for these things seemed important, starting with truth before stepping ever-further from it. "May I come in?"

***

Back at the hotel, Jacob showered again and placed a call to Anabel. They spoke of Gabe, who was out with her parents, and when she inquired about his father, he lied and lied well, and loathed himself for the ease of his duplicity. Yet all the while, he brimmed with the same vitality as ever he had since they'd met. Not owing to anything she'd said on the call—for if anything, her words were perfunctory, her tone tepid—but simply to the fact that she'd always stoked in him a reaction like no other, and, he'd long ago come to understand, forever would. A sensibility cellular in nature: she was the love of his life; this he knew in his blood and in his bones. The one person for whom he'd been procreated into existence—blood and bones and organs and musculature and tissue—his, in its precise assembling, that he might those decades hence meet and love this woman who, until recently, had professed a devotion no less profound. And so, he brimmed with this imperative and wanted to tell her he loved her, for so he did. Not to persuade her toward some starry end, but simply because it was truth, of the most unassailable type. Truth had become an inestimable, if faltering, beacon upon the fringe of this fathomless sea.

"Jacob. Jacob?"

He channeled back from his ruminations. "I'm here."

"I asked if you'd heard the news. I mean, I doubt it, being out there, but didn't know if you got local news on your phone or anything. An officer was murdered outside of Sub Rosa last week. A stabbing. They think they got a look at the guy before he ran into the park. Can you believe that? I was going to tell you the other day when you called, but Gabe was so anxious to talk. So scary that something like that could happen here, you know?"

He started to reply, but his throat caught.

"Jacob?"

"Yes," he said. "Very scary. How good of a look did they get?"

"I don't know," Anabel replied. "Hopefully good. I hate the thought of a killer at large."

After a few formalities regarding phoning again soon, and hopefully getting to talk with Gabriel, the call ended.

Morse, thankfully, had agreed to see him at his home later that evening. Jacob staggered to the bathroom and bent over the sink, woozy. He turned the faucet on and splashed water onto his face. He looked haggard, unkempt. Hadn't shaved since the start of all this, was going to do so before heading to see Morse, but now, as he rubbed the slightly graying stubble, he thought better of it. Not that they were apt to put out an APB and description here, of all places, but still. He would let the beard grow. One more obfuscation in this affair grown full of them.

***

"It's a simple home," Reginald said, welcoming Jacob in. "Anything more would defeat the purpose."

Jacob stood blinking in the yellow shaft of illumination supplied by the waning sunlight from an aft room. He clutched a notepad in one hand, and had a pen clipped in his breast pocket. The anterior space in which they stood was windowless and spare—no lamps, no television, no outlets. Reginald had spoken aptly. Adorning the far wall was a simple cross, a nondescript clock, and what looked to be a wood-carved plaque inscribed in Latin. Jacob stepped closer.

> *Deus, Pater misericordiárum, qui per mortem et resurrectiónem Fílii sui mundum sibi reconciliávit et Spíritum Sanctum effúdit in remissiónem peccatórum, per ministérium Ecclésiæ indulgéntiam tibi tríbuat et pacem. Et ego te absolvo a peccatis tuis in nomine Patris, et Filii, et Spiritus Sancti.*

The long hand of the clock orbited with a soft, rhythmic swoosh, like an old man's slippers in a hallway. Jacob squinted through the gloom and perceived the wooden plaque had been in some way fractured, the last phrase—the *Et ego te absolvo a peccatis tuis in nomine Patris, et Filii, et Spiritus Sancti*—dangling askance. He stepped to the wall, and could see that the item was in fact constructed in a segmented, detachable manner. It occurred to him that it was most assuredly not his place, but he'd been overcome of late with an abiding compulsion to set things in place.

"Leave it, please," said Reginald.

Jacob turned around. It had taken minimal dishonesty to wrangle an audience with Morse. He winced at the notion: a vampire welcomed by an unwitting host. He asked Reginald where he was from.

"Small town in the states. I'd doubt you'd know it."

He'd told Reginald he was a writer, and this of course, was true. He told him he was researching missionaries for his new book, and Reginald had, with neither animation nor intransigence, assented to an interview. His host gestured to the simple, wooden table, and Jacob nodded his thanks and sat.

"I'll fetch some iced tea," Reginald said. He shuffled away toward the small kitchen, grimacing a bit as he went.

When he returned with the tea, they sipped from their glasses, ice cubes clanking softly like chimes.

"Did you hurt your back?" Jacob asked.

Reginald studied the slow orbit of the cubes in his glass. "Been bad for years," he said.

"Sorry to hear," said Jacob. "Would surgery help?"

"I reckon so." Reginald sipped his tea, set it back down, his gaze still set upon it.

"But you do this work—this charity—full time?" He shook his head in admiration. "How long have you done it?"

"Long," said Reginald.

"That's amazing," said Jacob. He sipped his tea, set it back down. "To devote your life to helping others."

Something lit in Reginald's eyes, but not a happy something. More like an unwanted light trained upon recesses of his consciousness preserved, until this moment, shadowed and undisturbed.

"You're a writer, eh?"

Jacob nodded.

"How the dear object from the crime remove, Or how distinguish penitence from love?"

Jacob lifted his glass to his lips, that in so doing he might obscure his own grimace. A current of shame shot through him; he'd allowed himself to grow optimistic this assignment would prove an easy one. Here was, after all, a selfless and giving man, having devoted himself to the noblest of causes to a degree achieved by few. Yes, Jacob harbored qualms about the religious aspects of the whole thing—the presumption involved in the quest to save souls—but as he lowered his glass and met the rueful eyes of his host, he realized he should have known better. In this man's case, the question of souls was clearly anything but settled.

He withdrew his pen, patiently, like a surgeon wanting to reassure his patient before the first cut. Another sweep of the room confirmed a dearth of photos, or any suggestion of family.

"Forgive me," said Jacob, his pen poised above the page. "Are you... were you—"

"She left me," said Reginald, swirling his glass. The cubes tolled thinly. "There was a tragedy."

"I'm sorry," Jacob said. "May I ask when that was?"

"Been thirty years."

"That's why she left you?" Jacob regarded his host with what he hoped the appropriate solemnity. "Because she couldn't forgive you?"

"Because I could not forgive myself."

And now Jacob waded into murky waters: insensitive to press the matter at hand, perhaps equally so to not tender a requisite follow-up. After a moment he inquired, "Any children?"

Morse's eyes flared darkly. His words were soft-spoken, but unequivocal, like one who'd just closed a door behind him. "We're done, I'm afraid."

This was no good. He'd clearly struck a nerve, and this, despite his desperation, evoked within Jacob jagged pangs of guilt. "I'm sorry."

Reginald stared into the floating prisms in his glass.

Jacob exited into the wan and failing light, striding across the sparse lawn to the dusty walk that separated it from the road. When he reached the path, he turned and regarded the home, the small, soot-colored structure so nondescript as to seem in the dying light scant more than some oblong husk. The few trees crimping toward the residence were hardly more substantial, skeletal and disjointed, their emaciated limbs slotted in shadow upon the otherwise featureless canvass of the house, conferring to the structure the appearance of a drab and lonely cell. And who was this man reposed within?

That determination would now be far tougher to achieve. He'd gleaned a little, but not nearly enough, and time was spilling away as if through a burst dam — only a day, but a day without gain was several lost. And so, he stood, rooted aimlessly like the skeletal trees, his shadow falling unremarkably among their own, thinking of two men, one not thirty feet beyond him, the other thousands of miles off, upon a mountaintop, in the company of dead men. He'd piqued something in both, something that seemed for a brief and elusive moment to span those miles like a subterranean cable.

Now that connection faded, submerging below the shrouding waters of hemorrhaging time and truncated missions. The shadows had bled into a darkened mask upon the home.

Jacob turned and shuffled along the path, each step raising hot clouds of dust behind him.

The air hung damp and heavy, and he stripped down when he returned to his room and took a long, cold shower. While he was dressing, his phone buzzed on the desk, and he went to it—a text from Justus, with no more than an address and a time. No matter the revolt it stirred within him, he'd no alternative but to acquiesce.

***

He arrived at 9:00 p.m. at his destination, not more than a mile from his hotel, but even in the shade of night, the air clung to him as he strode. The house to which the coordinates led him appeared residential upon his approach, but now he observed two other men, then a third, striding quickly, intently, a touch uneasily, and so he knew. The door pulled open and a pretty thing with tired eyes and tawny complexion smiled wearily and motioned him inside.

The fore room had a table, and several couches, upon which mostly young and mostly pretty and mostly tired-looking women lounged in various states of undress, drinks in hand, smiling coquettishly at their male suitors, businessmen most, Caucasians all. Most of the ladies appeared Indian. One of the men's shirts was partly unbuttoned, his hair disheveled. A crimson print of lips visible upon one cheek. Another man leaned into his girl and whispered something, his eyes rutted in a miasma of inebriation and—for the moment—unsated lust. The girl smiled and inclined him by the back of his head toward her breast, upon which he smiled like a comforted child. The girl checked her watch.

The woman who had let him in took his hand and led him into an adjoining room, where behind a bar stood a hulk of a man, polishing glasses and wiping the countertop, a cigarette dangling limply from a corner of his mouth like the protruding tail of an unfortunate rodent. The woman gestured to the bar, smiled. "A drink," she said.

"No thank you," said Jacob. "I—"

"The man says you should have a drink," the woman politely continued. "Your friend. He is upstairs. He says you will have a drink and come up to see him." She motioned again to the bar, behind which the animated mountain had paused in his tidying and regarded Jacob dispassionately.

"Whiskey and soda," Jacob said.

The giant set about his duty with not even a nod.

Jacob eased up to the bar and reached for his wallet, not wanting, despite his host's exhortation, to run afoul of this particular barkeep.

The woman grabbed his wrist, tugged at it gently, and shook her hand. "No money," she said. "Take your drink, and I take you to your friend."

Friend. The word hung in the air as conspicuously as the smoke, as equivocally as the painted faces, the honeyed declarations.

They ascended a steep, carpeted stairwell, the ice clinking in Jacob's glass as he followed the woman, whose slender hand whispered up the balustrade as she went, her figure shapely and undulant beneath her tight and florid dress. With her heart-shaped backside inches from Jacob's face, a flurry of shame welled up in him, and he quickly looked down.

They plateaued into an ill-lit hallway, heavily perfumed by a panoply of scented candles, no doubt intended to displace the more unsavory musk that lingered. A thin, naked woman materialized from the obscurity, propped against the wall smoking a cigarette, her long, dark hair spilled out over her small, pointed breasts. The woman leading Jacob spoke sharply to her, and she muttered something, took another drag, then lowered her head and disappeared behind a nearby door.

"Here," said the host, stopping at another door at the end of the hall.

Jacob's face crinkled as certain unmistakable sounds resolved into distinction from behind the door. "I think I should wait," he told her.

"Your friend says you are to go in," she said. "It is okay." She gestured with one hand to the door, nudged him gently forward with the other.

He regarded her momentarily, then placed a tentative hand upon the knob.

Satisfied, the woman swept about and disappeared back into the gloom.

Jacob took a drink. Paused. Took another. Turned the knob.

Were he being truthful, he would have to admit the safe and careful execution of his life had in the last years been done to excess—Anabel was surely right. Perhaps Justus was right as well. Jacob had inured himself, and so too, he hoped, his family, against pestilence and peril, lechery and liability. He'd viewed this as his duty, but failed along the way to realize it had been too much, become its own pathology. But if he had, by virtue of his frailties, swung the pendulum too far, said pendulum at present went blasting past him in the opposite direction, wresting from its moorings and careening wildly into the dark and carnal depths of some unreckoned hinterland.

Justus was facing him, nude and athwart a petite and panting woman, pistoning back and forth in rapid-fire, either hand dug claw-like into the girl's sides, like she was some grunting beast of burden. He grinned at Jacob. A cigar smoldered in an ashtray on the nightstand beside the bed. The girl raised her eyes briefly to Jacob's, but what trace of humility he thought he saw, fizzled quickly away beneath a tide of resigned ardor. Her breasts swung pendulously, and now Justus reached and cupped one of them roughly as he rode, twisting and pinching the nipple. The girl arched her back and groaned, the tallow light framing her lithe figure in golden hue in the otherwise shadowed room. With his other hand, Justus delivered a flurry of slaps to her round and gyrating posterior, the sound reverberating through the room like the crack of a whip.

Jacob felt himself becoming aroused, cursed himself silently, and angled himself slightly from view.

"Come in, come in," Justus exhorted, motioning with his head, for his hands remained occupied, to an easy chair on the far side of the room. "Finish your drink."

Jacob did, wished for another, looked at turns at his glass, his shoes, the nondescript walls, as though their plainness belied in fact some key and elusive cipher. Anywhere but at that scene not ten feet from him, which played out in the edges of his averted vison and through the grating staccato of their activity. When perhaps ten minutes later they had finished, Jacob permitted himself to glance back to the bed, where the two participants had collapsed into a glistening tangle of naked flesh.

Justus reached to the nightstand for his cigar, lay back and drew deeply upon it, a dragon's eye of fire flaring crimson at its tip. He withdrew it from his lips and glanced over at Jacob. "You saw Morse."

"Yes."

"Do you have enough?"

"I don't know. Maybe not."

Justus nodded, puffed a few times more. "A determination you must make."

"Is there anything else?"

Justus grinned from the bed. "You injure me," he said. "I am looking out for you, after all. A brief reprieve from your travails. Would you care for a girl? You can have any here that you wish." He indicated with a crook of his head the young woman beside him. "This one, if you'd like."

"Hey!" The girl rolled to her side and rested her cheek upon Justus' chest. When she raised a thin and manicured hand to his cheek, he sprang from the bed, tossing the girl aside in his wake. She scrambled to her hands and knees and looked up at him fearfully.

Jacob put his glass on the ground beside his chair, rose. He wanted to go the girl, cover her up, stand between her and this insidious figure poised glaring on the bedside opposite.

Justus gestured at her presently and she slunk from the bed, breasts heaving, the black tuft of pubic hair slick and matted beneath her navel. She grabbed a few lacy undergarments from another chair and slipped soundlessly from the room.

"What in God's name is the matter with you?"

Justus, still working the cigar and stepping into a pair of trousers, regarded him almost quizzically. "Again, with him?" He stood, slipped on an undershirt, tucked it in. "You have other things to concern yourself with." He finished dressing, motioned Jacob to the door. "Let's get another drink."

Jacob groaned, and followed.

***

He was drunk, and in the company of strangely persuasive dead men.

Call him, said Parsons, who'd taken up residence rather impudently on Jacob's bed, arms crooked behind his head on Jacob's pillow. *Everyone needs a friend.* He tried nudging Flint with the toe of his boot, but the boot merely melted into Flint's thigh like intersecting pools of water. *Ain't that right.*

Dead Flint paid no attention, and instead stared wistfully at Jacob's boots, as he had that first night at the diner.

Hell, said Parsons. *You ain't got no use for them now.*

Call him, said the officer, startling Jacob, who whirled around in his seat. The officer was immersed — literally, the lower half of his spectral frame having submerged within the cushions — in the sofa chair in the corner of the room. *And do you think perhaps you could get rid of these miscreants?*

Flint looked up from Jacob's boots.

What the hell did he call us?

Parsons smiled and waved his hand. *Don't mind him.*

Jacob gestured at each of them with his glass. A spot of whiskey sloshed over the rim and onto the floor. "You're not here," he said.

Another wager you're willing to make? Parsons eyed him. *How you been doing so far?*

We gain things and lose things along our way, said the officer, attempting feverishly to prop himself up on the armrests of his chair. *We are in the end only that which we've retained.*

You better hope we're here, said Parsons.

"Otherwise, I'm crazy?"

Otherwise, you're lost.

Jacob closed his eyes.

Chapter 14 – Calvary

He set his alarm but slept through it, had requested a wake-up call but slept through that, and had he not failed to put on the *Do Not Disturb* sign and been awakened by housekeeping at 10:30 that morning, who knew how much of the day he might have squandered. He dressed quickly, eschewing a shower, and set off for the mission.

Morse would not see him, as conveyed to him by the mission directors, politely but clearly.

He forged his way back through the molten heat to his hotel, where he got lunch at the café, then returned to his room. The laptop beckoned, and he thought for a moment he'd take a stab at the Morse submission, but felt disingenuous and ill-equipped to do so. Instead, he fell onto the bed and stared at the twisting threads of shadow upon his ceiling, courtesy of the window-side bushes and noonday sun. A breeze kicked up and the branches swayed, provoking the shadows, which writhed upon the ceiling like macabre marionettes, at one point appearing to Jacob like a lasso. He thought of the horse and rider, and thought it would be likewise nice if he could corral and bring to heel the necessary clues, pull through these twisting threads. This was the last thing he remembered before slumber again prevailed.

***

Philip was finishing dinner with colleagues but suggested they meet at the park nearby. It took Jacob ten minutes, and he sighted Philip on the opposite end of the grounds and started toward him, when a text rang in—hopefully Anabel, maybe even Gabe. He slipped his phone from his pocket.

Fuck.

Making friends, I see.

Jacob looked up and swept his gaze across the park.

Involve others at their own peril.

Jacob pocketed the phone and decided he might yet be able to retreat from view, but no, Philip had spotted him and was hailing with great exuberance. Jacob drew up his features as they approached one another from either end of the path that bisected that section of park.

Philip winced slightly as they shook hands, but smiled and waved away Jacob's concern. "Not to worry," he said. "My circulation issue, like I explained in the car." He held his hands before him and shook them out. "Thumbs prickling a bit, is all." He nodded along the path before them. "Let's walk."

They did so beneath the streaking hues of another dying day.

"Did you get to the mission?" Philip inquired.

"I did," said Jacob.

"Did you find what you wanted?"

"I'm not sure."

Philip seemed to accept this.

Jacob watched their shadows range out cartoonishly upon the pavement as they walked, protracted, spectral versions of themselves, testing the integrity of the path ahead. He glanced at his companion as they paused at the edge of a large pond, which fell out glimmering before them in the last light of day like a vast teardrop. At its far end, the waters tapered into the base of a small ridge. Upon the ridge snaked a narrow stream, which fed in turn into a large, wooden barrel. The barrel was already near full and lurching, ready at any moment to send its contents coursing into the pond below.

A family stood nearby, two adults and a small boy, who stood pointing at the barrel.

Something caught Jacob's eye and he squinted through the twilight and observed a snow-white swan swimming in leisurely orbit directly beneath the barrel. Surely, Jacob thought, it was familiar with the pond and would abdicate the spot shortly, before the wall of water crashed down upon it. Jacob eyed the barrel: small crests of water lapped at its rim. The swan appeared oblivious. Jacob shook his head, not for the swan's predicament, but his preoccupation with it. He'd more pressing concerns, to say the least.

Philip began to say something, but at that moment another shadow washed over theirs. Neither sound nor movement had betrayed his approach, but here he stood.

"Good evening." Justus bowed his head, count-like. "I hope I am not intruding. Off upon my evening constitutional, and I am always grateful to happen upon fellow Americans, if I detect correctly."

"Not intruding at all," said Philip, shaking out his hand before extending it. "Philip. This is Jacob."

Justus shook Philip's hand then turned to Jacob with glinting eyes. "Justus," he said, extending his hand.

At the far end of the pond, the swan continued its pirouette. Above it the barrel canted and lurched.

He makes a swan-like end, fading in music.

They resumed walking, three astride upon the path, Jacob in the middle. A late-setting sun and whispers of the day that was lingered over the land. A tall structure hove into view just ahead, imprinted within the dusk, and bearing atop it the palely lit face of a great clock. It cast in shadow an inverse rendering of the hour upon the stone path: 3:15, its 8:45 counterpart illuminated starkly upon the rounded timepiece.

"Genesis 3:15," Justus said. "The first promise of a Redeemer, of He who would die for our sins." He chuckled and glanced at the other men. "If you are inclined toward such beliefs."

Philip eyed their guest. "Are you not?"

"I think it's a stirring notion of sacrifice," said Justus. "An innocent dying for the sins of another. There is, of course, another take on that hour now projected before us."

Philip raised an eyebrow. "Oh?"

"The Devil's Hour," said Justus. "Believed the inverse of the time Christ died at Calvary."

They paused a moment as a small cluster of rats scuttled quickly across the path.

Philip regarded Justus with the look of someone upon whom a certain understanding had been only in that moment conferred. "A rather dark take on our savior."

"Your savior," Justus said.

They resumed walking as night came on like a wave, displacing the day that was, until the fast-failing light flared out in a last, spectacular ellipse—a world yielding. Jacob looked for the moon saw none; he looked for stars but saw none.

Beneath this dome of blackness, Justus grinned most amicably, most terribly, his eyes a mirror to that dark world descended.

Philip reciprocated the smile, and Jacob cringed at the innocence of the gesture. Across the pond and scarcely visible, the swan maintained its course, the barrel swaying impossibly above it, as if restrained by a tremulous and unseen hand.

Do it! his mind commanded this phantom puppeteer. *Do it and be done.*

"Fair enough," replied Philip. "We must all choose our path. What is it then, might I inquire, in which you put your faith?"

"In man," said Justus, almost quizzically. "'Fate,' according to Sophocles, 'has terrible power. You cannot escape it by wealth or war. No fort will keep it out, no ships outrun it.'"

Jacob thought he could still hear the faint dimpling of the swan at the far end of the pond. Any second now would come the torrent of water. Any second. His head roared with the inevitable percussion. The moon had at last breached the smoke-colored clouds, pale and circumspect, like a slowly opening eye. Its luster cast the figures of each man into long and twisting shadows, which slithered out before them like peculiar specters.

Justus's eyes glinted back the moonlight. They had nearly completed their circuit around that section of park, three men and their adumbral twins. A smattering of wayfarers had appeared here and there as they'd gone, but none visible now. The night fell quiet, and even the towering imprints of the trees seemed to shrink back against their own enormity.

"Like as the waves," said Justus, "make towards the pebbl'd shore, so do our minutes, hasten to their end."

And so, thought Jacob, *it comes to this.*

Had there been time, he might have wrestled with all sorts of horrific contingencies, but there was no time. He stepped between the two men and extended a hand to Justus, met his eyes squarely.

"It was nice meeting you," he said.

He waited. A barrel teetering.

Justus regarded him, and now a smile crept across his features, tinged with approval. He took Jacob's hand. "The pleasure was mine," he said. He held a hand to Philip.

"Have a good evening," Philip said.

When Justus had gone, Philip consulted his watch, and gave Jacob a nudge. "Up for a drink?"

Jacob nodded. He most certainly was.

CHAPTER 15 – DISCIPLE

He awoke the next morning hungover and possessing the sort of determination unique to such manner of infirmity. He must see Morse again; he hadn't gotten enough. It wouldn't be easy, but he must try, and then he must craft a convincing case and submit it, for time was running on, like the rivers upon whose shores this city had risen.

He went to the café, and when he consulted his phone, there was Justus with another text. Jacob grimaced and cursed under his breath, and took his coffee back up to his room.

> *See Morse no further. You ran afoul of his hospitality, plus you must be penalized for your interference at the park (admirable though it was)! Bring your submission to me tonight, by the river, under the Nivedita Setu. 9:00 p.m.*

He set to writing. Wrote and deleted, wrote and deleted. Got more coffee. Got some food because he hadn't eaten, and barely made it to the bathroom in time to vomit. Returned to the desk.

In the end, there blinked upon the screen a text whose economy belied the effort expended in its composition.

> *You instructed me to rely not upon my writing ability but rather that truth I would*

discover. And so, my case for Reginald Morse is neither fanciful nor protracted. Clearly, he suffered some manner of trauma and loss, as clearly did Danny Marcus. These are things surely known to you. And surely, you'd know it to be false were I to tender some romantic tale of him overcoming these things and living happily ever after, of how he serves the Mission owing to the faith and serenity of his own heart. He can find neither forgiveness nor hope; his faith has been shaken, his heart tormented. He has made of his life a prison, his service his penance, hardly a happy life, but I submit to you this: it is his life to live. His life to live and his choices to make, and if this endless atonement is the path he must walk, then who are you or anyone to deny him? Perhaps this self-recrimination is deserved (though I tend to doubt it). But even at that, his choice, his road. Where is it decreed that happily-ever-after is the endgame we all must seek? And no matter what compelled his service, he has given it, years of it, toiling away to help others, countless others. Reasons be damned — this is more than most do. Leave him to his exile, to his service, to his road. Leave him.

He printed the submission in the business center and headed on foot for the Hooghly, at the iconic bridge Justus had specified, and arrived early. A distant region of otherwise blackened sky flashed ghost-white beyond the structure, which loomed pitch and outstretched like the slatted, beseeching wings of some monstrous fowl. The skies rumbled.

Years ago, he'd read "A Sound of Thunder," the first known literary treatment of Lorenz's Butterfly

Effect, that notion of minute changes in one state of nonlinear systems, impacting events in later states — a butterfly in Mexico causing a hurricane in China, and all that. This idea gnawed at Jacob, and the fact that it did gnawed at him further still, for the circumstances in which he was mired did not seem the grand culmination of some smaller, incipient event. Flash and rumble repeated, and he wished the fleeting luster would confer upon him but a sliver of wisdom, illuminate some hitherto veiled thread. Perhaps he'd been looking at things all wrong. Perhaps he was living Lorenz's notion in reverse, and these circumstances, these flapping of tiny wings, were not compelling him toward some profound moment, but were themselves woven by some prescient occurrence of erstwhile past.

He forded his way down a slope of reeds that whispered at his passing, until he reached the sandbar that ran down to the river. Every few moments in the still night, the muted flap of small fish breaching sounded from the shallows. Moonlight had lent to the surface a lucid, shimmering luster, a motherlode of diamonds spilled forth from benefactors unknown.

A barge appeared now from the gloom beneath the bridge, announced by brazen beams of yellow light that fell out over the surging blackness, causing the river to appear somehow ablaze. A company of honking waterfowl soared upward into the cover of night like rousted trespassers. A few smaller vessels drafted behind the barge, upon one of which a man stood starboard smoking a cigar. Between puffs, he fell to silhouette, until the ember flared again, like a cycloptic, demon eye. Did it spy him there at the river's edge, an itinerant soul awaiting some baptism of this unholy hour?

Behind Jacob loomed the hot city, night fallen but offering scant relief, a stark city at once old and young, for what was age in a city boiled to the essence of its dwellers? An essence discoverable in the crumbling fountains of dusty malls, where children played, where men would kill for a pittance, and where, in the missions, charity and penance permeated. All of a minute and that minute of a day, and that day gone down to the dust it had raised, as the dwellers of that city would go down to dust as well—a question only of time.

Jacob regarded the moon upon its suspended perch—pale, painted world, sending tides asunder, setting wolves to doleful song.

He closed his eyes and listened to the river. *Back to the sea.* He thought of Anabel, to whom he would always return. *But what of that river turned back? Politely diverted. Our currents once ran as one, but there is no room for you now.*

Jacob's eyes flew open. Justus would be here imminently, and lives hung in the balance, but all of it felt in this moment displaced by the tide of his bereavement. By his realization that, like the river, some things ran on, and the most grievous losses appropriated from one's heart a levy compounded in advance of all despairing yet to come. He felt something now, and turned from the river and peered back toward the subsiding city. He narrowed his eyes and watched as Justus swept like a gale across the expanse between them.

Tell the wind and fire where to stop, wrote Dickens, *but don't tell me.*

A wind arose and his papers flapped, and he secured them and regarded Justus's approach.

Something caught his eye from below, and he looked and saw the rats had come once more, scuttling past. Reviled creatures, bearer of plagues. Among those things that plagued Jacob grew now an unnerving consideration: that this man and his ordinance, deplorable both, had nevertheless instilled in him an ardor greater than he'd ever known. This man had hauled him from his comfortable inertia, hauled him, perhaps, on account of it. He'd marooned him unto this feral breach out from which he might only claw contingent upon becoming something feral himself.

Justus drew closer, now a stone's throw away.

Jacob unrooted from his spot and strode toward him, and they came face to face.

"Why these goddamned field trips?" Jacob demanded.

"Manners, please," said Justus. "The Bhāgirathi-Hooghly is sacred to Hindus, its water thought holy."

Jacob stared in disbelief. "Is that what you think this is? Something holy?"

Justus shrugged. "A fair question. Time will tell, perhaps. But I believe we dishonor a place and its people if we discount their history. And this place—here, where we now stand—teems with it." He swept his gaze about. "The Comnial Wars of the eighteenth-century. The Battle of Plassey Palashi. The earlier wars against Maratha raiders. As the river runs here, so ran their blood."

"Thanks for the lesson," Jacob said. "You'll forgive my lack of interest, under the circumstances. Unless there's some clue there that'll help me out of this nightmare."

Justus looked wounded. "The greatest of clues," he said.

Thin cries sounded above them, and Jacob looked up to spy a silhouetted flight of birds wheeling in the pale darkness. The river thrummed past, obsidian waters whispering the passage of all things.

"Nightmares," continued Justus, "are but a dream. Where you find yourself, and where we stand, is anything but. It is real, as those who stood and fought and bled their lives into the sands beneath us, were real. People rise and fall, as will us each. There is only the question of when and how. No greater wisdom I might confer."

Jacob stiffened, fighting to stave his rage. "Perhaps you think I should be grateful, but perhaps it's you who should be. I should kill you where you stand."

Justus listened politely, then nodded. "Whatever your will, I shan't begrudge it. There now, see? How you must feel. Willing to kill now. Have killed. Can you tell me, honestly, have you ever felt more alive? As those who rose and fell upon these banks surely felt, and same the world over. For truly, when night falls upon another day, those trivialities with which we preoccupy ourselves fall away too, and all that shall be registered is who has lived and who has died, and so again each day to follow. So," said Justus, perfunctorily, "you have called upon your subject?"

"You know I have. You obviously have followed my every move. You see I've got the papers."

A river breeze broke over them, setting briefly aflutter the articles in question, which rippled audibly in his hand.

"I do indeed," said Justus. "May I have them, please?" He extended a hand. Jacob thrust them over, and Justus narrowed his eyes in examination.

"You're going to read it here, in the dark?"

"Why not the dark," said Justus. "Even in the most garish light, how many of us truly see?"

Jacob's lips drew back. This man and this commission were loathsome enough without such reveries. Justus now strode toward the riverbank, papers in hand, and Jacob frowned and followed.

When he reached the banks, Justus was already kneeling at the lapping waters, some strange and dark disciple. Jacob's eyes widened as Justus extended the papers toward the water, like one setting afloat a Japanese lantern.

"Jesus!" Jacob rushed to the water's edge, but it was too late. His papers had set off upon their journey, crinkling in at their edges before skimming away atop the rolling darkness.

Reginald Morse, this is your life. Penned into witness, exiled into watery interment.

Justus rose.

"You didn't read it! You're rejecting it?"

Justus came alongside him and looked out over the water. A foghorn intoned mournfully from somewhere upriver, and a chorus of baying dogs rejoined almost instantly. Another barge issued forth from the chasm beneath the bridge, its lights an eye of startling illumination upon the dark run of the river. Large moths and other insects swarmed into the hot white beam, and now from the underbelly of the bridge descended a coven of bats, a coil of thrumming wings and ravenous cries that imprinted into the arc of illumination and set to feasting.

"I saw that which I needed," said Justus. In the dark patina of his gaze hung twinned, gray moons. "You have done well for our Mr. Morse. Better, perhaps, than he has done for himself."

"What game is this?' said Jacob. He put a hand in his pocket and grasped the jasper. "To pass judgment? Bad enough that we crossed paths, but what did these people do to deserve this? They already have their demons. They certainly don't need to be plagued by you."

Justus turned to face him. "Splendid!" he cried. "These are right and proper questions, and if properly pursued, shall serve you well. Too often we chase answers all the while oblivious of the questions. You have done well, and may move on to the next leg." He turned and strode back up toward the reeds that bearded this stretch of shoreline.

Jacob watched him and felt the smallest ember of hope kindling within. Nothing grand, for hope had changed for him, no longer fluttered in the airy realm of what might be, but hunkered down in desperate consideration of what might not—a matchstick in a cold, dark room. But still, it was something. This would put him on schedule.

"Oh!" Justus called out.

Jacob squinted to where Justus stood silhouetted against the dark and sleeping city.

"I nearly forgot. You are comporting yourself admirably thus far, but our purpose would hardly be served if it is accomplished too easily."

Jacob's jaw quivered.

"Your timeline has now been altered," Justus called. "Ten days now, not fourteen."

Jacob felt Justus grinning in the darkness as he watched him turn and recede into the night. He clenched his fists, the rage appropriated as much inward as without, for now he knew himself guilty of a grave miscalculation, of grievously misapprehending the nature of things. Almost immediately had he realized the danger this man posed, and the breadth of it, the depth of it. It had upended him utterly, overwhelmed him like a great tide, but here was where he'd erred. A tidal wave rushed right at you, straight on, and Jacob had come to regard Justus as right before him, coming for him, even permitted himself contemplation as to how he might, if and when the moment presented itself, defeat this straight on and pernicious threat.

But now he saw it. Now he knew. Whoever and whatever Justus was, he was more than anything like the wind, as destructive at turns as any wave, but far more furtive; as apt to take a wayward turn as to rush straight over him, like ancient winds that had beset him on the mountains, funneling straight down on him one moment, and lashing this way or that the next, even disappearing in a blink. Impossible to get your head around, much less your hands.

He stood unmoving for several minutes upon the colorless shore, where blood once ran, and he thought perhaps he heard it now, whispering to him, urging him from his station.

Chapter 16 – Alibi

He'd always been fascinated by the lines between things. Once, as a child outside playing with friends, a cloudburst had opened and they'd scattered for shelter, but then stopped not a quarter mile off, deer-eyed and blinking in the sunlight that suffused them. They could see the periphery of the ring of rain—could touch it, and did—inches from where they stood. Perhaps it ought not to have struck them odd—storms were finite, after all—but it mesmerized them each.

It wasn't raining as he neared the house at 710 Evergreen, but it looked as though it might at any moment, and the contrast between the pallor shrouding the home and the radiance just beyond, was striking. Justus had provided the address for Rose Tierney—the only of his four subjects for which he had done so—and Jacob scarcely doubted there was a catch. Nonetheless, he'd taken the opportunity to take some precautions, build some cover. He'd searched her name and thankfully gotten an immediate hit, and after some digging learned her family had moved here a nearly a quarter century ago. Her father was a minister. And so now, here Jacob was, the blurb he'd found printed off and folded within his trouser pocket should the need for an alibi arise. That was entirely possible, given the dubiety of his mission, as well as his staggering exhaustion: with two connections along the way, the flight from Kolkata to Cape Town had taken a full twenty-four hours.

It was a simple house—ranch—quaint and well-kept. An older couple hurried past in dark coats and hats, walking a darkly coated dog. They nodded to Jacob and kept their heads down, bracing for the inevitable rain. A large, black as coal raven swooped down from the grayness onto the mailbox, minced about, flourished its wings and settled. It stared at Jacob. He stared back. It croaked at him, a shrill sound, cautionary, but he proceeded past the mailbox and staring bird, and crossed the line of the property.

It would not be the last warning he would ignore.

When he rang the bell, the front curtains fluttered, but when he looked it was merely a cat of striking merle coloration, with suspicious, emerald eyes. It arched its back, regarded him, and skulked away. No answer at the door. He waited a few moments, rang again, waited.

"Hello there!"

Jacob raised his head. The greeting had not issued from the house.

"Over here!"

A woman of perhaps sixty rose from a garden and strode toward him across the yard adjacent.

"Looking for Rose?" she said, smiling.

"I am," said Jacob. He extended a hand. "Just visiting."

The woman rubbed her hands together to shed the dirt and then shook, small in his hand, but certain. "I'm Natalie, Rose's neighbor." She laughed. "Obviously."

He smiled and said, "Jacob. Do you know when I should come back?"

Natalie dabbed at her forehead with the back of her sleeve. "Not really."

Jacob nodded. *Damn.*

"But," said Natalie, "I know where she is."

***

When he arrived at the bookstore, he sat in his car and dialed home, his mind so sluggish that he couldn't recall whether his phone would show where he was calling from, expose his great lie, expose him. No time... *ringing.* And lie he would, as lie he had. Amazing, the proliferant nature of duplicity. How readily it bred. It? Him. He was the liar. He felt sick. *Ringing. Ringing.*

Now the machine: *We are not here to take your call,* said his wife's voice.

Shit. He'd called home, where they no longer were. He hung up, cued up Anabel's cell, and dialed. *Ringing.*

What time is it there? What time is it here?

Ringing. Now a *click.*

"*Hello —* "

"Anabel! It's—"

"*I can't take your call right now.*"

Shit again.

"*Please leave a message and I'll get right back to you.*" Pause. Pause. *Beep.*

"Anabel, it's me, Jacob. Not sure what time it is there. Sorry, it's been crazy, but I should be home in like a week. Is Gabe doing okay? Are you? I mean, not doing okay without me, I'm sure you are, I just mean... I.... Anyway, sorry. I miss you guys. I love you. Both of you. Tell Gabe that. And that I'll see him soon. Thanks. Okay then... bye."

He entered the bookstore and stood looking about amidst the smell of coffee and printed pages, a heavenly aroma to any scribe. He didn't know why, but he headed for the poetry section and turned a corner, and there she was, so easy to tell from her photo, except for the wheelchair: the photo was a headshot, so there'd been no way of knowing. Her head tilted in examination of titles, and a slate-black tress spilled over her face like a waterfall. Bathed in the filtered windowlight, her eyes were what first caught his, wide and forest green, searching.

"Do you always stare at people in wheelchairs, or are you about to hit on me?"

Jacob knotted inside; not the start he wanted. An older woman down the aisle looked up from the selection in her bird-like hands, and regarded him reproachfully.

"I'm sorry," he said, voice lowered. "But I think you might be whom I'm looking for?"

Those eyes sized him up, took him in. "I think we've all heard that one before," she said. "That's not really your best line, is it?"

"It's not a line," said Jacob. He took a slow step nearer. "Rose Tierney?"

"You better have a particularly good reason for asking."

He couldn't help but smile. Her voice, even in admonition, was alluring. Siren. The old lady eyed him, and he eyed her back until she returned her attention to her book. He returned his own to Rose.

"With respect," he said, "I think I do." He nodded in the direction of the café. "Buy you a coffee?"

Rose pushed back from the books and swiveled in her chair to regard him. Something danced behind those eyes, perhaps to say, 'this better be good.' "Sure," she said. "I confess to being mildly curious." She headed toward the café, and he followed. "They know me here," she said as they went, not looking back. "If you're a creep, I'll have you thrown out."

"As well you should."

He bought two coffees and they found a table, and Rose lifted her mug and blew across it, eying Jacob with an indeterminate blend of wariness and intrigue. She poured a dollop of cream from the carafe and stirred it twice around. When she released the straw, it continued unaided several moments upon its centrifugal pass. When it ceased and lolled silently against the side of the steaming mug, she lifted her eyes to a small music box adjacent them on a shelf of mementos and, smiling softly, thumbed open the lid. A cherub-faced ballerina poised at the ready, arms entwined nimbly above her head, and one leg crimped out ninety degrees and bent-kneed from its upright twin, and from the hidden workings of the box rose into the air the dulcet tones of *Air on the G String*. The ballerina, upon this cue, slid adroitly into her routine, posture impeccable, gliding in porcelain perfection.

Rose blew across the rim of her coffee and eyed him through the small twist of steam. "You know it?"

"Bach."

Her eyes glinted. "In fact, no," she said. "Though most would guess as you have. Wilhelmj arranged the second movement of Bach's Orchestral Suite. Number Three in D Major."

Jacob nodded his appreciation of this fact, blew into his mug, sipped.

"Everyone just accepts it as Bach," Rose said. "But details matter, yes?"

The ballerina completed another pirouette as he met her eyes. "Yes."

Her mug clinked lightly as she returned it to the table. "Well, what say we start with some of yours? How did you know where to find me? And, um, *why* did you find me?"

The café reverberated with a ceaseless grinding—coffee beans, smoothies—and a litany of orders at the ready. Yet there in the filtered sunlight, with the steam rising from their mugs, the tiny dancer making another pass, there seemed only to be him and this woman, and Number Three in D Major.

"Your neighbor told me where to find you," he confessed. "I looked for you at your house."

Rose had begun to raise her mug again but paused it now, the steam momentarily shrouding her features. "Oy, Natalie," she said. "Well-meaning. She looks out for me, and Oz too, my cat. Probably only other person I'd trust him to." She chuckled. "God love her. Presumes the best in everyone."

"And you?"

"We'll see. How did you get my address?"

"I'm a writer," Jacob said. He gripped the piping mug with either hand. "Doing research for my novel."

"What's it about?"

"Loss. Perseverance. Hope."

"Ah," said Rose, sipping her coffee. "So, what better place than this, then? Come to see if we are in fact aptly named."

"Perhaps," said Jacob. He sipped.

"Well," said Rose, "that's all pretty romantic, but what the devil does it have to do with me?"

He drew up a breath, exhaled deeply. "I'm not sure it does," he said. "But that's how I stumbled across you. Looking for Americans who had moved here, trying to learn their reasons, learn their story."

He held her gaze, anxious to do so, but more worried about looking away. How to best dress up a falsehood? What to say, how to say it? How to look in that moment of its saying? The anatomy of a lie. *Christ.*

"Stumbled across me?" Rose leaned back, folded her arms. "Fair warning, friend, you may be losing me." The ballerina had eased to a flourishing stop, the music fading as she did so. Rose flipped the box shut.

Stumbled. A fitting word to die upon. "That's how such research goes," Jacob said. "You look up one thing and get routed to another, link within a link, stuff like that. I couldn't retrace each step if I tried, but your family came up. From there, I just looked up your name and found your address." He shifted in his chair and withdrew from his pocket the blurb he'd printed, and slid it across the table.

Rose narrowed her eyes, striking even in this failing moment, and cast them back and forth across that page he'd given her. At length, she looked up, shook her head, and pushed the paper back across the table. "Well, I'll be damned," she said.

Not you, thought Jacob.

Rose nodded toward his left hand. "Married man, I see."

His eyes fell to his ring. He could not be certain just then what registered upon his features, for this topic and this moment defied any semblance of construction, but something must have shown.

"Something of a story there?" Rose said.

He met her eyes again. No derision.

"She left me," he said, quietly. He sipped at his coffee, but quickly lowered it, as it had grown cold. "Not long ago. Nothing official yet, not divorced, but she moved in with her folks for now."

"I'm sorry," Rose said, and she sounded it. "Do you have kids?"

A smile broke its way through the ligatures of his sorrow. How could he not smile at any thought of his son? His hand went reflexively to his pocket, around the jasper. "Gabriel," he said. "Gabe. He's eight."

Rose smiled, and Jacob nearly flinched at its solicitude, not mirthful or expansive, but befitting the moment: tinged with empathy for the doubtless impact upon the boy, but also with affirmation of the unrivaled grace that was a parent's love for a child.

"This has got to be hard," Rose said. "Being away right now."

"Yeah," said Jacob. "It is."

Rose nodded, swirled and watched the cooling liquid in her mug, then regarded him once more. "Okay," she said.

Jacob regarded her. "Okay?"

"I'll talk to you. Be your subject. Whatever you need."

Jacob smiled. He resisted an urge to take her hand. "Thank you."

"But not here," said Rose, pushing back for the table. "Not now. You'll come over for dinner tonight, say around seven?" She eyed him. "Unless you've other plans, of course."

He shook his head.

"Good," said Rose. "Now, how about you tell me your name?"

"I'm so sorry," he said. "Jacob."

Rose lifted a hand, and he grasped it. "Nice to meet you. You'll forgive my caution, but I think I need you to prove it."

"Excuse me?"

"Prove it, that you are who you say you are. Show me your driver's license, please."

He nodded and fumbled for his wallet. "Of course." He held his license out to her.

"Jacob Fallon," she said, and peered more closely. "You've come a long way."

She grabbed her mug, wheeled over to the café counter, and clinked it down. After speaking briefly with the barista, she pivoted back to Jacob. "Thanks for the coffee. See you tonight. You apparently know the place."

CHAPTER 17 – COLLATERAL

He stopped at a grocery store near his hotel and bought a Pinot Noir, then headed to see Rose.

When he rang the bell, she pulled open the door after a moment, and a soothing, savory aroma wafted over him. He handed over the bottle. "Thank you so much for having me."

Rose wheeled back toward the kitchen, heeled closely by the cat that had regarded Jacob so coldly a few hours previous, and which at present glanced back every few moments at him with expressions of similar censure.

"Come on," said Rose. "I'm finishing up, so you can open this and pour for us."

He followed her into the kitchen and, upon seeing him enter, the cat scowled and arched and leapt upon Rose's lap.

"Oz!" she admonished, but she laughed and caressed the feline before gently returning him to the ground. "It's his eyes," she told Jacob. "That's why I named him that. Emerald City and all, you know?"

Jacob smiled and held up the bottle. "Where?"

Rose pointed. "The drawer right in front of you, and the glasses in the cabinet just above."

Jacob pulled open the drawer and withdrew the corkscrew as the cat stepped and shied.

"It's okay, Oz." Rose attended to a boiling pot on the stove. "He doesn't take too well to other men in my life, I'm afraid." She laughed again, though it sounded a touch less mirthful.

"Is there one?' Jacob said. He'd worked the helix into the cork, drilled it down and tilted it, applied pressure, and pulled. The resounding pop sent Oz flying upon the counter, where he growled softly and regarded the proceedings with rapt eyes.

"Oh, Oz," said Rose. "It's okay, love." She turned her attention to Jacob. "A tad forward, such a question, wouldn't you say?"

Jacob had placed the bottle upon the counter—a safe distance from Oz—and was retrieving two glasses from the cabinet Rose had indicated. He met her eyes. "Yes," he said. "I reckon it is. Sorry." He poured the glasses.

"Besides," said Rose, taking up his left hand. "You're the married one. I think before we commence my interrogation, you perhaps ought to tell me the full story there."

She relinquished his hand, and with it he retrieved and handed her a glass. He extended his own. Rose smiled—and damn it all if that didn't set his heart to galloping—and clinked her glass against his.

Dinner was divine, not just for the sumptuous meal but for the ease of their repartee. Jacob spoke of his family and joy and grief, and the tenderness in Rose's eyes felt to him a measure of intimacy he hadn't until that moment realized he'd been for the longest time bereft. Their discourse steeped with empathy and warmth, and this, along with the wine, suffused the evening with endearment. He'd answered Rose's question as fully as possible, but of course did not bestow her with full truth. He could not. He'd left out Justus and how Rose's life and that of three others hung in the balance. He omitted it, as if some collateral aspect to his story, backstory at best, and he read in her eyes that she read this in his—that he was holding back—but she didn't press him. After helping clear the dishes, he and Oz followed her to the living room. She pulled up to the couch, and when she began to hoist herself out of the chair, Jacob flinched—wanting to go to her, to assist, but uncertain if he should.

"Thank you," she said, having either seen or otherwise discerned his inclination, "but I've done it a thousand times."

"Of course." He stood uncertainly, regarding the two chairs opposite the couch.

"Oh, come on," said Rose, indicating the space adjacent her.

Jacob and Oz eyed the spot, and then one another. The cat leapt suddenly, staking first claim, but quickly abdicated upon Jacob's approach, and slithered beneath one of the chairs, eyeing Jacob contemptuously.

"Oh, Oz," said Rose.

Jacob sat, rigid and equivocating. Matters most grave swirled about—life and death matters, entire futures, beyond merely his own—yet what presently benumbed him held each of these things for the moment at bay: the matter, quite simply, of what, here on this couch beside this woman, precisely his next move ought be. He was a boy again, frozen by the prospect of his first kiss, or more, and his heart pounded, and he wondered if he should put his arm around her or inch closer.

Rose turned to him and resolved this question unmistakably. Her lips went to his like the smallest fall of rain, brushing over them like a whisper, before trailing away to the nape of his neck. He closed his eyes and returned her kisses, touching and caressing her, his hands traveling her body as his own awakened and pulsed, despite the exhaustion that pervaded it. From the corners of his clenched eyes, he could feel a hot wetness and he worried of her reaction, but from Rose sounded the most poignant of acknowledgments, and she kissed his cheek down which the tears had traced. Had she inquired of their nature, he could not have said—whether guilt or salvation or some measure of both—but she did not inquire, and instead placed her cheek flush again his own. If the stubble he'd permitted to grow irritated her, she did not show it. Their hands intertwined, and in this manner they sat, bathed in the soft light of the now-risen moon.

Each time a consideration beckoned, he ushered it away, that he might a little longer indulge the raw simplicity of this moment. Not that it was simple, not really. Blood and flesh were roiling, rousing. He was hard and knew she saw it, and felt it too, this galvanizing of his entire body, and he felt a flickering of embarrassment, but just a flicker, for his arousal was, right then, infallibly a part of him, the truth of him, and he felt suddenly and somehow certain Rose would not approve contrition.

She moaned now—guttural, yet tender and disarming—and turned to kiss him again as her hand trailed down his body to his manhood.

His tongue found hers and he pulled her to him, astride him, and their breathing was rapid and staccato, yet harmonized perfectly in exploration and delight, and any misgivings he might have suffered, about if and how she might engage such passions, quickly melted away as they melted into each other. How foolish he was to have forgotten the immutable way of those things most basic. Her body was her body, the use of her legs be damned, and she grabbed the back of his head with both hands and bit gently into his lower lip while working her hips with surprising agility, and he felt badly for his surprise, for here she was as gliding and graceful in her way as the porcelain ballerina that had so entranced her that afternoon at the bookstore. He moaned beneath the press of her most intimate flesh, that heavenly nexus of her inner thighs and womanhood, and he thrust up to meet her, and so they entwined, and he was sure he heard his heart along with their breathing, and he smiled at this harmony.

He gently took Rose's face in his hands. "You're beautiful," he said.

A smile lit in her eyes and she brought her lips again to his, searching them out, searching him out, and their tongues danced — hot and wet and undulant. When after some time — time a most elusive quarry in the throes of such ardor — they came up for air, Rose smiled and nodded at the living room window. Curtained, but no doubt conveying quite the shadowed spectacle.

"Bedroom," she whispered. "Carry me." Her tongue glided ever so lightly across the lobe of his ear.

He wrapped his arms around her and maneuvered from the couch. As her tongue continued its flickerings, he wanted her right there, but he moved toward the bedroom.

"Always ask a paraplegic before carrying them," Rose whispered. "It's like tossing a dwarf — you never toss a dwarf without permission."

Jacob blurted out in laughter, and had to pause mid-stride. It made him want her more. Rose laughed too and kissed him, and they remained there a spell, laughing and kissing and laughing again, and it was only when this subsided that Jacob took the opportunity to resume his march to the darkened quarters of her room, and he did not turn on the light but instead sank with her onto the bed, Rose rolling off him momentarily from the impact. They laughed and she slithered back atop him, and there was only the sound of their communion, that and what Jacob thought to be the furtive patterings of a displeased feline slipping stealthily into the room.

Chapter 18 – The Twelve Apostles

He thought maybe they slept at some time in the night, but they were awake when the sun came up, and together watched it flare across the eastern rim of the world, that which they could glimpse. Vast shafts of translucent light shone, and these in turn spiraled upward until they disappeared into a medley of burgundy clouds. They hadn't had sex, though they wanted to. But he couldn't go that far and, seeing this, Rose wouldn't let him. They'd pleasured each other otherwise, and kissed and confided the evening through.

He learned Rose's family had moved here not just because of her father's work, but because of her, because of something that had happened when she was ten years old—a tragedy, of which she did not elaborate, and which he did not pursue. There was the church in need of a minister, there was the surpassing beauty of the place, and after what had occurred, who among them could argue a change of scenery and fresh start weren't precisely what they needed?

And now, in the soft light of morning, he pressed upon this matter, which he understood he ought rightly leave inviolate. Sacred were those frontier places of a person's soul, places of joyful light, or baleful darkness. You could not let yourself into such a place. At best, you might stand on tiptoes and polish away a section of frosted windowpane for a fleeting glimpse inside.

Even then, you must not tarry, for no trespass was more egregious. Rose's head was nestled perfectly on his chest, rising slightly with his every breath, and he kissed the top of her head and inquired after that which he mustn't, about what had happened those years ago.

"You ask something I cannot give," she said softly, and ran a finger through the dark curls of his chest hair, her eyes glazing with a faraway look. "Such is the nature of buried things."

She turned over now, so that her chest rested on his, and regarded him.

Jacob nodded, guilty over having asked, guilty over this tryst, guilty over so much more.

Rose looked into his eyes, took him in. "Must you truly know?"

He nodded, for how he did.

"There may be a way," Rose said.

"Anything."

"You've a journey ahead of you."

Truer than she knew.

"The Cape," said Rose. "My happy place, as they say. Table Mountain. Can hike, or take the cable cars up. About twenty-five dollars. Best sunsets in the world. Some people bring champagne and toast the moon. I like to light a little candle, kind of my own little vigil."

"Sounds beautiful," Jacob said. "So — "

"I wouldn't send you up there just to see the moon. There's something else... when we first came here... something that will help answer your questions about me, I think. Something I buried up there, when I was a girl."

He could feel the slow thrumming of her heart against his. "You want me to unbury it?"

"You are compelled to, it would seem. I am willing to let you."

He nodded solemnly, waited.

"I'm not so sure I could get you there, though," Rose said. "It's off the path. Quite a ways off. The flattop—the tabletop—where you let off is what everyone knows. It's what's on all the postcards, and it's lovely. But if you are up for this, Jacob, then you're going to have to be ready. You'll be heading off the top into wild country, but nature, for all its beauty, wields power beyond which we tend to respect. You walk in clouds up there, like walking in a dream--some say like walking through heaven. But those same clouds are just as apt to collapse as not, and then it's a white-out and you can so easily become stranded, become lost."

No more than at present.

"It'll be crowded where you let off," said Rose. "At the upper station, with shops, restaurants, viewing stations, walking paths. Enjoy these, take your time, especially with the views. There's nothing quite like them. But to find what you're looking for, you'll need to head for the Back Table, all the way across the plateau. Use Maclear's Beacon as, well, a beacon. It's the highest point on the mountain, towards the eastern end of the plateau. It's a stone observatory built a hundred fifty years ago. The range along the Atlantic coast is called the Twelve Apostles. Get to the Back Table by the time the sun has set about forty-five degrees above the sea. Sunlight will fall over the land, and where it bisects the tree line, that is where you must follow. It is one of the most diverse ecosystems you'll ever see—forest, wetlands, flowers, waterfalls. And the Fynbos—Fynbos everywhere."

Jacob raised an eyebrow. "Fin--?"

"Fynbos," said Rose. "A pervasive vegetation, many different types in the Cape. It's everywhere up there. You'll be amazed by the diversity. Wildlife too, so be careful."

"Thank you. So where—"

"That will be the hardest part. There is a monument there, a stone cairn, really something to behold. Wait for sunset, and where the sun's last rays flare over the tower, follow that finger of light into the forest at the far edge of the plateau. Maybe a half mile in, more or less. It was so long ago. Three decades, in fact. The sun sets at different times and angles different times of the year, of course, so I may be way off. Father had to carry me. We came to a waterfall and then a cluster of orchids— disa uniflora, their proper name. A beautiful orchid, sprung up in seeps along the waterfall. It was like being in a fairytale."

Jacob smiled at the wistfulness in her eyes.

"But my fairytale had ended," she said, coming back. "And I felt it a proper place to bury that part of my life which had been taken. It is there you must look."

"Thank you," said Jacob, softly, unable to escape the gnawing uncertainty of his motivations.

"When will you go?"

He met her eyes. "Today. Soon. Now."

She studied him.

"You'll need provisions. Let's have breakfast, yes? But let me give you some water and protein bars to take, and some candles too, and matches, should the mood strike you up there. Just don't get lost and miss the last car down. Can be a treacherous hike if you take the wrong path, especially at night."

"So noted," Jacob said. He took up one of her hands, pressed his lips to it. "Thank you."

"And a shovel," she said.

For a moment, a skein of dark scenarios arose within the wearied theatre of his mind, grim and spectral visages entreating him.

"Well, just a little spade," said Rose. "If I don't have one, I'll borrow one from Natalie. She's a pretty die-hard gardener."

"How deep must I dig?"

"I don't really recall," Rose said. "It was so long ago. But I can't imagine it's terribly deep. I was only a girl."

"You want me to bring it back—whatever it is?"

At this, Rose wriggled and maneuvered herself until she was propped up beside him, and took up his hands in hers. "Heavens no," she said. "In fact, you must make me a promise." She regarded him, perhaps that she might read the answer in his eyes. Satisfied in what she saw, she bent to him and brushed her lips over his. "You must rebury it. No matter what you find, you must rebury it. Promise?"

She sat back up, and he saw the glistening in the corners of her eyes, and felt the same forming in his own. Framed there in the sunlight, naked and beautiful and smiling through her tears, she looked angelic. He moved to her, and she closed her eyes and smiled as he pressed his lips ever gently upon the wetness of first one eye, and then the next.

"You have my word."

She extended her arms and pulled him toward her. "Remember to return to the cable station before the last car. You don't want to try to make your way down in the dark. More than a few have perished trying."

He nodded and caressed her cheek.

"It'll be a tight window," she said, "for I have given you sunset as your marker. You must find the spot and work quickly. Then make your way back to the station before last light."

"Thank you," he whispered, and their lips found each other once more. "I will."

***

The cable cars accommodated far more people than he'd anticipated — he estimated about fifty in his — and this possibly translated to hundreds of visitors at the summit. This could bode in his favor or against: it would be easier to blend into and slip away from multitudes, yet so too would their presence increase the odds of being discovered in his furtive act. The lower station was itself nearly a thousand feet above sea level, and soon as their rotating car commenced its ascent, they were treated to panoramas of staggering majesty.

Their intended destination first apprehended his attention, a great and rising monolith, ringed by vast cliffs and plateauing at its summit more expansively than he realized from town. A good two miles across, they'd said, flanked by two other mountains: Devil's Peak to the east, Lion's Head to the west. A distinctive gorge bisected the cliffs leading up to the summit, and Jacob could see several hikers at various points along its ascent. As the car rotated, a glimmering bay eased into view, and a cluster of islands, then the Cape itself.

When they shuffled out of the car at the upper station, he couldn't help but feel invigorated by the crisp mountain air. Colder, cleaner, the salty bouquet imbuing him with a visceral sense of connection with the natural world. He checked his watch: just past six, maybe an hour before sunset. Another car unloaded behind him, and its occupants disembarked and fanned out into the various clusters of visitors. Some ambled between restaurants and shops, some gathered around the assorted viewing stations near the precipitous edge of the summit, and still others set forth toward various farther destinations along the plateau.

Jacob squinted across the sprawling expanse — two miles to the opposite end — cinched up his coat, adjusted his pack, and set out.

His father had always found a walking stick, and encouraged young Jacob to do likewise, when they'd gone camping or hiking. Jacob had continued the habit ever since, even as his father fell from his life, and he'd passed the habit on to Gabe. He spotted a fallen branch perhaps four feet in length to the side of his trail, and picked it up. The bark was loose in spots and peeling at the end, but it was of good reach and sturdy, and besides, he didn't plan on being up here longer than a few hours. He'd brought his backpack, but there was only the spade, some protein bars, water, the candle and matches, and Anabel's book.

Life felt different up here, simultaneously closer and more remote, away from it all but right on top of it, so distant a vantage but so absolute. More than disquietude had gathered above. He hadn't paid them much attention upon his ascent, the orographic clouds of which Rose had spoken, but hovered overhead, blood-red in the crucible of dying light, they loomed like the underbelly of some vast satellite. Less an assemblage than one incalculable layer, they seemed to extend the length of the plateau, ranging across the sky to Devil's Peak, which, it was said, owed its legend to a smoking contest between the old pirate, Van Hunks, and the devil himself. The clouds formed from the undying remnants of their fabled encounter.

The tablecloth of the mountain again offered a mixed blessing, sure to mitigate the chances of his discovery, but equally apt to complicate his search. He quickened his pace, glancing upward every few moments. The descending haze had enshrouded the stone cairn at the eastern end of the summit. Maclear's Beacon, the materials had said, constructed in 1865 for trigonometrical survey, was the highest point on the plateau. Jacob squinted through the funneling mist to see the base of the monument already obscured, but its uppermost portion pierced the cloud cover, and perched upon it were a handful of visitors, posing for pictures alongside the spire that jutted from its crest. Standing in clouds. Jacob regarded it wistfully, this sudden Olympus. This world apart.

The plateau, he'd learned, was comprised of five-hundred-million-year-old rock, and the quarzitic sandstone across which he treaded was fissured in spots with steep, gray crags, perfect for breaking an ankle. He strode quickly but carefully, watching his footing now, not the sky. When he finally neared his destination, he paused and took in his coordinates. It took a few moments and considerable squinting to gauge things, but soon it became manifest, an incandescent lane intersecting the periphery of foliage that bearded the edge of the plateau. When he reached the tree line, things darkened considerably, and he paused to let his eyes adjust.

The terrain sloped more immediately and precipitously than he'd anticipated, and he scolded himself for such guilelessness — this was a mountain, after all. He must proceed even more delicately than was required across the cobbled plateau. He'd learned quickly at the Beartooth the capricious nature of such places, how one step might take you from one world right into another, wholly different in landscape and conditions. To wit, this slope down which he now eased was a thicket, and he used his stick both for balance and to part the bramble and branches impeding his path.

Something apprehended his attention at present, something not seen, but heard—an unmistakable whooshing. Rose had mentioned a waterfall, and Jacob closed his eyes and tried to ascertain its locus. It required but a moment for the sound to distinguish itself, the unmistakable rush, and he made his way in its direction.

Five minutes later, he emerged into a brief clearing, and was buoyed to find the waterfall. The water pooled and fell, steadily but not torrentially, in the seeps that composed it. Rose had said it was buried near one of those seeps. It. Whatever it was. He was to look out for a cluster of orchids—red orchids—though whether he indeed stood in the correct spot, or the topography had remained in any way comparable to those decades ago, was anything but certain.

He stopped ten feet from the falls and looked skyward. The vast overlay of clouds hung almost tangibly overhead, appearing from this vantage less part of the sky than sky itself, gray and uncertain. He scanned the seeps until, tracing his vision down to the far base of the waterfall, he detected a crimson bloom. He stepped closer, minding his footing, as the proximity to the falls had slicked the soil considerably.

There. A cluster of orchids. Disa uniflora. Bright and vivid, here in this cold and darkening frontier.

He treaded gingerly to the florid cluster, cast a quick glance about, then slipped the backpack from his shoulders. He unzipped the pack, withdrew the spade, and glanced about once more. No sign of anyone, but the rush of wind and water would surely inhibit any sound of approach. And what, precisely, did he fear? Was it criminal to dig a hole?

And not your first.

He squeezed his eyes shut and threw his hands to his ears, that he might exorcise these voices and focus on the task at hand. There would be time later for such compunction, for all manner of rebuke which awaited him. After one more look around, he dug.

The soil turned over more readily than he'd anticipated, given the season, probably due to the proximity of water. He unearthed a roughly three- by three-foot radius, a foot deep, unrequited, and paused, his breath fogging into the space before him. Maybe he hadn't dug far enough. Rose had said she hadn't buried it too deep, but then, how much had layered on top of it through all those years? If he were even in the right spot.

Jesus, what if I'm not.

Something caught his eye, and he glanced down. A blue-crowned lizard edged toward the hole, but paused upon sighting him, one tiny-clawed leg crimped mid-air and unmoving, nervously awaiting Jacob's next move. They regarded one another in that manner unique to all encounters in the wild, wherein almost instantly a fundamental understanding is conferred. The lizard had no interest in the biped, understood it was helplessly outmatched. Less certain was the biped's respective interest. The lizard blinked but remained otherwise motionless: if this act failed, it would spring into flight. Such was the way of things. But a new variable had come into play—another creature had for the moment stolen the biped's attention, and the lizard seized the occasion to dart off.

This latest arrival appeared some kind of rodent, with conspicuously long incisors, but the longer Jacob looked, it took on a more mammalian countenance, well-tufted and gray, short tail, a rotund body perhaps two feet in length. It seemed to be chewing something as it watched Jacob, not with those vaunted incisors, but with its molars at the sides of its jaw. No remnants of food, though, so perhaps the chewing was done in nervousness.

I mean you no harm, he could assure it. *I am only here to find something buried, then be on my way.* When he turned to resume his work, it scampered off.

Jacob plunged the spade back into the earth, turned it over, and again, until he had fashioned a nearly identical aperture as the first, growing more despondent with each repetition until, on what he'd determined would be his last effort, the spade clinked—lightly but clarion—against something lodged in the soil. Jacob fell to his knees and dug around the edges of what appeared a rectangular, wooden depository, maybe a jewel box. His heart thrummed. He extracted the chest from the earth, shook off errant crumbles of soil, and lowered it delicately to the ground, for those contents possessed within, if not themselves fracturable, represented nonetheless an inestimable trust. The box was snapped shut in front with a small, brass latch, and Jacob nudged his thumb beneath it and paused, once more stayed not by what he might find, but that he'd been entrusted to find it.

When the box opened, a faint, musky redolence lifted from within, and Jacob thought he perceived for the slimmest of moments something else arise with it, scarcely discernible, but there—a faint rippling in the air, then, gone. He squinted, shook his head, and

regarded the contents of that which he had exhumed —
papers, and photographs, and a drawing by the hand, it
would appear, of a capable child. The photographs, and
the drawing too, presented this girl in various athletic
activity, but principally gymnastics, and around the
neck of the girl in both rendering and photograph was
draped an opulent medal. Jacob lifted one of the papers
closer, a press clipping: *Ten-year-old Rose Tierney,
champion. Rose Tierney, daughter of a small-town preacher,
prodigy. Rose Tierney, Olympic hopeful.*

Jacob lowered the items gently back into the chest,
careful not to expose them to the wetness he felt
trickling down his cheeks. The child's accomplishments
were remarkable, but these were not what had most
apprehended his attention. No, it was her eyes, the light
and vitality with which they brimmed, the hope, the
expectation, the formative sentience of all that awaited.
The awakening of a dream.

He sat there for some time, unaware of time, just a
man on a mountain assimilating wordlessly the story of
a life. When at last he did look up, he was surprised at
how dark it had fallen, and consulted his watch. He'd
promised Rose to honor her ritual of lighting a candle
and toasting the moon, which, even through the dense
brush, he could see had risen, enormous and glowing
against the midnight blue above Devil's Peak, fixing
him there where he knelt. He had to go. He relatched the
chest, returned it gently to its resting place, grabbed the
spade, and began shoveling the mounds of dirt back
atop the chest.

After refilling the hole a few minutes later, he
smoothed the spot over with the spade and patted it
down. He layered back on some of the grasses and sod
that had covered it, then rose, gazing a final moment

upon this hallowed ground. He squared the backpack on his shoulders, and faced about to begin the ascent back up to the plateau.

Except, no. A wall of mist hovered in the place where the path had been. He'd not detected it in the slightest as he'd dug, not that one typically thought of mist in that manner, in a manner of detecting, but he thought of it that way now, for there it poised, shaped-up before him, a quiet specter slipped into a room. The clouds, those orographic clouds, and slowly now, as through to beguile him, the wall began to unfurl and expand, shrouding the mountain and all things upon it, so that Jacob could no longer even discern the moon, so prominent mere moments ago. Here then, the tablecloth of the mountain; here then, that smoking testament to a pirate and his unholy foe.

The moon had moments previous afforded more than ample illumination, but Jacob paused now, for the descended layer had subsumed all visibility. A whiteout, of which Rose had forewarned, and as the mist drifted over him—clammy and textured and vaporous—a new and primal understanding arose within him, of those cunning ways of darkness. There he stood, in sightless radiance, beholden to this creeping otherworld and its province, grown with each passing moment infinitely more macabre.

The evening might as well have been midnight pitch, though Jacob knew there remained the glinting streaks of waning day. He knew there to remain at various stations upon this mountain visitors such as him, and so too what other life this place might hold, both flora and fauna, and all manner of cliffs and stones and crags so fathomless to seem as portals to the bowels of the earth. He knew each of these things and more to endure in their place, but for the moment, all life and all things stood marooned in this dominion at once insubstantial and immobilizing, suspect worlds unto themselves. Jacob understood immediately the nature of such a world: that he was its denizen for the duration of its choosing; that even his darting contemplations were dangerous things in such a place. More than all of this, his rising dread that if there could be one thing worse than this solitude so eerie and absolute, it was found in what might yet shape itself out of these spectral depths to invade it.

No choice but to wait it out. The Beartooth had imprinted upon him the danger inherent in the architecture of any mountain, and he dare not amble forth based on a sketchy recollection of whence he'd come. To exacerbate matters, vertigo set in presently, courtesy those smoking, hypnotic layers of fog. He could detect no sign of the world beyond, these gossamer plumes his only world for now—his floor, his walls, his roof—yet a structure most uncertain and illusory.

He retreated gingerly the few steps he'd gone, and sank back down against a silver tree, amongst the bed of orchids. Gray and vaporous filaments curled about the stems, slithered away, and reconstituted with larger segments. Jacob leaned back, propping himself, audience of one in this dry-ice theatre in the round.

***

And now shaped up before him a phantom troupe, begotten souls of despairing countenance at this latest manifest of their fitful purgatory, at the indignity of this tenuous and arbitrary subsistence that is the whim and folly of this man's conscience. This wayward ensemble last convened in his room back in Kolkata—the officer, Parsons, and Flint—regarding this new setting for what they might make of it, before realizing they were as one with it.

The officer seemed the most piqued, drifting over to Jacob and boring through him with the enmity of those hollows where once were eyes, entreating answers. *Why have you abandoned me to the company of such men? And what sort of man are you? To leave me cold and dead on the sidewalk like an animal, justice denied me, truth and peace denied the wife and child I leave behind?*

"I'm sorry," said Jacob, for truly he was, but no words on this day would stand as atonement. No explication would subdue the restiveness of a forsaken haunt.

Beyond them, Flint and Parsons glided stealthily about, appraising perhaps what plunder they might yet appropriate. Some said all sins are forgiven, the slate wiped clean, the worst of us expunged by the hand of grace upon our passing, but it occurred to Jacob that death in its finality might only serve to carve into perpetuity our most defining parts. Come sinners and saints and all between; you have in your choices set out before you your road eternal.

So it is written, and so it shall be.

And so, says the officer, *may your road be attended by company not of your choosing. No peace afforded you, while our peace denied.*

At this, Jacob nodded, as his incorporeal callers disaggregated back into the obscurity from whence they'd sprung. But this parade of haunts had just begun, apparently, as now shaped up before him she to whom his heart had for so many years belonged, substantiated out of the ether to regard him. He wondered now: *Is this not what love is, love and all such notions? But a wishful conjuring, as apt by nature to reclaim that very thing it has bestowed?*

Questions for now left wanting, for Anabel stood before him, and he braced for the adjurement that surely awaited, and was most assuredly deserved. He had been intimate with another, and he trembled in anticipation of her rebuke. But in those eyes no such thing appeared, only the most benign detachment. If there was the slightest trace of censure, it was that she had been in this way summoned, that it was not so much her grace for which he was desperate, but his own.

Any such trace and all sense of disposition faltered now, draining away, much to his despair, for he longed to be near her, but she was dissevering away before his eyes — going, going, gone.

She wasn't there, he told himself. *She wasn't there. No more than Flint or Parsons or the deputy — one of many prevarications to which this nebula lays claim.*

He could see too readily that steep descent, here where all rules frittered away like wind, tumbled away like stones down a mountain. Oh, for a bout of madness, that it might for a moment allayed this terrible sentience that pierced him with its ceaseless refrain.

She wasn't there, she wasn't there, she wasn't there.

This fallen thunderhead had not so much affected the air as displaced it. Like walking in a dream that was no dream, and so he did not walk, must not walk, for the injury or worse that might result. But what was injury to him, this him he had become? What, truly. What misstep and descent more treacherous than those for which he was already culpable? A twisted ankle, a broken back, when death itself immaterial beyond the impact on those others tethered through no fault of their own to his fate? Injury, then, assumed new bearing. Pain revealed a fathomless reach, not bones nor breath nor blood its measure, but only the untouchable distance between ourselves and the ones we love.

But still, for those loved ones and even those strangers whose fates he held, he must demure, be patient, wait out this obscurity. He hunkered back down amidst the orchids, the red disa, waiting for this false world to dissipate, that he may return to that world scarcely more certain, but which entreated him nonetheless.

Straight ahead, he exhorted himself. *Look only straight ahead, that you shall not falter beneath this fallen sky. Focus. There is only that before you.*

Yet something beckoned from the edge of his perception, drawing his eye. A butterfly, the Mountain Pride, on which these orchids so utterly depended. Suspended, wings flared black and white and orange and brown, in such variegated pattern as to suggest some primeval cipher beyond the knowing of all men. Come to do what it must, inexorably. He watched it a moment further, then closed his eyes. Waited.

CHAPTER 19 – STRANGE ALCHEMY

He thought he must have fallen asleep, so much time had elapsed by the time he opened his eyes, but he couldn't be sure. One thing was certain: he had missed the last cable car back down. This was no good. This was very, very bad.

All the shops were closed, poised darkly save for the dim glow of auxiliary lighting, but perhaps some staff remained inside, tidying or locking up. He'd apologize profusely, and simply explain he'd meandered off path, lost track of time, and gotten caught in the white-out. Couldn't have been the first time.

Fifteen minutes later, he'd rapped at each locked door, and some windows, unrequited. *Bloody hell.* He withdrew his phone, eyed the number listed on many of the signs, for park emergencies, and....

Of course. No signal.

Time was time, and his was fleeting, but somehow the futility of his circumstances seemed to exacerbate it. He needed to act, to embark upon a treacherous descent in the darkness, against which countless signs warned, or lose more time and face whatever risks might be associated with staying the night atop the plateau.

He decided upon the latter. Whatever he might face up here, he would at least contend with upon level ground, rather than chance veering off path and plummeting unseen distances to his demise. A stand of silver trees beckoned in the moonlight, and he set off in that direction.

He worried of snakes and God knew what else in the tall grasses beneath the trees, so he lay down for the night on a stone shelf nearby, rolled his jacket up and rested his head upon it, staring up at the rounding darkness, a starlit sea into which he might go hurtling at any moment, and no witness present to protest. Yet he could feel the uncontestable draw of this great, spinning rock, restraining him there with redoubtable exertion, that he could not slip its bonds, ordaining him to what purpose might yet be his. Andromeda winked from her wayward station more than two million light years away, named for she chained to stone in sacrifice. Perhaps as he. The brightest star to the naked eye, yet not a star but close a trillion, snaked the firmament in elliptical shaping, a galaxy itself.

We see what we wish to see. Who has two million light years to spare? And what now is time but the accounting of things which must be done.

In the enormity of this quiet, the wash of unwanted truth broke over him. Like those cresting waves he couldn't see, but knew broke ceaselessly beneath him at the foot of these cliffs. These strange flutterings of his implacable heart grew—in this world gone aberrant, a development more aberrant still. This should not have been, this stirring of parts of him subterranean and grown cold. In all that he'd forfeited—things he'd had and things he'd been—no ballast save one had kept him afloat. Were he a soul gone wayward, his body little more than some puppeted husk, what compelled him was devotion to wife and child, and should this devotion be in the smallest manner impugned, he shuddered at the notion of what he'd become. He regarded the stars for what truths they might provide, his mind awash in rising sacrilege. Yet how often throughout the centuries had sacrilege borne out as truth, had man in its yearning enwrapped itself in intoxicating layers of delusion? This strange alchemy had long been anointed and long since named: love. The word skittered away like the muted sounds of the small life passing in the darkness around him. Was love anything more than our chemical prostrations, a hapless obeisance evoking surely the perplexed derision of those onlooking gods, if such gods there be? Were we truly to believe, in the quiet void of such depthless nights, that the Fates in their wisdom had ordained to each of us a soulmate, sprinkling a speck of serendipity, that we might in our travels encounter them?

The sky, a vault of burning lights, bequeathed him not the slightest answer, begging only more inquires. Suggesting from their celestial vantage the sad gullibility of the world below, and he shapeless and prone in the dark remote of this alien place, he in his husk recoiling at the thought of the emptiness within. Fearing suddenly that he should be shucked down to his essence, and no essence there'd be; instead, only a bleeding out of man's posturing, and trailing this a primordial ooze of blood and hunger and wantonness, that for all its distaste evoked from the world a grudging acknowledgment of its gospel.

And yet, when the tide of these realities at last retreated, he remained anchored there with the same truth as ever, that which never ebbed, which sustained and depleted him, at once his scourge and his salvation. Prostrate beneath the eye of a watchful moon, itself occupied in its ritual conducting of those far greater tides below. Oh, for the refuge this might have granted, stranded here upon this darkened summit, reprieved even briefly from the urgencies of his ordeal and the recriminations of his own mind. Splayed there upon this spire, a plaintive offering, restrained from his task and unfettered by all distraction, he'd become infinitely more assailable. A great and terrible light thrown upon him, in the tract of this pervading darkness, revealed this charlatan he'd become, this mountebank, this non-him, taken up residence in that hollowed space inside.

It was colder on the mountain than the mid-fifties below, but he had a jacket and it hadn't been that bad. Even with the fading hour and falling sky, when the last streaks of sunlight succumbed beneath this cloak of mist and a chilled wind swept across the plateau like phantom stallions, he tugged his collar more snugly upon his neck, jammed his hands into his coat pockets, and soldiered on.

Prone beneath this starlit theatre, night full on and the air crackling around him, it occurred to him he might have gravely miscalculated. His breath hovered like small clouds above him, a lost child beneath this latticework of unseeing stars, which in their brilliance illuminated the heavens, but whose light from such remove fell upon the world cold as stone.

He thought for a moment how amazingly quiet it was, given the environs, but quickly realized it wasn't quiet at all. Various cries pierced the air, sporadic rustlings whispered through the grasses, and frenetic wingbeats thrummed overhead. Far below intoned the unequivocal sea, tuning all things around it, great conductor of this strange and feral symphony. An indispensable adaptation, the ability of humans to selectively filter and attend various sounds and stimuli, but how in this alien world to know upon which to focus? So many professed a desire to be at one with nature, but it occurred to him, lying there in this pitch and breathing world, where things with teeth seemed to be awakening by the moment, that the only way this was possible was if it swallowed you whole.

He hadn't at first noticed the murmuring and quiet movement within the ring of silvers, which formed the periphery of his encampment. A dimpling within the leaves, which he took first for wind but, now that he peered more intently, took on the telltale impression of something animated. He reached into his pack for a protein bar, took a few bites, slid it back into his pack, and rose quietly. The trees had registered as another piece of this shadowed world, but now that he'd zeroed-in and his eyes adjusted a bit, they glimmered in the moonlight, pale and apparitional—elegant, ghostly limbs. He'd thought perhaps a snake or bird responsible for the activity within, but the eyeshine glinting back at him was of such character and proportion as to suggest something quite larger. He swept his gaze over the space around him, in search of anything he might appropriate as a weapon, on the off chance he'd need to defend himself.

Surely, that was a stretch. He turned on his phone's light and inched toward the trees. The night seemed docile enough, but still the sea seemed in fuller throat, out here in the boundless dark, a colossal waterfall laid flat. He'd felt it, too, where he'd lain, pulling at the submerged bedrock of these mountains with their own gravity.

Jacob's attention remained on the trees, where he'd spied the movement and eye shine. Something was in there. He could tell this not by what he saw, but what he didn't. The moonlit branches offered quite the presentation, a beguiling overlay of shadow and light, but where he gazed, the pattern broke, imbued by a different sort of darkness, its nature for the time concealed.

When Jacob neared within ten feet, the breeze seemed to stop, and things grew quiet, and the branches seemed to crimp inward. He directed the phone's light that way. The eye shine briefly flashed before fusing away within the phone's illumination. Now materialized, incrementally — for Jacob's mind was fighting to piece together what his eyes beheld — the dark and matted torso of a large and incongruous beast. A baboon, and now Jacob vaguely recalled warning signs on the way up. It was sitting cross-legged, like a large child, its body tufted in dark, silvery fur, its long tail curled up beneath the branch on which it sat. Its ears were pointed, wolf-like, its muzzle long and black, and it looked at him and, for a moment, appeared friendly enough, like a dog, but now its lips drew back from the muzzle to reveal a set of fangs that Jacob understood immediately could kill a man.

Jacob inched backward, not wanting to alarm the creature with sudden or demonstrative movements. He would get his backpack and retreat from this location, and take his chances making his way back down the mountain. The baboon eyed him, and he eyed it back, trying desperately to recall what his father had told him to do should he ever encounter a bear. This was no bear, but he'd no other frame of reference, and now the thing was easing forward in the branches, so that it might pounce, were it so inclined. Jacob thought he remembered that it was best in these situations to stand tall and hold your ground, but then, maybe you were supposed to play dead. Hell if he could remember. He would keep backing slowly away, grab his pack, and go.

When his feet found purchase upon the rock shelf, he reached behind him, not turning his back on the baboon, but his grasping search was to no avail. *Shit.* The animal had paused in the canopy, so Jacob permitted himself a quick glance behind him in order to relocate his pack. It wasn't where he thought he'd left it. A baboon he hadn't detected in the slightest had laid claim to it and dragged it a few feet off, and now crouched staring at him with bared fangs. He flinched, and the animal barked and scrabbled backwards with the half-zipped pack. The matchbook and candle Rose had given him went skittering. The wrapper of the protein bar was lodged between the baboon's teeth, and as it worked its mouth frenetically about, the wrapper disappeared.

Hell, thought Jacob. *There are more bars in the pack.*

These of themselves were of no consequence to him, but they were to the hunkering, agitated beast, and surely to any more of his klan that may catch wind. This also meant all else in the pack was now in jeopardy. The spade had served its purpose and could easily be forsaken; so too the remaining rations. But the book.... his Anabel book.... He intended to give it to her someday, maybe no day soon, and almost certainly not as some plaintive gesture meant to ply her into reconsideration. He'd do near anything to get her back, but it seemed somehow more important to preserve this testament in the event he did not, to preserve that most abiding piece of himself even as, especially as, so many other pieces continued to slip away. He reached for the backpack.

The baboon reared and snapped and clutched it to its chest, and Jacob quickly took a step back. The animal bared its fangs and glared with flashing eyes, and once more Jacob struggled to conjure whatever sage wisdom existed for quandaries such as this.

Stand tall. Yes, he was pretty sure that was it. *Stand tall and gesture and vocalize aggressively.*

"Ah!" he cried, feigning a charge. "Ah!"

The baboon flinched and shied, then reared again and snarled, trying to pull the pack farther away. Jacob feigned again and the baboon emitted a series of sequenced barks. One. One-two-three-four-five. One-two-three. And then one long, drawn howl into the darkness.

The darkness answered.

The breeze had picked up again off the sea, and upon its gusts now arose a discord more haunting than the wolf cries he'd heard upon the Beartooth. These were not mournful, but angry, menacing, and of far greater number and proximity than Jacob had by any means bargained. He lifted his eyes to the copse of Silvers. Each of them seemed alive now in this strange substantiation, this spectral interplay of shadow and light, disjointedness and coalescence. From each canopy glowed like coals the eye shine of beasts such as the one poised gnashing before him. They crept forward in the blackness, apparitional within the shadows.

Jacob executed a very slow turnabout—he estimated a dozen baboons, at least, and who knew how many additional lurking beyond his sight. The one with Jacob's pack barked again, a staccato calling, and its brethren answered again in a piercing cacophony. Some had slipped from their branches and crouched on the ground not ten feet from Jacob, and fully presented in the luster of the moonlight, they were large and darkly coated, each baring its fangs. Jacob's eyes scanned feverishly over the immediate area for any sign of a weapon. Futile, he knew, but he was moving on adrenaline now, his body seemingly possessed of its own sentience, keenly aware of the gravity of the predicament it now confronted. The shovel could help—it wasn't of great reach but sharp—yet it remained within the folds of his pack. He must under any circumstance retrieve his book, and in so doing could then of course retrieve the spade, and then—

A baboon behind him grunted and shrieked, and Jacob whirled in time to stay its charge. "Ah!" he screamed, waving his arms wildly about. "Ah!" The baboon scampered back and rejoined its troupe, scowling at Jacob all the while. The baboon with the pack yammered, and Jacob whirled back around, and it screamed and feigned and retreated farther. Jacob scanned the grounds once more. The stick—his walking stick—was all he had. He shot over to it, scooped it up, and swept it around in his pirouette. The baboons closest him screeched and leapt back. More had materialized from the trees, and filed in behind those most proximate to Jacob. He checked his phone, keeping the stick raised as he did. Still no signal.

One of the baboons screamed and feigned. They had him surrounded. Another growled and lunged, and Jacob bellowed and parried it back. The end of the stick was somewhat fraying, but still retained something of a bite at its tapered end. It had to be now. He must drive off the baboon behind him, retrieve his pack, and fight his way out. Maybe they'd stand down once he'd reclaimed the backpack. He would give them the remaining bars and make a run for it. There was little chance they viewed him as a meal. They wanted his food, that was all, their hostility owing to that and probably fear, so surely once he'd given over the bars, they would let him pass.

But he must have his book.

He turned carefully back to the baboon with the pack, making a pass with the stick, all around him, as he did so. The baboon snarled, attempted once more to flee with its prize, again to no avail. Taut with adrenaline, Jacob summoned his nerve and leapt forward with his stick, and the baboon dropped the pack and scampered back several yards, where it turned and feigned and snarled. Jacob fell to his knees, one end of the stick tucked under his arm, and unzipped the pack. He fumbled for the protein bars, found them, and turned and tossed them in the direction of the converging troupe. The inner ring of baboons screamed and shied, but then quickly fell upon the offerings, tearing and biting at them and squabbling amongst themselves.

Here was his chance. He felt for his book, closed his hand around the binding, felt for an instant that jolt of purpose which had for so very long defined him — felt, despite Anabel's departure and the direness of his predicament, that blood elation found in obeisance to the gospel of one's heart. He felt these things purely and entirely, marveled at the ability to do so in these circumstances, thought how love, in all its glory and all its pain, was surely the most enduring of things.

The larcenous baboon charged again, and Jacob cried out and parried it, but dropped the pack in the process. The crush of baboons behind him yammered and seemed nearly upon him, so he spun and bellowed and swung the stick, driving them back again for the moment. When he turned back, the thieving baboon had pilfered the pack once more.

He was exhausted, and growing woozy. He must take one step at a time, now, with the utmost dedication, that he might live to see the next. A primal focus —

caveman, food, shelter, fire. His head was spinning as the baboons feigned, and Jacob parried again, then paused.

Fire.

The packs of matches lay strewn on the ground between him and his pack. He eyed the end of the stick, just dead and frayed enough that it might catch, but how to steal even the few seconds needed to try. He must reclaim the backpack, but the snarling beast that had once again claimed it seemed ready to defend it to the death. The rest of the troupe seemed ready to beset Jacob at any moment, too, and if he lowered his guard to effort the lighting, they surely would. But he must have the pack, for he must have the book.

He cried out and thrust at the baboon, but rather than release the backpack as Jacob had hoped, it snarled and retreated, pack in tow. The baboons behind Jacob snarled and feigned. He executed another flailing pirouette, again sending them back, again but for the moment. His legs were unsteady, his strength fading fast. Another pirouette, and the animals fell back, and in this briefest of reprieves, he snatched up one of the scattered matchbooks. He would need more time to attempt a light, so he spun again, brandished the stick, and yelled. The baboons fell back, feigned and snarled, including the one with the pack, and now Jacob saw that in its retreat it had swung the bag such that the book had fallen out.

A chance.

But first, the matches—he must attempt a light. The troupe barked and began to creep back. The mountain seemed to have roused, a chorus of hoots and howls echoing in discordant harmony with the jawing baboons, like the impenetrable wailings of a terrible madhouse. Jacob slid the stick back toward him, upright like a staff, so that the end he'd been pointing now rested before him, face-level. With his opposite hand, he pulled at the fraying strips, rotating the stick around and peeling them down. He yelled again at the creeping baboons, yelled and feigned, then fluffed up the strips until they resembled something of a bedraggled wreath. He wedged the stick in his armpit, struck a match, and groaned as it promptly snuffed out. He struck again, tried awkwardly to cup it this time, and the match caught and flared ever briefly, but extinguished again.

Come on. Come on!

He glanced around him at the baboons, which seemed momentarily stayed, uncertain of his ministrations.

It wasn't going to light like this. He didn't detect much wind but he'd spent enough time on mountaintops these last weeks to understand there was always wind, felt or unfelt, a ceaseless turbulence reminding of the precarious stasis between heaven and earth. He needed a greater flame, and for that, greater tinder, and he needed it now. Another sweep of the stick, and then he leapt forward toward the bandit baboon and bent and snatched up his book.

He scampered back, as had the screeching primate, performed another sweep, and lodged the stick once more under his arm. He dropped the book to his feet, crouched above it, and withdrew a match. Everything around him continued to swim.

He felt the animals moving closer again, and he bellowed and rose up slightly on his haunches. He sank back down now, full on to his knees, maneuvered his hands into as much of a cupping posture as he could muster, and struck the match—a flare, then gone.

Shit!

He flipped open the book so the pages would be more quickly accessible. A second gained could make every difference. The words upon this arbitrary selection registered vaguely in his consciousness, something about loving the mother she was, something about how it made him a better dad. Perhaps one day, long from now, should he live to see it, the irony of the moment would overtake him — he'd risked his life to save that which he was about to burn — but for now it settled somewhere within him, aching dully. That ache would no doubt sharpen at some point in the future — to a measure no less grievous — but now there was only the narrow prism of his task, the matter of striking the match and catching a light and protecting it and transferring it to the pages.

Were he not so exhausted, his hands might have shaken, but he seemed glazed into a dim focus, and they held steady, the match took, and he kindled it gingerly to the lightly tufting pages of the book. That the baboons might at any moment beset him while he was poised in this vulnerable state had not entirely escaped him, but it was because of this, not in spite, that he redoubled his concentration. The flame bowed and shied at the edge of the pages, flaring briefly translucent before beginning a slow advance across the pages. The paper curled, blackened, crackled softly in dying throes, and Jacob carefully lifted the book and flared the next few pages, that they might become similarly engulfed. His mind registered vaguely the subtle shift in the vocalizations of the troupe — still agitated, still aggressive, but also curious, alarmed.

Jacob lowered the book to the ground, slowly, so as not to be burned or extinguish the flame, but also for the solemnity of the moment.

O for a Muse of fire.

He stood and executed another sweep of his stick, and the baboons, which had yet again begun creeping back toward him, yammered and fell a few feet back, watching. Who was this strange being, and this mystifying fire dispelled from his fingertips, for the only fire they knew was that wrought by lightning, some having witnessed it, all having understood it from the first, from the blood tapestry of their lineage. They understood its power and its pain, and so it was that when this mad and bellowing biped whirled once more about, the tip of that weapon he'd been brandishing now frightfully ablaze, a great terror arose amongst them and they cried and slunk slowly back, some scampering back up into the cover of the Silvers.

Jacob exhaled and glanced skyward. *Deliver me from this mountain, and I'll ask no favor more.*

He cursed himself softly for beseeching a benefactor in whom he scarcely believed, and entreating covenants neither was apt to keep. He glanced about to see most of the baboons had retreated into the trees or huddled together just beneath. Jacob retrieved his torch. It was waning some, and he dipped it into the flaming remnants of the book until it flared back up. It wouldn't last long—perhaps twenty minutes from the looks of it—but what did he know about the lifespan of improvised torches?

There was much he didn't know, but life had of late become much more about the look and feel of things. Either way, his flame would extinguish soon enough, and if it did not, he must extinguish it, as it would have burned its way down the length of the stick. When he could use it no longer, he would power on his phone and use the light, but for now he must wield the torch to ensure his passage from this expanse, at least, to fend off any of the baboons that might still accost him here, or along the way to the path that wound back down the mountain. Hopefully, none would besiege him once he reached the path. *If* he reached the path. They were likely used to visitors there, knew they were no food source, probably even considered them a threat. And Jacob had conceded his pack, given over his rations, and so hopefully they desired nothing further of him.

He raised the torch and stood in the firelight, a weary sentinel. The baboons still chattered and barked, but held back now, no longer feigning, the air freighted with an uneasy détente. Jacob eyed the burnt book, what little of it remained. The fire had consumed it wantonly. Black and orange embers crackled into the air, and a pungent musk hung about its smoldering ruins. It was burning out fast upon its stone bed, but he could not chance an errant ember, which might find its way to the dry grass, so he gingerly placed the heel of his boot into the lingering flame and ground it down. The fire hissed and thick plumes of smoke shot from beneath his boot before escaping skyward in dark, fading spirals. Jacob stepped aside, checked for embers, and spying some, stepped back atop them with both feet and ground and tread about as might one stomping an assortment of hybrid, glowing grapes. When at last the fire died, he stepped back and looked a final time upon the smoldering residue, upon this smoked-out pyre, upon his book of dreams consumed.

When he turned about, the torch brandished high, the baboons that remained on the ground shrieked and fell back. He'd glimpsed the walking path, one of them, anyway, on his ride up, and was pretty sure he could intercept it a little ways down from here. He guided the firelight toward the tree line, glancing behind him once more and pricking his ears, and, as satisfied as possible that the baboons were not in pursuit, then eased into the brush. He figured to reach the path engaging a roughly forty-five-degree descent. The baboons did not appear to be following, but this only from what he could see, and what was to keep them from setting after him at any moment, particularly once the torch died out? And what other manner of life or obstacle awaited him along his descent? Beyond the borders of the firelight, the mountain pressed in upon him, so that as he proceeded, he did so within the narrow prism of his hard-fought incandescence, this modest box of light outside which the world became not more luminous, but darker yet.

It wouldn't be easy. His legs were first to alert him, conducting up to his brain the burden induced from this unnatural gait. His path immediately obscured by foliage, he mustered his reserves to keep the torch high, away from this sprawling tinder. He peered ahead within the modest scope of visibility, one arm extended to ward the clawing reach of jutting brush, tapping as might an equine with his foot upon this uncertain terrain. The blueish smoke trailed into his own chilled plumes of breath, so that each step was like traversing the portal of some gauzy netherworld. In this manner he proceeded for a considerable period, the distance no doubt incommensurate with the duration, the hazard of his descent compelling a tortuously halting pace.

He wanted to check his phone for the time, and perhaps there'd be a signal now, but what use would that even be? How could he describe precisely where he was, and to whom? Would he hunker down in this lost world, in this thicket, awaiting rescue from some helicopter or jeep? He needed to get to the path.

When perhaps thirty minutes later, at last he spied it, something primal exhorted within him. He'd come down another mountain. No way of knowing, really, how many remained. He staggered on, another fifteen minutes or so, until the parking lot appeared, an oasis in this ghostly desert.

He stumbled forth from the tree line, sighted and slunk cautiously toward his vehicle in the otherwise abandoned lot. When he reached his rental, the earth seemed to cant up wildly toward him, and he braced himself on the vehicle. After several draughts of breath, no one of which felt assured, he straightened back up and regarded the mountain a final time, that darkly imprinted leviathan. Having endured where most men would have withered away. Not just yet, he thought.

He fumbled for his keys, found them, and half-collapsed into the vehicle. There was work yet to be done.

Chapter 20 – Distillation

Back at the hotel, he grabbed his laptop and collapsed onto the bed. Justus awaited, and so too, therefore, Rose's fate. He longed to go to her, to embrace her, thank her for all she had shared, not least of which that he had just hours ago unearthed upon the mountain. He wanted to shield her from the iniquity looming just overhead. This longing evoked in turn an equal distillation of confusion and rebuke, for who was he if not the loyal husband and father? What was he, if his heart had so easily strayed? *Strayed from she who has forsaken you.* Yes, this was true, but no, it was no excuse. And yet....

Stop. Bloody hell, stop. Lives hang in the balance. Think. You must craft your submission, craft and send it, and hope like hell it is accepted. Then go to her, but make haste.

He wrote.

> *Rose Tierney must live.*
> *This I think you know.*
> *She has endured a great many things, beyond whatever occurred in her childhood, and of which you are doubtlessly aware. I am not certain precisely what occurred (though I suspect you are), but I do know whatever happened robbed her of her dreams, robbed her of so very much.*
>
> *Again, all this you know, right? Of course, you do. Why else is she on the list? You know it, and so it behooves neither of us for me to recount occurrences, but rather to acknowledge her courage*

and resolve in all the time since. More than just that specific dream of her childhood, there were other dreams too, dreams we all have, whatever their manifestations – of love and work and life, infinite really – that were either altered or snuffed out entirely. And, from what I've deduced from my limited vantage, her family did not make things easier for her. Still she persevered, and not just with courage and not just with strength and not just as this incredibly intelligent and erudite being, but with something more, something which, even from my vantage, is impossible to miss.

She has a light, deep within her and illuminating all around her. Have you been around her? For her sake, I hope not, but if you have, perhaps even you couldn't help be taken in. Do I insult you? Truth will out, as you have so adamantly insisted, but it took me in. Whether because of my vulnerability, and whether my allowing it bespeaks my own moral failing, in any case, it bespeaks nothing but esteem for her. Judge not, that ye not be judged, yes? She does not – unlike some – judge, but rather gives a little light to one in such desperate need of it, despite those dark spaces in her own soul. I can think of few things nobler. For one from whom so much has been taken, must be granted all possible remaining freedom. She must be left alone to live as she sees fit. To live. If there exists any trace of justice in that most perverse of minds, you will see this. If you cannot, then take me in her stead. Rose Tierney must live.

He paused a moment, then sent it. He inhaled deeply, exhaled deeply, welcomed the tides of slumber pressing upon him, though no peace, he understood, would they bring.

Chapter 21 — Falling

When he arrived at her house, he knew he looked frightful, what with the exhaustion and injury. After ringing the bell, he straightened his clothes a bit and ran a hand through his hair. No answer. It might take her a moment, he realized. His eyes traced down to the bottom of the front curtains, in anticipation of feline-induced movement, but the curtain was still. No sound came from within. He waited... rang again.

"Hello!"

The neighbor, Natalie. The scene unfolding much like it had the day previous, distant though that now seemed.

"Hi," said Jacob, turning fully about.

"She's gone," Natalie said, closing the distance between them.

He started to thank her but something had arrested his attention, something squirming in her arms as she approached. Oz.

"Did he get out?"

"What?" Natalie glanced at Oz then back up at Jacob. "Oh, no, he didn't get out. Rose went away for a while. Did she not mention it?"

Jacob swallowed and took an extra second to find the words. "No. Did she say where, or when she'll be back?"

Natalie shook her head and frowned. "She didn't." Oz squirmed and purred and arched his back. "Only that it would be a while and would I look after this sweet guy."

Jacob forced a smile. "Okay, thank you." He turned to go.

"Wait."

He turned back.

Natalie regarded him with a strange expression, stroking the back of the purring feline. "Is everything all right?"

Jacob swallowed, hoped she didn't see. "I'm sure," he said.

***

He parked in the lot and headed as he had the day previous for the cable cars. Abutting the lot, small ridges of the mountain base fell out to either side, and protruding from one a craggy shoal some ten feet or so off the ground. Jacob perceived through the twilight something rising atop it, dark and odious. Justus's form and then features materialized, a terrible pestilence conjured out of the gloom. Jacob felt his jaw working, his gut churning with animus, but he headed dutifully for the shoal.

Justus stood and withdrew from the pocket of his vest his timepiece, and dangled it above Jacob. "Your submission is approved," he said, smiling perniciously. He looked from Jacob to the cable station. "Ah," he said, eyes glinting. "The game within the game. Make haste on wing of this favorable verdict, or tarry further, owing to some noble motive with which you ply yourself."

"My game to play," said Jacob, meeting Justus's eye. "You said so yourself, remember? The deadline is the deadline, and I do as I wish within it."

Justus snapped the timepiece shut and repocketed it. "Right you are." That grin.

Jacob whirled and strode toward the station, loathe to abide Justus a moment longer. Nor would he occasion a glance back; no need to watch him disappear back into the gloom, conducted by that darkness like so many lampless roads.

He paid his fare, boarded, and stared out the glass at the world falling away, at that stone world canted up before him. The few other passengers stared too, chattering among themselves. When they reached the top, Jacob stepped out, shielded his eyes against the flaring sunset, and regarded the lay of things before him, as he had the day before this, time being the strange thing it had become.

The summit sat vast and sprawling, but he knew where he'd find her, if find her he would. Not on the western edge, where throngs gathered with cameras and phones in hand, immortalizing the sunset, the cotton candy sky with incandescent streaks of berry, magnum opus of the day that was. At the edge of his vision, sun and sea met in blazing confluence at the rim of the world. Gold fire suffused that quadrant of sky beneath the violet canopy, straight down to the black-inked horizon, from which laid out that tremulous cobalt world. The sun itself dipped now into that watery realm, but hardly extinguished: it simmered there, emboldened, placid and recumbent beneath the smoldering eye of its ebbing sire.

He spied Rose on the eastern rim, the lone figure in the distance, shadowed quietly in the pale wash of a stone-faced moon. He strode toward her rapidly, something knotting inside him as he went.

She, seeming to sense him before it seemed possible he would be heard, wheeled partly about. "I thought you were leaving."

"I thought so too."

"Come to save me?"

"Maybe myself," Jacob said.

"Come closer."

He did, and was taken somewhat aback upon discerning the sheer drop-off just feet from her chosen spot. Night had already arrived on this side of the mountain. The sea lolled darkly, and dark shadows of gulls floated against the dusk. Something of the secrets of such places occurred to Jacob just then, that their greatest magic resided not in their own majesty, but in their ability for one perfect moment to make the rest of the world vanish, illuminating the principals on stage as all else fell to silence and obscurity. There remained just him, and just Rose, and their truth, in all its terrible beauty. The space around them fell to a sort of dusky blue, the sort of shadowy light that, in its dimming of the farther world, brought into stark relief that which resided just before you. Within the shroud of this spectral glow, he regarded Rose, palely lit and sublimely beautiful, and she regarded him—sole proprietors of this moment and of this place.

"Did you find it?" she asked him.

"I did. And reburied it, as promised."

"Thank you. No misadventures, I trust?"

He paused, uncertain any longer what qualified as such. "Nothing I couldn't deal with."

Rose wheeled closer. "Good. I hope, now that you have seen it, you understand why I couldn't just tell you. Why the effort behind burying it—not the physical effort—required effort to unearth."

Jacob stepped to her, lowered to one knee, took up her hand, and said, "I think I do. I wouldn't presume to know a fraction of what you've endured, but yes, I think I understand."

The wind picked up, whipping up the sea below, the slap of crashing waves so relentless as to be almost soothing. A formation of cawing gulls wheeled into view, dark and furtive shapes, before diving.

Rose turned back to the ledge. "It's a view like no other. You afraid of heights?"

"Afraid of falling."

Rose smiled. "Maybe you would fly. I come here sometimes and think what it would feel like to take wing and be free, even for a moment."

Jacob inched closer.

"Of course, Father wouldn't see it that way," Rose said. A bitterness tinged her words, like the saltwater breeze that broke over them presently. "He always said to keep the faith. It was practically an order. Others would tell me too. Well-meaning, most of them." She traced a finger along the arm of her wheelchair. "It's always those whose faith is yet tested who are quickest to implore you to hold fast to yours."

Jacob listened. One didn't do much else when someone was unburdening themselves in such manner, but her words, in content and tenor, sounded to him like the end of something.

"So," Rose said, "Father would call that sort of freedom a sin, but what of the sin that stole mine away so long ago?"

Jacob eyed the narrow gap between the ledge of the summit and the black wheels of the chair. "But are we not told that is precisely what faith is — retaining belief despite of, perhaps because of, those tragedies that befall us?"

"We are told that, yes." Rose smiled wryly and gestured at the precipice before them. "But she who accepts blindly things told — in the face of things lived —

is but a lemming who would, if so exhorted, plunge, swaddled in faith, to her demise."

The wind quieted, and Jacob rose and stood alongside her. The sea seemed to expand exponentially in just those few feet, calling, pulling, a vast, solvent arbiter of all things beginning, middle, and end. He saw himself and Rose as if from a distance, the two of them gazing out to where the darkening edge of this watery world met the thinning horizon in a nexus of otherworldly tincture. He was a decent hand at description, but understood those moments that most profoundly called for elucidation were the very same for which no words could ultimately suffice. He blinked away the vantage of his mind's eye, returned to himself.

"Back to the sea," Rose murmured.

"Rose—"

"I like you," she said, and his heart thrummed as she touched his arm. "In this short time, I've come to like you. That says more than you may know."

Jacob stood silently.

"We're not too far from where the two oceans meet," Rose said. "The warm water Agulhas current meets the cold water Benguela and turns back on itself. That's an interesting thing, don't you think?"

Jacob squinted out along the far plane of the sea.

"Dias named this place Cabo das *Tormentas*," she said, emphasizing this last word. "Cape of storms. Was only later the name changed to Cape of Good Hope."

"Pretty big difference," said Jacob. "Storms and hope."

Rose glanced up at him. "Is it?"

Rose's pupils shone with twin reflections of the moon. It lent to her eyes a celestial glow, the image so lucid that Jacob could make out the dappled surface, but even that bled quickly away into the emerald architecture of her irises. She took his hand and pulled with gentle insistence, and he lowered once more to a knee so that he might meet her gaze straight on. In those moonlit eyes he now glimpsed his own, as she, he knew, glimpsed hers. Truth will out in a place like this, a place long scrubbed clean of dubious and fragile features, smoothed down to its essence by those elements that prevailed, and one who came to know such a place understood any attempts at the slightest pretense would find no footing, but careen away along those polished routes carved out through the millennia.

Only truth remained, as raw as nature, in that small and closing space between them, between their burning gaze and seeking lips, beyond all judgment. Still, he knew, if for no other reason than the late hour of his undertaking, it was a space he could not cross. He withdrew his hand from hers, slowly and contritely, and unzipped and reached into the new backpack he'd purchased.

"I brought you something," he said.

He'd not wanted for this moment for her to have to bother with batteries and unboxing the thing, and so he'd put in the batteries and had it ready in the pack. As he withdrew it, the lid fell open and Air on the G String alighted upon the sea-kissed breeze before the item itself was even in view.

He moved to give it to her, wanted to see her eyes, but they were closed, lifting her along what causeways the music had for her determined. She turned her palms out to him, whether to receive the music box or his own hands, he was not certain, but he felt it must be the latter. He set the box down, and when he placed his hands in hers, she smiled and held them fast.

"See," she said, her eyes slowly opening. "I like you for things like this. It's the little things, yes? The details."

A fuller darkness had settled upon them and the sea thrummed steadily below, the unfettered wind skimming across it in a great whisper of the world's secrets. Through the darkness Jacob saw that Rose was crying.

When she opened her eyes and saw his concern, she shook her head and smiled and said, "No, no, it's okay. It's all so good."

"Then you'll come?" he said, squeezing her hands. "You'll come with me now?"

Her smile faded slightly, but the light remained in her eyes. "Where?" she said. "And for what? You still must leave, yes? Miles to go before you sleep."

He started to answer, stopped.

"And you have a wife," she said. "And a son. Return to them."

"I told you," Jacob said, "she left me. Yes, I still love her, but—"

"Jacob." She leaned toward him in her chair, and he felt the warm kiss of tears upon his hands. "You have given me much in this short time. Please allow me to give something to you."

"You already have," he whispered.

"Something more," said Rose. "And you can do with it as you will." She squeezed his hands and smiled again, but when she spoke again her voice was tinged with a great solemnity. "From what you have told me, there may be little hope with Anabel. I hope I'm wrong, oh how I do, but from what you've told me, I fear your hopes—and your heart—may be dashed."

"So that's what you leave me with? Accept the loss and let it go? That one day I'll find new love? She was the love of my life, Rose. Not temporarily, not until the next. Her. I neither seek nor warrant the slightest sympathy, for the blame rests at my doorstep, but if she is gone forever, then so too is all hope. You would have me accept it, bestow me perhaps with some epiphany of perspective that will help me move on?"

He started to withdraw his hands, not for any antipathy but the shame of his petulance, yet Rose held fast. "I'm sorry," he said.

"You don't have to be," said Rose. "And you don't have to move on. Your devotion is perhaps the thing which endears me to you most. You don't have to move on. Maybe you can't. Maybe you can give your heart to no other, and if that part of your life is over and your heart beats out in vigil for the rest of your days, then so be it. Embrace it. Who am I to say?" And here she pulled him closer still, so that their faces nearly touched. "Perhaps you can't move on, but you must *go* on, and in your heart, I think you know this to be true. You go on because you have a son, and you must give him all that you can—you and Anabel both. You must show him that even when things like this happen, life goes on, not without pain but in spite of it, not easily but nevertheless, and you must model courage and resolve and gratitude for all those things for which you remain so abundantly blessed. Gratitude that while your heart may be broken, there are in fact worse fates. You must get up every day and meet that day. Don't begrudge yourself your pain, for it is real and runs deep, and may do so for the rest of your days, but please—please, Jacob—do not permit it to paralyze you. You have a choice in that. Not everyone does. It may not be the way you dreamed it, the way you imagined, but you have chapters left to write."

It occurred to him there in the darkness upon that windblown summit, that sometimes the most proper response is none whatsoever. He regarded her and hoped his eyes conveyed the gratitude he felt, and they were silent a good while until at length he said, "But I wish there was something more I could give you."

"You can."

He'd penned enough words through the years to know life's greatest meaning lived in the spaces between. And there was little doubt of the meaning here.

"Rose...."

"Please." She squeezed his hands hard now, urgently. "Jacob, if you've come here to save me, however noble, you must know that when you fly off tomorrow I can simply return. Or the day after that, or the next. It is hardly your job to save me, but I'll say that you've done so in ways you may never know. If you truly desire to give me one thing more, then give me the greatest thing, that thing which has been robbed of me in so many ways."

His heart thundered so that even the ocean in full throat seemed to lull a moment in deference to the matter at hand.

"Freedom," he said.

She smiled. "To do as I so choose. Mayne not tonight, maybe not tomorrow. Maybe never. But to have the choice."

Jacob closed his eyes and listened to the sea, breathing its salty bouquet. When he opened them, Rose's were right there, and she touched his cheeks with angel hands and pressed her lips to his. They were wet and salty too, and in this confluence grew wetter and saltier still, and they tasted of one another their essence, their sorrow and joy and an intimacy borne of acceptance unconditional. No more to be said, and when their lips at last disjoined, their foreheads pressed gently together, and they squeezed each other's hands.

When this was done, Jacob handed her the music box, stood, and walked slowly back toward the cable cars.

***

Night. Cold mountain air pooled in the valley in a vast overlay of fog, smoking out of the forests and across the fields and over the roads, so dense that even his high-beams bored only such visibility as to make it appear the pavement was unspooling anew, scarcely ahead of his passage.

It was, however precarious, beguiling. Beautiful. He cared not a bit for it, not owing to some apprehension of its illusory nature, but on account of how viscerally it reminded him of his own. A great device, the mist, in all manner of storytelling, whether as a compelling touch of description, or perhaps establishing mood, a palpable sense of foreboding. Of what lies beneath. What evil lurks in the hearts of men? He feared not the answer, for already had evil reached through the veil to find him.

When the fog of his own soul cleared, it was not what might be found that haunted him, but what might not. The fog hid not his soul, but *was* his soul, and when it spired away at last, it would leave behind nothing, and never again return.

CHAPTER 22 – CLARION WORLD

When he woke that next morning, he withdrew from the manila envelope the last of the photos Justus had given him: the child's.

Her eyes, bright and moonlike, had arrested him from the first, speaking to him from an ancient, clarion world, spun of an innocence he could not again know. She regarded him through the strange and glossy film, entreating him, forging wordlessly some vague but implicit contract: *Make things right.* He'd known even then, in the drunken brume of that smoke-addled bar, that he must do just that. His hand trembled as he clutched the photograph and met her eyes, and for a moment he shifted his gaze in shame.

He thought were Justus there, he might be unable to keep from killing him on sight. To have imperiled a child, to have involved her in any manner in this ruinous affair.... But here again Justus had played another insidious hand: unlike the previous three subjects, there was no name, no location, no information whatsoever. It occurred to him to upload the image to a search engine, in hope of a hit, but he would first have to scan it.

The hotel had no scanner, but told him the library would, and he set out accordingly into the awakening day. He walked, to the apparent disappointment of the hotel's mustachioed doorman. A cab might have saved him ten minutes, but fruitless would they be if he didn't manage to shake the torpor that plagued him mind, body, and soul.

Get the blood moving. Awaken what determination might remain.

He'd snatched a cup of coffee on the way out, and he raised it steaming in the dew-kissed air to his mouth as he strode. It breached his lips simultaneous to his foot misstepping upon a crumbled bit of sidewalk, and he exclaimed as a larger than intended dollop coursed past and went searing down his throat. Too hot, it somewhat scalded his lips and throat.

Good. This is good.

When it was his turn at the library, he set his coffee upon the counter, produced the photograph, and asked if he might have it scanned.

The librarian, a diminutive, bespectacled woman, eyed first the cup, from which had dripped a pellet of condensation, then the phototroph, and then him. "Do you have a card?" she asked.

"I do not. Do I need one to scan something?"

She said he did not and they regarded each other silently a moment, and he lifted the coffee and mopped its leavings with his palm, and she looked disapprovingly at the filmy print this left, and told him to please follow her.

The first attempt was unsuccessful, and the librarian looked up at him like the failure was his.

He peered over her shoulder at the screen. "I think it defaulted to a PDF," he said. "Does that sometimes. Could you try maybe setting it to a JPEG?"

She returned expressionless to the screen and moved the mouse this way and that, and inquiries about file size and pixels and what not flared, and she dispatched them and moved the mouse, and a minute later asked him what email address to use, and he told her, and she typed it in.

He thanked her, found a table, set up his laptop, and found the email. He clicked open the image. The girl regarded him: *What took you so long?* He saved the image, left it open upon the screen, a witness to his machinations.

He went to his search engine, clicked the camera icon, and clicked upload image. It twinkled on the screen, darkening, this strange summoning of a digitized soul. He watched, and the girl watched him, as her clone materialized onscreen beside her. Both now entreated him. Unsettled by it, obliged somehow to both, he harbored a feckless loyalty to the first, for she was the progenitor of this unsolicited spawn. And yet, not even. There was the original photo, sheathed neatly in the envelope so given by Justus, laid beside him on the table. Of course, the child herself, somewhere, awaited unwittingly his intercession, as all children await unwitting the intercession of that world to come.

Some thirty minutes later, he'd no luck whatsoever—no name, nothing at all evoked from the adjuring image. He turned from the monitor, cursed softly, withdrew her photo and studied it. A strange sound reached his ears, and he looked about and saw an old man muttering over his newspapers a few tables up, inspecting them with, of all things, a magnifying lens.

"Sir."

The man kept to his reading.

"Can't find a good pair of reading glasses?"

The lens paused upon its odyssey, and the man looked up with an expression about as amiable as the librarian's, then turned disjointedly in his chair. "No," he said, his voice like a saw in a log. "If it's anything to you."

"No harm intended," said Jacob. "I think it's ingenious, actually." He nodded at the assemblage of photos and papers before him. "I was just thinking I might do well to borrow it a moment, if you'd be willing. See if there's something here I'm missing."

The man regarded him a moment, then extended the implement toward him. "There's always something we're missing, son."

Jacob nodded, rose, stepped over to the man's table. "Obliged," he said. "I'll only be a few minutes."

The man waved a dismissive hand. "Where am I going?"

Jacob smiled and nodded again. "Thanks."

At his table, he trained the lens over the girl's cherubic features — looking for what, he could not say. Perhaps some epiphany would imbue him with the recognition needed to set him on his way. But all he saw was a deepening of what he'd already seen: a beautiful, wide-eyed child in whose suddenly prominent pores, in the now nuanced strands of cascading hair, emanated an innocence as crystalline and perfect as a first snow.

But who was she? And where on this great and listing rock might he conceivably find her?

Her features nor her cherry-colored dress provided the slightest clue. He swept the lens about the photo, and again, deliberately, paused every few moments as might a beachcomber wielding a metal detector in search of a hit. Nothing stood out, just a few discolorations and distortions, owing perhaps to age and the haziness of the sun-dappled porch on which the child stood.

Jacob sighed, rested the lens upon the table, and stretched his arms behind his head, numbed with exhaustion. When for a moment he closed his eyes, he nearly drifted to sleep. He started and leaned back over the table, and as he did, the bank of lights above him caught the photograph anew, and then he saw it. Briefly. A fleeting blossom of discoloration that, for the first time, occurred to him as something more. He felt eyes upon him and looked up to see the old man studying him, and he nodded and picked up the lens and bent back over the picture, closer this time, face pressed flush to the lens in examination of the illusory, brick-colored smudge. How mad must he look to the child, bent wide-eyed and cycloptic over the oval glass above her? The blemish blurred and he sat up, blinked, and shook his head. The old man did likewise and returned to his papers. Jacob returned to his perusal.

There.

An inch upon the photo above the girl's shoulder, perhaps a foot above, to scale, appeared diminutive markings — numbers   and   letters   too — scarcely discernible and etched, it seemed, in some Lilliputian hand, shrouded within a vague and phantom border. Jacob's eyes narrowed. Not etched upon the page. *In the page.* Part of the page. Impossible. Now, as he settled into the best possible vantage, his eyes widened and his spine ran cold as the rendering shaped into the first flickerings of coherence.

666-

IS NO GOD

Jacob broke from the lens and bolted upright, his head flooded in a confluence of discordant waters. These were things in which he did not believe. A chill rode up his spine, and it occurred to him that fear knew no grander victory than bursting upon the theatre of man's disbelief.

His mind churned as Medusa coils roused gnashing unto the breach of new realities, for none of what his eyes beheld squared with anything he'd ever known. He raised his head, blinked again, bent anew over the lens, as if it would be gone, this most ghastly of emblems. Although, would this stand him now in any better stead? The appearance then vanishing of this fiendish mark? Better to be haunted or mad, or so far along either road as to render moot the difference. He was no closer to revelation, and still the hourglass flowed, appropriating away more than he cared to reckon. His eyes locked helplessly on the photograph, which pulled at him until he felt what little stamina remained might spill away, drawn away in obeisance.

"Huh."

The murmur registered vaguely. And again, louder. A clearing throat. When he looked up, the old man stood peering past him with furrowed brow.

"Find what you wanted?"

Jacob set the lens down and rubbed his eyes. "I don't think so," he said.

The old man looked from Jacob to the picture. Back again. "But you found something."

Jacob glanced at the photo. "Yeah."

The old man held out his hand. "Let me," he said.

Jacob stared dumbly a moment before blinking again and nodding and handing the lens back over.

"By the looks of you, I'd say you seen a ghost," the old man said.

Jacob glanced about to see if anyone were in earshot. Seeing no one, he lifted the photograph with a slightly tremulous hand, and extended it to the man. "Perhaps."

The old man cocked an eyebrow, took up the photograph, and raised it before his squinting eyes. In this manner he remained for at least a minute, his craggled face scrunched up and petitioning. Apparently unsuccessful, he now lifted the glass to the photograph, one eye clenched shut, the other peering hugely from behind the lens like a madly inquiring cyclops. Another minute later, he lowered the lens and photograph and gestured with both to Jacob.

Jacob carefully grasped both items and placed them on the table as before.

Back at the main desk the librarian eyed their activity with a sort of feline lassitude.

"No wonder your color, then," the old man said, nodding toward the photograph. "Perhaps a ghost it is, but the devil's in the details, young man. Always is. And it's not his hand at play here, despite what you have just seen."

Jacob nodded, glad to hear it, if not entirely convinced.

"I seen it," said the man, glancing edgewise at Jacob but otherwise retaining his focus on the object in question. "You believe in that sort of thing?"

"I don't," Jacob said, and he didn't. "Probably not. Maybe. Maybe in some ways different than most."

"There's only ways different than most," said the man. He raised a small and weathered hand to his mouth and coughed, a rough sound, coarse. "There's only the way we believe things, and no one else believes them quite the same."

"Even if I don't believe it," said Jacob, "I see it. You saw it too. And I can't explain it."

"Look again," said the man, turning to head back to his own table. "You're looking too much at the thing." He was shuffling down the aisle now, but his words trailed back to Jacob. "We do too much of that: look at a thing, and just that thing, preoccupied with whatever's right before us. But life's more than that. There's what's behind it, beside it, all around it, leading up to it. Many pieces to the puzzle. We won't get far only looking at one."

The man had reached his table and eased back into his chair, diminutive and hunched. He looked up at Jacob a final time. "Bring back the glass when you're done."

Chapter 23 – Secrets

It has appeared out of nowhere, the storm, and still seems a far way off, shelving blue and billowy in the distant west. Whether it has anything to do with the rougher currents, the boy is unsure, but what worries him more are the looks being exchanged between the adults at either end of their raft. The raft is coursing faster and rougher, the river lapping up and over the sides. The children at first laugh and look on in excitement, even as the adults tell them to hunker down and hang on.

"Maybe the lifejackets," the man at the back of the raft calls out.

"Best they stay down and hold on," the boy's father says.

When they hit the rock, the boy has a sliver of time to realize that's why his father had just cried out, "Jesus Christ!"

He's flung backward in the raft, and bodies tumble over him, and one of the men is shouting that a few kids are overboard.

"I got the boy," one of the men shouts, and there are a tumble of bodies and the boy is swallowing water and the river is bouncing and the sky is rising and falling crazily. The last thing he remembers is his father's voice, so frantic in its intonations that it frightens the boy to his core.

"The girl," his father cries again and again. "The girl...."

***

When Jacob awoke, a number flashed into his head: 2999. He'd discerned the 2 — inverted like the rest of the numbers and letters—upon closer examination, upon discerning the faint shape of a plastic screen window he'd somehow missed until then, and which obviously reflected the markings emblazoned on the front of the house: 2999, Dog on Site. The t and e hadn't shown, but of course this was what it was, and then he'd also seen the letters below, substantiating like reappearing invisible ink. RonaM euR. Rue Manor. And finally, now, a stroke of luck: when he entered the address, his jaw dropped—Franklin, just a few towns over from his own.

He hurried to the airport and arranged passage home. Although there were hours until his flight and the flight would be a long one, he was happy to be headed back.

When the plane lifted off, he fell benumbed with the opiate of inordinate considerations. How many days were left? Two? Three? None? He thought it might be two. Could he find the girl in time, and succeed in this final elucidation? There was the consuming prospect concerning Rose—was she alive? Dead? What did it say—what would it forever say—of him that he'd gone on his way in the face of her possible demise? That she'd so exhorted him did little to mollify the crushing apprehension and addling exhaustion.

He ached to go home first, even briefly, being so very close, but he resisted and rented a car and drove straight to Franklin. To 2999 Rue Manor. It felt odd employing the mapping technology, when on pulling up to his destination it looked and felt very much like he'd gone a considerable way back in time. The dated ranch home, tired and gray, retained the same weathered porch as in the photograph. Jacob's heart accelerated as he parked the rental and strode toward the front door, uncertain what he would say, what lie he would tell, but exhilarated he'd found the place.

He knocked, and after a brief silence, small footsteps sounded on a creaking floor. When it pulled open, a hunched and gray woman stood peering out at him with an expression neither welcoming nor hostile, but bespeaking a detachment commensurate with years. The girl's grandmother, perhaps? Or maybe mother, pending the age of the photograph.

"Good morning, ma'am," Jacob said. "Sorry to bother you. My name is Jacob and I had a few questions about the house. May I talk with you a moment?"

"She won't speak," said a voice from the gloom beyond, an old voice, pleasant. A slow shuffling of feet on the threadbare floor ensued, like sifting sand. "A mute, she is, but mine at that." A wrinkled, gray face evinced from the darkness, then a frame shrunk by years to a childlike stature. The skin caved to eyes gaunt and cratered, but those eyes still gleamed. The man touched his wife gently on the shoulder.

She regarded his hand and, after a last glance at Jacob, shuffled back into the darkness.

"What can I do ya for," said the man.

"I'm looking for someone," Jacob said.

"Fair enough." The old man watched Jacob with the patience of one settled in for quite a spell. "Aiming to tell me who?"

"I'm at something of a loss, I fear." Jacob withdrew the manila envelope from his jacket. "I've only a photograph."

The man's eyes remained on Jacob's, unjudging.

This instilled all the greater his desire to proceed as honestly as possible. Again, something in his stomach turned as he withdrew the photo of the child and handed it to the man, who accepted it with a rumpled, slight hand.

The old man raised it before his straining eyes. "Why that's what's her name, Midge," he said suddenly, turning back to the shadows. He held the photo up to his wife, who sat a few feet away on an easy chair in the foyer.

She stared impartially a moment, but then her eyes widened and her gaze shot from the photo to Jacob, and then to her husband, and she quickly crossed herself, rose, and shuffled from sight.

Jacob stared after her a moment before turning back to the man in the doorway. "I'm sorry," he told the man. "I—"

The old man dismissed him with a flourish of the hand. "It's all right," he said, "but now I remember too." He lifted a crooked index finger to his temple. "Get to be my age, it takes longer and longer sometimes."

"No worries," said Jacob, though a reservoir of it had begun to churn within him. "Do you know her?"

The man's face crinkled forlornly as he handed the photograph back across the threshold to Jacob. "Knew," he said. "We all did. That there's sweet little Grace Luctus. Lived here with her family before we did." He shook his head. "Such a tragedy."

"Oh," sputtered Jacob. "I, um.... She's... gone?"

"She's at Bane and Lux," the man said quietly, and nodded.

Jacob regarded him a moment, more questions begging, but a current of discretion welled up within him and so he carefully replaced the photo, and nodded in return.

"Thank you," he said. He turned to go but paused, unable to help but think a little something more was owed. He angled back toward the man, who leaned in the doorframe as if part of the place, watching him with the same acceptance as before. "Did you want to know why I was looking?"

The old man smiled wistfully. "That's another thing that comes with years," he said. "People will tell you what they want you to know."

Jacob nodded again, met the man's gaze. "I want you to know," he said, "but truth is, I'm not so sure even I do."

The old man braced up from the doorframe and extended a withered hand. "Well then," he said as Jacob took it up, "I wish you Godspeed."

***

"Don't get no funny ideas, there."

It took him a moment to register the sound, so lulled and ogling he was at this strange wasteland, where fell out before him a sad copse of fallen crosses, overrun stones and long untended grass. Here and there an unearthed plot appeared: empty graves awaiting tenants, or perhaps enterprising dead who'd found no rest upon this pitiable range, and clawed up and gone forth in search of more reputable quarters. Small birds stepped about and cried in the wan and shadowed twilight. He'd known, soon as the old man had told him—known, but told himself he could be wrong in his surmise, that it could be a house, a house where little Grace had gone to live after moving from Rue Manor.

"I say, don't get no funny ideas there."

Jacob turned and shielded his eyes against the dying sun.

A cop, somewhat paunchy, regarded him with narrow, suspecting eyes.

"Forgive me," said Jacob, "but what funny idea might one get at a graveyard?"

The cop shuffled forward, raising plumes of dust from the rutted road. A keyring any dungeon master might envy jangled upon his hip. He removed his cap and gestured with it to the graveyard. The last light of day gleaned off his bald and beading dome.

"You'd be surprised," he said. "I'm the sheriff." He ambled alongside Jacob, and they peered out together. "Kids. Well, teens, I mean. Get drunk and party here like was they own house while their folks are away. Drinking, defacing them stones, having sex right there like they's on a goddam sofa."

Jacob smirked and said, "Well, I'm not here for any of that. Just passing through."

"Yeah," said the sheriff. He mopped his brow with his pale blue shirtsleeve. "Ain't we all though."

Jacob gestured. "Doesn't look like the place is kept up."

The sheriff angled a glance at him and said, "You ain't from around here, then."

"Petra," said Jacob. "Two towns over."

"Well, then maybe you heard. The place gone outta business a few years ago."

Jacob cocked his head. "How's that?" He frowned at the paucity of the place.

"Old man Lassiter," said the sheriff. "He owned the place, and his family before him. Gone back centuries. But business died down—well shoot, I shouldn't phrase things that way. Business slowed, and he started losing money and, hell, he up and closed, same as any other."

Jacob's eyes swept over the ruinous expanse.

"He used to say, Martin—" The sheriff turned to Jacob "—my name is Martin. He used to say, 'Martin, people just ain't dying like they used to.' Always lamentin' exercise and healthy food and what not, and I'd tell him—" Martin grabbed Jacob gently by the elbow to ensure his attention. "—I'd say, Lassy old boy, you may be right. People don't die like they used to. But you still as hell have got you the one business in town where customers is a sure thing, one day or another." He relinquished his grip on Jacob's elbow. "You know?"

A raven flew from the leaf litter and alighted on a rounded, smoke-colored headstone. It minced to and fro before settling into stately repose.

"Yeah," said Jacob, and Martin glanced edgewise at him. "I know." Jacob nodded toward the decrepit graves. "But certainly, there is some precedent, some etiquette for this sort of thing. Care or transport of their bodies?"

Martin shrugged. "Only such etiquette that money can buy. Those with means up and got their loved ones—dug 'em up or had 'em dug—and took them yonder to God knows where. Other cemeteries, but none such here—ol' Lassy had the only graveyard in town. Maybe they been took to other towns, maybe some to yours, or maybe some ended up in their own backyards."

Jacob winced and gestured toward the smattering of intact graves. "But what of the others? Those without means? What do they do?"

"Yeah, that's the thing all right," said Martin. "It's a dang shame. Theys who couldn't pay to take 'em elsewheres, or couldn't bear to see 'em dug back up like that, had no choice but to leave 'em."

Jacob grabbed the gates with either hand and peered in. The chains rattled lightly from his touch, and the raven chirped its agitation. "Well, what do they do?" Jacob said. "How do they visit?"

Martin's hand went to his hip and he jangled the impressive constellation of keys. "They's got to ask me," he said. "They set an appointment and I open the gates for 'em to visit. Sometimes I get called away and I have to close it up and they have to try again anothern time."

"Called away?"

Martin shrugged and said, "Sure enough. The living are ripe full of emergencies." He snuffled. "Or so they think." He gestured to the graveyard as the day's last light gilded the forsaken grounds. "But the dead ain't got no emergencies, at any rate."

Jacob was not so sure. "Still though, they have rights. It's a case of respect, and decency, no? Are there not laws which govern this sort of thing, when a proprietor abdicates a business like this? Special codes which go into effect?"

Martin looked at him somewhat askance. "I'm not sure about no pro prior," he said. "But if the dead have their own code, they sure ain't tellin'."

I wish they would, thought Jacob.

"Well," said Martin, returning his hat atop his perspiring forehead. "Unless you needed anything...."

How he did, and Martin seemed just guileless enough for him to chance it, but something stayed him. Strange, given his desperation, but there was the matter of endgames, and if he set this lawman onto his scent by revealing any more than he ought, all could come crashing down.

"No," he said, turning from the gates. "Thanks. I'll be on my way."

"Well." Martin extended a hand. "You have a good day, sir."

They shook. "You as well."

Jacob turned and headed back to his car.

***

A lurid sky hovered, vast tracts of cloud cover on the move, smoke-gray in parts, deeply bruised in others. The alabaster moon edged in and out of view, bright and ghostly beyond the passing veil, submerged at turns within the depths of this inverted sea. Now it returned, then sank again, now back, just barely, a seashell luminescence. Every few moments came a reframed sky.

Come what will, thought Jacob.

When he cornered slowly back onto Bane and Lux, he shut the lights off and rolled under pale moonlight toward the front gates of the cemetery, the black oaks tall and crimped and reaching on either side. He could hear leaves crunching beneath his tires, and when the wind kicked up, it went about the trees like a whisper, setting aflutter what leaves remained, some spinning briefly against the blue pitch like crazed bats.

He angled the vehicle onto a far and shadowed corner of the grounds and, hands thrust into his pockets, strode briskly back toward the front gates. Furtively. Everything was a gamble at this stage, an ever-shifting calculus wherein a few moments wasted might be chanced for a greater allotment saved. But no luck. Martin had upheld his duties; the gates were locked. Jacob shook them plaintively, moaning as he did so, like an unrequited haunt. His head lolled against the cold and unforgiving iron. Perhaps he had enough? If the child was here, then wasn't that enough?

Of course, it was not. Not for Justus.

He peered through the moonlit shadow. He could walk the periphery, testing for weakness, but that would take time and could prove fruitless. No, he had to climb.

One of the procession of oaks lining the grounds like brooding sentinels. He based his selection on the relative proximity of lowest branch to trunk, up which he shimmied best he could, chafing his hands and thighs as he went. He swung out onto the thick, protruding branch, clasped his arms and legs around it, and scooted forward. The charcoal sky lurched above him; the bowed arms of the fencing jutting below him like claws. When he'd cleared them, he gingerly unwrapped his legs from the branch and let them swing back down. He took a few breaths, then unclasped his hands and dropped to the earth like some fallen gargoyle.

Moonlight fell over him like a floodlight, and he slunk into the darker reaches of the grounds. He started to reach for his phone — for the light — but thought better and proceeded solely by moonlight. He moved slowly, arms outstretched as his eyes adjusted, like a Frankenstein monster wandering back to his rightful home, escaped at last from the cursed ministrations of his unwanted sire. He paused at every headstone, even those degenerate, to squint through the gloom for testament of who slept below. When at last he found it, he knelt and touched her name with his palm.

Grace Alice Luctus, beloved daughter and sister,
March 5, 1980 – June 11, 1988,
God's sweet angel called home too soon.

In this manner he remained for some time, bent and kneeling and hand outstretched, a midnight penitent, his palm cold against the stone. The marker to his left had crumbled into oblivion, but to his right one stood in fair shape, and his eyes grew wide as its inscription resolved darkly into view.

Here rest James and Suzanna Luctus,
died of a broken heart,
August 24, 1988.

And there it was: two stones, a smattering of words, three lives come to pass.

The air was pristine, if cold, possessing a brittle feel, like slowly fracturing glass. At length, he straightened up from the stone and rose, his bones aching in this jilted parcel built on bones itself. His sight was obscured by plumes of his own breath, obscured by the welling moisture in his eyes. His angst owed less to the desperation of this moment than the heartbreak of a child lost.

And what now? What revelation might you possibly conjure, scribe? What sleight of hand. For no mere plot twist shall now suffice, no grand Rubicon.

Not man, nor beast, nor mountain had vanquished him, yet here he stood upon the threshold, unknowing and uncertain, as unmoving as the dead.

He thought he'd best depart this place, drive back home and conjure the best submission possible, extract from any reservoirs within him what facility might remain, but only now did it occur to him that he hadn't any viable means of egress. He felt his weary frame, already contracting against the cold, slump further still, and he sank back to his knees, his back to the child's stone. A great lassitude fell over him, and he folded his arms and hugged himself against the chill, closed his eyes. Things pressed in upon him, things arriving, as he knew they would.

***

The cold has deepened, and he shivers but does not rouse from his slumber against the stone, sees himself from on high. He feels in his sleep for what covering there might be, but his hands find only a latticework of garish cobwebs, the sort sold to Halloween revelers. He sheaths himself, cocooning for the viscid warmth.

Now the dwelling spirits drift forth from out the shadows, coin of the realm for all days to come. Approach this swaddled figure, raise him up, these non-corporeals, by force of will unique to the indignant dead. The earth beneath him tremulous, shifting, falling away, dark waters rising in its wake. He is trussed up in his cobweb suit, Sunday best. Limbs splayed flush against this sacred stone, come before this patronage of peers, those who row into the onyx waters of this fallen world. Strange and spectral oarsmen sallied forth for this the hour of midnight judgment. Through gauzy lens he watches a giant, moonlit hare lope uncertainly across the heavens. Put down your bow, Orion, I'm only grazing here.

From just beyond the chimerical tree line, a hint of smoke appears.

"Dad," he says, and sure enough, his father stands behind an oak, just yonder. "But, Dad, there is no earth. Where do you stand?"

"Damn," his father says, his light gone out. "I don't walk on water, son, if that is what you're thinking."

Now a different voice rises, familiar, a pall on this place itself bereaved. Faceless, yet presiding, the voice comes as an icy wind: "As for the charge against you, how do you plead?"

His mouth works sluggishly about, but no words will come. He paws plaintively at his wrappings.

"My client," intones another now, "would like to know the charge." There stands another Jacob, his own counsel, dapper-dressed and full of verve.

"Trespassing," hisses the reply, "in the first degree. How does he plead?"

"Not guilty!" says the accused, clearing his mouth at last. "I've come to visit, not to stay. I'll take my leave now, if it's the same to you."

His father, silhouetted in the shadows, shakes his head forlornly.

"Let me take it from here," advises counsel.

The hallowed shrine against which incipient Jacob rests, swivels like a carnival ride to behold the cemetery gates. NO TRESSPASSING, rears a sign of billboard proportions, somehow missed on his way in.

"It faces in," whispers counsel, "not out. You are not accused of trespassing on this day, but rather each day preceding it."

"Prosecution calls first witness!"

Jacob swivels back and his heart, entombed as the stone he rests on, craters as he watches his father skim forth across the waters. "Dad?"

His father plucks the limp smoke from his lips and pokes the index finger of his opposite hand into the swaddled torso of the accused. "Trespassing also the body of my son," says he. He fumbles again through his own pockets. "Damn it all, does anybody have a light?" Finding none, he pokes again and resumes his hectoring. "Imposter," he spits. "Fraud. What have you done with my son?" He leans over Jacob, their faces inches apart.

Somewhere in the darkness, the clang and rattle of chains ensue. Open locks, whoever knocks.

"My son," says his father, again and again. "My son."

Badgering, Jacob thinks. Why does counsel not protest?

"My son. My son...."

CHAPTER 24 – DESECRATED

"My son? Can you hear me? My son."

As one world receded, his mind and body slow to breach that world returned, his eyelids bore that world's weight. But there, a fleck of consciousness. Here another. Eyelids struggling, but now a stitch of fire from morning dawned. His eyeballs cowered, but nowhere to hide as the curtain began to lift. A face peered back at him, a father of a different kind.

"A curious place to spend the night," said the priest, his face awash in benevolence and concern—a somewhat weathered face, older. "Are you all right?"

Jacob blinked and worked his lips, which along with his tongue felt thick and anesthetized, like negotiating taffy. *Am I all right.*

The priest, observing this, withdrew an ornate silver flask from the black layers of his cassock. "Water," he said.

To cast out that which afflicts me.

Jacob drew back against the stone, but the priest chuckled.

"Forgive me," he implored. "It's just tap water. You look parched." He gestured with the flask.

Jacob affected what he hoped was an appreciative look, and the priest lowered the flask to his mouth and canted it slightly, and Jacob felt the water flow past his leaden lips and down his gullet. He propped himself up and swallowed best as he could, but some of the water dribbled from his mouth and down his chin and cheeks, and the priest produced a kerchief and dabbed at Jacob's face, as he might a child, repeated the process, and then once more.

Jacob finally sat up flush against the stone, wiped the back of his hand against his mouth, and said, "Obliged."

The priest nodded, capped the flask, and returned it to the folds of his vestment.

"How did you get in?" Jacob asked, peering about. He pictured the priest scaling the crimping gates, glancing furtively about before hurtling into the graveyard, arms flared beneath his robes like some giant, prehensile bat.

"I might ask the same of you," the priest said, smiling gently.

Jacob nodded, blinked, struggled to his feet, dusted off his rumpled, dirt-clotted clothes, and breathed in his own reek. "I climbed," he said. "Not to do anything. Not steal anything. Was just something I needed to see."

The priest nodded. "I would reckon so. As for me —" Here he reached once more into the folds of his garment. " —I find a key most useful."

Jacob rotated his neck to work out the stiffness. Day had broken, a golden tide, and he raised a hand against the glare. He peered about for Martin, or any sign of the law, but there was none. He eyed the glinting key. "How did you get that?"

The priest eyed him curiously. "Do you suppose by some nefarious means?" he said, but quickly smiled. "That would be a story. But the truth is, I visit each morning to bless this sacred place, by man forsaken, but not by God. I have been given dispensation toward this end."

Jacob nodded, glad to hear it.

The priest regarded him. "Did you find it?"

"I'm sorry?"

The priest returned the key within his ensemble and gestured over the grounds. "That which you sought?"

Jacob angled back toward the hallowed headrest. "I didn't mean to fall asleep," he said. He glanced at the priest. "She may need extra blessing. If I've desecrated things."

"We all need it." The priest nodded wistfully toward the girl's stone, toward the flanking stones of her family. "You knew them?"

"I think I'm supposed to have," Jacob said. "I doubt that makes the least bit of sense to you."

The priest stepped closer, knelt before the tombs and crossed himself, thrice over. "Life is joy and sorrow, death and rebirth, many things." He rose, grunting quietly under the toll of his years. "What matters is whether it makes sense to you."

"I don't know." Jacob narrowed his eyes upon the inscriptions — a chiseled telling, a hazard at truth. Where life had fallen, these markers stood in testament... until they fell as well.

The priest regarded him benignly. "There seems to be a story there," he said.

Jacob looked up from the stones. "Yes," he said, his throat dry again, coarse. The priest removed the flask once more and offered it, and Jacob nodded his thanks and took it and drank. "There is at that. But stories are everywhere. I don't presume to burden anyone with mine."

"It is no burden."

"Only because it's your job. You must listen." Jacob returned the water. "No offense intended."

"None taken," the priest said. "I would only ask you consider the possibility that I don't listen because it's my job, but that it's my job because I must listen. If that makes any sense." A smile.

"It does," said Jacob. "But still, I'm not sure I can."

"Don't think of it as confession," said the priest. "We are just two men talking in a graveyard."

"My time is short."

"Yet still you linger. Something you must know."

Jacob turned back to the headstones.

"Ah yes," the priest said. "A story there, at any rate. Not happy, either." He took a sip from the flask, then pocketed it. "The kind which tests our faith."

"A test I fear I fail," said Jacob. He met the priest's eyes. "Even so—" He gestured back now to the stones. "—theirs is a story I must know."

Faint sounds from town now echoed in the distance. Yet the space around them remained still, a benighted obeisance to this place unwaking and bereft.

"Let us walk then," said the priest, voice lowering, like he might be overheard by those who slept unknowing beneath their feet.

It was a more expansive property than Jacob had realized. A procession of rows fell out before them, each in much the same manner as the previous, a macabre and disheveled amalgam of an unknown—a well-preserved stone here, a crumbling marker next. Beside these rested a few unearthed graves. Beyond the rows ranged out a modest copse of cottonwoods, toward which Jacob and the priest now walked.

"They were a good family," the priest said. "About same age as me, the parents were. Two beautiful kids, a boy and girl. Good family, churchgoing. James worked in the mill. Suzanna taught school. Well-respected folks." They reached the periphery of the trees, immediately cooler and darker there in the shadowed parcel. Leaves crunched lightly underfoot. "Thirty years ago," the priest said, "give or take."

Something piqued within Jacob at this, but he couldn't say what.

The priest reached once more into his vestment, for whatever sanctified munitions abided within.

Some men are holy, thought Jacob, *and many more are not. And for even those qualified, see too how they must arm themselves against the iniquitous?*

But the priest had withdrawn no more than a cigarette, and now a lighter, and he smiled at Jacob with sheepish mortality and said, "Something's gotta kill you, huh?"

For which Jacob found himself strangely appreciative, this little slice of unambiguity, the chance to speak to something stark and unmistakable, not elusive and gray. He nodded.

The priest expelled a tight plume of smoke in the direction opposite. "A helluva thing," he said, drawing again. A wind picked up and dislodged the dangling ash from his cigarette, and he stamped quickly after the scattering embers. "Dry season," he said. "Wouldn't that be the rub, uh? Priest sets cemetery on fire."

Jacob glanced down, and noticed his laces were untied on one shoe. He nodded back toward the rows as he bent to re-lace them. "What happened?"

The priest peered through the haze of his exhalation and said, "A tragedy."

Jacob froze, on one knee. His mind shot back to that night on the Beartooth, with Marcus.

I'm not some tragedy, Marcus had said.

The priest dragged on the cigarette, held it, exhaled. "Church trip, actually, rafting, for kids from churches of some of the neighboring towns. Two of the fathers were their guides, one from Petra. Capable men, good men. Both were. But something happened."

Jacob fumbled with his laces, but his thoughts were preoccupied. He saw Morse now, in his mind's eye, imprisoned there in a cell of his own making, back in Kolkata.

There was a tragedy, Morse had said. And of course, there was Rose, and whatever awful thing had robbed her of her legs, and her dream, so long ago. *Three decades, in fact,* she'd said. Same with Marcus, same with Morse. Jacob tightened the laces and pulled them through, then rose on trembling legs.

The priest laid a steadying hand on his shoulder. "You all right?"

"Please go on," Jacob said, solemnly.

"It was terrible," said the priest. He frowned in painful memory. "The men were experienced, knew how to guide a raft, but it had been raining the days before, and when they got to the bridge in Petra, the river was swollen beyond anything they'd seen. They capsized, and everyone went into the water. They got to almost everyone, including the son of the guide from Petra. One girl was badly hurt. They tried to get to everyone, but the river was too strong that day, too fast. They lost poor Grace."

Jacob gasped, struggling suddenly for air. He braced himself on a nearby Cottonwood.

"You okay there, son?" asked the priest.

Jacob nodded. "I'm okay. It's just... I'm a dad, and I can only imagine...."

The priest put a hand on his shoulder once more. "I know," he said. "I know. It's a hard thing to take in. Would you rather I stop?"

No," said Jacob, unequivocally. "No. Please, go on."

The priest eyed him somewhat quizzically a moment, but continued. "The whole town was crushed." His cigarette had died, and he tossed it to the earth and crushed it under his heel. "Such a sweet child. It killed her parents, literally." The priest's hand made a motion toward his mouth, where a cigarette might be. "They killed themselves not long thereafter." He stared out ruefully along the rows. "God says it's a sin, yes, but how can we not feel compassion for their anguish? The loss of one's faith, the loss of a child... surely these stand as the greatest of bereavements."

They stood silently.

"We both have things to get to, I imagine," said the priest at length. "Life must go on."

"What was she like," Jacob said, after they'd walked a while. "Grace?"

"All things love and light," the priest said. He stopped and turned to Jacob. "Everyone she touched, everyone who was ever around her, lit up. Everyone talked about her, about that angelic heart, that compassion beyond her years—thinking always of others. You couldn't not smile around her, no matter your mood. She was the reason we live, and even the faithless were reminded with her laughter that we all have a soul." He priest stopped and gripped Jacob's arm with a gentle resolve. "You know?"

Something welled up within Jacob and he could not for the moment reply, but the priest seemed to find the answer in Jacob's eyes. They continued on. When they reached the Luctus stones, Jacob stopped and the priest, who had kept walking toward the gates, turned back and paused. Jacob stood in front of Grace's grave and regarded it languidly, inadequately, the unqualified pilot of whom Kipling spoke.

A jangling of keys came now, the tolling of the gates, as they were swung back open by the priest. Jacob turned.

When they'd gone out and the priest relocked the gates, they stood a moment peering in. A corner of sky had discolored, a welling gray, and the wind picked up, tumbling in from the river and raising in the swaying cottonwoods a crackling among their remaining leaves.

"One more thing," said Jacob.

"Of course."

"The family... you mentioned another child... a boy?"

The priest did not at first answer, and in this, Jacob had his answer indeed.

"He was the one who found them," said the priest. "His parents. Can you imagine? And he was a doting brother, so protective of that little girl."

"That's horrible," said Jacob, struggling to find his voice. "What happened to him?"

"We took him in," the priest said. "The town. The church. Everyone. Grandparents were dead, no relatives we knew of, so different families took him in for a spell while a permanent home was sought. Family services wasn't like it is today, especially in a small town like this."

"No child should endure that," Jacob said. "It must have been devastating."

The priest eyed Jacob. Then his gaze traveled back to the headstones as his hands wrapped once more around the iron gates. "Yes," he said. "Of course, it had to be, but that was the thing."

Jacob's own gaze volleyed between the priest and the stones. "What?"

"God works in mysterious ways," the priest said. "So too with grief. Especially for a child. Each of us mourns uniquely, sometimes in ways that might seem strange or unfathomable to another." He released his grip on the gates and turned back to Jacob. "The boy never cried, not once, not that anyone saw, anyway. He withdrew, yes, was quieter than before, but went about his life like the whole thing never happened. He accepted whatever home he was sent to, went to school, lived his life, never once mentioned his family or what had occurred. The school at one point had him talk to a psychiatrist, one who worked with kids, and he was confounded by what he observed. It was the same thing those of us in the church saw too."

A few vehicles rattled down the street.

"What did you see," asked Jacob.

"A child with surpassing judgment, beyond that of most adults. He possessed a calculation and remove so calm and dispassionate, so devoid of malice and animation—things that would have been quite understandable had he been so consumed—as to be chilling. The times any of us—including the therapist—inquired of him about the tragedy, he would only and quite coolly reply, 'Death is a part of life.'" At this, the priest reached into his robes and with a quivering hand withdrew a cigarette and placed it in his mouth, where it quivered too, then plucked out the lighter and fumbled with it near the tip of the cigarette, but it would not catch.

"Let me," said Jacob, grasping the lighter and sparking the flame.

The priest nodded his thanks, accepted the light, repocketed the lighter.

"It was as though he now understood the nature of things," the priest said. "The nature of man. It was as if he'd always known." Another car rolled toward them, and the priest angled his body away, obscuring the cigarette, like a schoolboy apprehended in a furtive act. When the vehicle passed, he stuck the cigarette back between his lips, drew deeply, exhaled. "Here we all were — psychiatrists, educators, men of the cloth — all of us commissioned in our way to the contemplation of this nature, all of us by and large confounded toward this end, and here was the boy with those icy-cold eyes, calmly revealing for us the way of things."

"What became of him?"

The priest had drawn the cigarette down to a nub, and he dropped it by his feet and crushed it out. "God as my witness," he said, "and He always is, I don't for the life of me know. I don't know anyone who does. What I do know is that things started happening in the town. Bad things. Pets gone missing, later turned up dead. People having accidents. Brakes going out on a car. Accidental drownings in a pond."

Jacob frowned. "He did it?"

"We didn't know," said the priest. "No one wanted to think it. Such thoughts seemed to go against our nature, to accuse a boy — much less one who'd suffered so greatly — of such terrible things. No one wanted to believe this could be in the nature of a child, to have done such things, even one who'd been so traumatized. But nature or no nature, certain things stand as crimes, and it became impossible for the law to ignore the possibility. And so, one day they came to see him."

Jacob waited.

"He disappeared," the priest finally said. "Vanished. No one had seen him go, and no one could find a trace of him, as if he'd rode out on the wind, and the wind wasn't telling."

Jacob nodded. He stared out into the graveyard a moment more, then extended his hand.

The priest stepped to him and gathered him in an embrace, grateful perhaps for this impromptu confessional, this reversal of roles. Or perhaps he just wished Godspeed to one so clearly in need of it.

When they stepped back, Jacob thought briefly he would inquire of the priest the child's name, but time was evaporating, and it occurred to him there was not enough of it to waste on such questions, the answers to which he already knew.

CHAPTER 25 – GRACE

Little else need be said beyond the unshakeable tenet that all children are innocent, that no child deserves to die. In this sense, the case for a child's life is made, indelibly, by her very existence. Grace deserved to live, to be alive now, happy and healthy and perhaps with a family of her own, and most assuredly did not deserve her tragic fate.

But I will say something more, not merely in hopes of succeeding in this abominable game, but because it is true. I will say something more about Grace. She was, so I heard, all things love and light. She possessed the purest innocence, and yes, in part owing her tender years, but more than that, far more. She carried a magic in her heart, a compassion beyond her years and beyond that carried by most, of any age. Therapists, social workers, teachers, clergy... anyone in these most noble professions yearn and train for that measure of discerning, of connecting, that this child possessed. She put the contentment and welfare of others before her own, and how rare a thing for a child – for anyone, really.

I saw it in the eyes of he who told me, which flickered upon recalling hers, and the sorrow at her absence. She touched the hearts of all who met her, lit them up, lit up the whole world around her. A rare soul, indeed, who so profoundly impacted so many in her time among them, and her time apart. All the smiles she would have evoked, all the comfort she would have provided... the joy denied to so many hearts. The things she would have done, perhaps the family she would have raised.

And, most certainly not least, the shattered family she left behind, whose grief and despair defied all chronicling. Their angel had been taken too soon, and from a parent's vantage, any time is too soon, but for this to occur in their lifetime so grossly incongruous, so antithetical, wholly counter to our blood level understanding of how life is supposed to unfold. They staggered through the aftermath as long as they could, but this was not long, and the grief was too much.

They now inter with their precious daughter, but left behind her older brother, his pain no less grievous, though his manner of grieving compelled him upon a very different road, a troubled road. I pause now in this recounting, for I've every reason to believe further explication is not required, and to proffer it would be insulting to Grace's memory, and to her brother's too. I believe you know the story, and in this case, at least, need not be persuaded on her behalf, but that I know it sufficiently too — feel it, best as I can.

To this I can offer but two aspects of testimony. First, I am a father, and my heart breaks at the mere thought of such a fate befalling my child. You have in this terrible matter exhorted me toward what I might discover about these four people, and in its doing, perhaps you have learned something of me. Maybe there were things you already knew, and which had evoked in you such disfavor. But in all that you've learned of me — and should much of it be disparaging, I might scarcely argue — you should by now be well aware that the notion — that intolerable notion of grave injury befalling my son — commands me most of all. If I am, and do, nothing else, my reason for being is to prevent such a thing, at any cost and by any means necessary. It is in this conviction, in this love of and fear for my child, that my sympathy is most deeply rooted. I don't know their pain, those who lost their sweet Grace, but can only imagine it, though, of course, it is the most unimaginable thing, the most terrible.

They are gone, but there was another, a brother, as again I much believe you know. Maybe he is gone too, in a way. For Grace meant the most of all to him, I believe – his guiding light, his star to go by, his to love, to protect. Loss does something to a person. Pain. And here now I speak to that second aspect that stirs in me such reverence and sorrow for that sweet, departed child, for Grace. For the truth is, part of me feels sympathy for her brother, and that truth owes directly to her, to whom she was and what she meant to him. She was clearly the best of us – of all of us – and it is in her name, in the name of Grace, that we must in our darkest hours rise to our best, in her name, and in her memory. Spare other innocents. Leave them in peace, even as it in so many ways eludes them.

Put away the anger and the pain. And if the pain can never be quite gone, then honor it, honor her, by walking not in darkness but in light.

Meet me at the Crooked River, upon the bridge. Daybreak.

Chapter 26 – Cucariva

He arrived there early, for he did not sleep, despite a fatigue so pervasive he couldn't be certain he was in fact awake, a benumbing correspondent to the phantom nature marking this ordeal from the first, an ordeal from which he had more than once prayed to awaken. But ever heard were the prayers of the faithless? He looked skyward, beyond the blanket of fog lingering above the river, beyond the shrouded outline of the bridge. The sky was too occupied with its circadian transformation to guide him, the sun as yet mere suggestion, but against the blue-black canvas shone Sirius of Canis Major, deep-set and aglow in the southern firmament. Maybe this was all he needed, all anyone needed, really. Not answers, for these were in the end as elusive as the cosmos, but simply, a light.

He'd chosen the spot, though he could not say why — a sourceless obeisance to a suspect marker. He stood at the riverbank, at the far end of the bridge that led from town. Dawn had not yet broken — it had not even occurred to him to wait for light of day — a meridian abiding no hour save its own. He could hear the current before spying it, streaming sightlessly like wind through trees, but now it materialized darkly into view, a coiling, coursing blackness against a world still more pitch. Fog rose off it like smoke. The high moon glimmered off the sinewy face of the river, suggesting in its blossom a dark and shrouded figure squatting within the gloom.

Justus, surely. Jacob's insides fluttered but he did not break stride. *This must be done.*

As he neared, the figure resolved into sharper relief, a vagrant, haggard and destitute, the underbelly of the bridge his home. The vagrant tottered to his feet, his dark rags fluttering up around him like gauzy wings.

Jacob paused, swallowed, his thoughts, like the river, coursing quickly, and like the river propelled by currents beyond merely those discernible. There was the matter which had compelled him here— finding Justus and engaging him in the climax of this pestilent affair—but now, too, there was this. This undercurrent had now risen, and dredged from Jacob's soul a most disquieting sentience. From behind the vagrant sounded the flutter and thin cries of bats. Jacob turned partly around and regarded the fiery cross-stitch at the eastern rim of the world, a new day rising, though not quite yet.

"I'm looking for a man," he said.

The vagrant's jaw, thin and angular, worked sluggishly about, the teeth discolored and few. An aroma wafted off him, and Jacob's nose pricked in anticipation of the stench, but instead his senses scrambled to process an odor strangely fragrant. Ambrosial. Like lavender. Strange. Yet not so strange as the eyes, which lifted now toward his own, a shade of blue such as Jacob had never once beheld.

"A man with gloves," said Jacob. "Have you seen him?"

The jaw worked again, until a rasping utterance dispelled forth, a dissonant, ancient sound.

"Cucariva," Jacob was sure he heard. He cocked his head, as might a dog.

The diamond eyes narrowed. "Cucariva." A skeletal hand slipped from its ragged sheathing as the vagrant gestured toward the river.

Jacob stared, then flinched. The embers seared into recollection, a resurrection of long-buried things.

Cucariva. *Cucariva.*

Crooked River.

Their eyes locked momentarily, but now Jacob's attention was drawn to the opposite shore, where stood Justus, draped in a dark and tapering cloak, regarding him in turn. Jacob took up the vagrant's hand in thanks, locked eyes once more. He began to step away, toward the gravelly embankment that curved up to the bridge, but the vagrant had not relinquished his grip. Jacob turned back and nodded, tried to extract his hand. He cast a glance to the far bank, where the dark figure he knew all too well looked on. The vagrant had not let go. Astonishingly powerful.

"If you please," Jacob said, pulling harder still.

The vagrant lurched forward, still possessing Jacob's hand, and pulled Jacob toward him. He pivoted slightly to place a spindly right leg just behind Jacob's own, enlisting him in some macabre and awkward dance, and Jacob not leading. The vagrant pivoted again, harder, to his left, and Jacob felt himself propelled through the air, before thudding to the ground like a felled tree. The shock and pain conferred a momentary incoherence, but as he rolled to his feet, his first thought was, *my hands are free.* He eyed the vagrant, this skeletal being who'd hurled him with ease, and beyond him, Justus, who'd turned and begun ascending the bank toward the bridge.

What is this thing shaped up before me? Must I, off all things, subdue this unhinged soul?

The vagrant swept toward Jacob—the animated amalgam of rags, the cadaverous frame, the astral eyes. His hands splayed out toward Jacob like uncrimping claws, exploding into his sternum and sending him flying once more.

He scrabbled to his feet as the vagrant advanced again. This time, he was ready, and he intercepted the protruding hands with his own, and swung the vagrant violently past him and hurtling to the earth, the next step in this mad ensemble. Jacob winced and held up his suddenly throbbing hands before him, smoking in the bluish darkness, burning, like he'd touched dry ice.

The vagrant in his composite of rags seemed to be twisting, reconstituting, and before Jacob could register the movement, stood once more before him, and advanced.

Jacob thought of Justus, how he must by now be upon the bridge, to do unto Jacob that which Jacob would do unto him.

The vagrant fell upon him again, thrust a hand once more into Jacob's chest, and sent him stumbling backwards towards the river.

He did not fall, but steadied himself, then with a guttural cry launched himself forward. They came together in a confluence of will, hands enjoined again and pressed between them, like strongmen of the colosseum. The vagrant pivoted again, attempting to place a leg behind Jacob's, but Jacob parried this time, side-stepped, shifted weight and, with every ounce of exertion he could muster, drove the vagrant backwards and to the ground.

Limbs akimbo and rags aflutter, the vagrant emitted an unearthly sound, sending another colony of bats screaming into the farther recesses of the bridge.

Jacob entwined the vagrant's legs in his own, collared his neck with one arm, pinned one arm with his other.

The cold fire of the vagrant's touch seared into Jacob's flesh, but he gritted his teeth and tightened his hold. He could feel the vagrant's free arm working, angling, seeking out that one blow that might turn the game for him, but this, Jacob knew, was futile. His vice-grip around the vagrant's neck would deflect and reduce the strength of any such blow, aided by his superior weight upon the prone, emaciated figure. But now he could feel the arm wriggling down his side, toward his waist. Jacob hung on, as little damage could be suffered there. He frowned as he felt the vagrant's hand stop at the jasper in his pocket, Gabriel's stone, and begin to press upon it with his fingers—uncomfortable, but a last-gasp effort, to be sure.

"Enough," Jacob said, breathing hard. He lifted his chin from the vagrant's chest to regard this most peculiar of combatants. Before he could ascertain the slightest clue, his hip, beneath the pressing finger of the vagrant, erupted in a spasm of agony. He howled and rolled off his adversary, untangling himself like a relenting python. He struggled to his feet, feeling instantly in his disjointedness that something had gone terribly wrong. When he stood and allowed his weight to settle, the pain exploded and he howled again.

The vagrant gathered to his feet.

Jacob inhaled deeply, gritted his teeth, and readied himself. The vagrant stepped toward him, and Jacob stepped to meet him, pressing a hand to his side to hold himself together. The hip was doubtlessly, if unfathomably, out of socket, but no time to wonder. His assailant raised a hand against him again, but as Jacob contorted his catawampus frame to parry the blow, he saw the hand upturning, extending, presenting a most curious object.

It froze him where he stood.

As a writer, and by virtue of this a man, he'd more than once pondered the way of things, the way of people, the way of life. He considered the roads that enjoined or eluded them, the meaning of things, or lack thereof, the good or evil in the hearts of men. He'd wrestled into the wee hours seeking reclamation for those souls he'd conjured unto the page, that they might—he might—set a good and proper course. No nifty answers, mind you, nor giftwrapped solutions, for life was not easy, nor were its denizens. But there were clues, if you knew where to look. There were those roads, threads, which might never be grasped surely enough to resolve into clarion certainty, but threads nonetheless, and maybe the secret, after all, was in the grasping.

But here before him, sitting like a jewel in the palm of this strange dweller, was his thread, awaiting only Jacob's grasping to bring this falling world to heel. He met the vagrant's eyes, where his world presently reflected, his course set out.

He reached for the object.

I have not held it for decades, but it returns to my grip like an old friend. It dangles elastically, that I might at the chosen moment draw it tautly back, as I've done countless times, but not once since that day upon this river. Now comes this rousing of a beast, of memories suppressed, the hauling of this bewildered, fomenting creature unto a stage so long forgotten. With its scrabbling claws the beast unearthed a great many more things, each as reticent to the light of day as the next. This vague tapestry, until this moment left fallow in the dark abyss — cold, dead markers of things gone by — now stands illuminated for the singular, if tenuous, constellation that they formed, a pictorial history best known by me, but not known at all, too close to the canvas had I been to see.

But one saw it, clearly.

He lifted his eyes, but the vagrant had already begun to shuffle back toward the shadowed chasm beneath the bridge.

Jacob turned and dragged himself up the hill.

They met full stride at the center of the bridge, an uncertain congress in the glare and shadow of this uncertain hour, not quite day but no longer night, that smallest of hours just before things begin to happen—before the birds sing and the breeze lifts from the river, before children rise and give voice to the waking day. A space between, and unto this breach they stepped, two men, arrived at last at final Calvary.

Count off ten paces, adversaries, then turn.

Yet Justus did not appear poised for a fight. He gestured at Jacob with something approaching concern. "A curious detour," he said, and nodded at Jacob's leg. "Injured along the way?"

Jacob frowned. Surely, Justus had seen. The comment must be yet another in his tireless repartee. Then again, what, any longer, was certain in any of this?

"I'm fine," said Jacob.

"Well then," said Justus, not unpleasantly. "I imagine you'd like to get down to it." Reading his answer in Jacob's eyes, he nodded and said, "So be it."

To a remote observer, they might have appeared the picture of concord: two men, weary from their common odyssey, conversing upon this theatre of nascent day. Jacob cringed, repulsed by the slightest notion of even perceived alliance. He'd as soon Justus set upon him, that things might at last be compelled to finality, and ebb whether favorably or otherwise into long-awaited denouement.

But his antagonist appeared inclined toward no such thing. Justus turned to his right, facing westward, where the receding dome of night arced over their sleeping town. The river ran on beneath them, as always did it run, sightless but inveterate. *Discharge your business, then,* it whispers, *and I'll press on.*

"On with it, then," said Jacob, shifting. His hip throbbed.

Justus regarded him in the anemic light. "What have I done but give you the opportunity to live? To truly live? To give that opportunity to Mr. Marcus, Mr. Morse, to Rose. An opportunity my sister never got. Each of you failed in your way to honor her through your actions, to show proper gratitude for the life she was so heinously denied."

"No," said Jacob, quietly. He ached to his core—his arm, his hip, even the cut on his hand from that night at his window—alleviated only by an exhaustion so numbing that he thought he might at any moment topple over into the murky depths of the river. That it was some manner of descent which awaited him, or upon which he had for some time now already embarked, seemed incontestable. None of it, however, mitigated his duty to keep on standing, just a while longer, to see this matter through.

"Accidents happen," he said. "Tragedies. They tried to save her. You know they did."

"You will in this final hour presume to tell me what I know? You, who have retreated from life, from knowing, in all of these years since?"

"I was a child," Jacob said. "I didn't retreat on purpose. My mind blocked it out, suppressed it."

"You speak of your mind as though some accomplice, someone or something distinct from yourself. Are we really anything more?"

"I like to think so,' Jacob said. "Even if I've lost touch with some of those things. But none of it changes the truth. They tried to save her. I wish with all my heart they had."

"Ah," said Justus, "but wishing cannot make it so, can it? What are you prepared to give? What recompense for a child taken? Your own child, perhaps? Easy now, easy!"

Jacob had surged toward Justus at this, the throbbing in his hip excruciating, but no matter.

"We've spoken of saviors," Justus said. "And the boy is yours. Your last redeeming quality, perhaps. I'll not ask for his life, but what if I asked for yours?"

"I would trade in a heartbeat," he said. "If I must. Won't go easy, though. My boy deserves a father, and the others deserve peace. They were children themselves: Marcus, Morse, Rose."

A great stillness hung over them as the gathering day seemed in a state of suspended animation, equal parts darkness and light.

"Your submission," said Justus, after an indeterminate silence, "is approved. Your task is fulfilled." He reached into his vest and withdrew a manila envelope, much as he had that first, terrible evening. "*Your* recompense."

Jacob warily extended a hand and accepted the parcel.

With that, it was over. Justus turned just as the light of morning calved over the bridge and the timber that lined the riverbanks, falling over them so that Jacob stood blinking as Justus disappeared into the now shadowed half of the bridge. The morning roused with its familiar portents: birds chittering, sky punching up, even the river thrumming into full throat as the fog peeled back beneath the surging dawn. Next came the sound of bustling households, braying motors, the morning's first commerce—a day like any other, by appearances, save for that dark figure immersing into it. He vanished like the wind, determined whether and when to reappear, impossible to conjecture.

And there, in that quiet slip of morning, Jacob's heart went back to the day—to the moment—Gabriel was born, his tiny, squirming, squalling miracle. His boy was at once so small and so big, the biggest thing he'd ever known and would ever. In that moment, we aspire to our best, and somewhere in our blood is forged a covenant, to safeguard this precious soul at any cost.

And like a firebolt, Jacob understood what he must do, even should it mean the forfeiting of his own soul, the becoming of that which he had, with such anathema, beheld. He stepped forward and called into the darkness, after the one who had, all things considered, just spared him with his grace.

Death roused warily, for contrary to popular belief, he'd long-since lost his verve for his calling. His work was incontestable, perhaps might be parried and delayed by intrepid souls, but in the end even they fell, and this being the case for all eternity, Death had fallen too, into a profound torpor. He'd seen it all and taken them all, harvesting an endless bounty of souls. He did so mostly without lifting an icy finger, for more often than not, those things that brought and sustained life, in the end, repossessed it—a failed heart, an addled brain, ashes to ashes, dust to dust. Death always won, and it mattered not how many new souls burst forth unto the world or how long they endured: each would perish, and each in the end would be gone infinitely longer than they were here.

It required, therefore, death of unnatural tidings to command his interest, and even these became in time so mundane as to quickly forfeit all appeal—accidents, disasters, insufferable luck or circumstance, too many to record and ever so pedestrian. No, only those things truly unnatural, unholy perhaps, could rekindle that dark ardor with which he once brimmed.

So it was on this morning that Death stirred, summoned by will of this listing man upon a bridge. *Someone dies today*, he heard him say, not aloud but nonetheless, death of course the most universal of tongues. And Death roused in that inimitable manner, not becloaked nor with scythe in hand, but shaped up rather out of each vestige of the world around—the night that was, the day to be. Death rose up like mist off the river, substantiated out of those lingering folds of darkness, set forth across the land like a helix of scuttling leaves—a cold wind come.

The wind picked up off the river, fanning this way and that, and broke over Jacob where he leaned on the bridge, as the world seemed likewise to be doing, unboxed and uncertain, and as Jacob watched, a sour thought curdled within him. Could it be that to Justus— that most malignant of figures—he was now indebted for hauling him from his refuge? The notion plagued him, but so too another, stark and incontrovertible, no matter to what depths he'd sunk. One thing.

Jacob pushed back from the railing, gritted back the fusillade of pain. "All or nothing!" he called into the void.

His voice echoed into the blackness. A flock of pigeons answered in clamorous report, fluttering from the underside of the bridge. Jacob thought for a moment he might have to wait, or set out in pursuit, this of course portending badly given his condition, but Justus strode from out the darkness like a summoned banshee. He crossed the space between them, and before Jacob could wriggle into whatever posture might afford him even a sliver of a chance, Justus upended him. The envelope went flying and another wave of anguish washed over him.

Now Justus was upon him, lording over him like a well-practiced garrotter, adjusting his gloves. He knelt over Jacob and, for the first time, his face was absent its composure, twisted now in a rictus of contempt.

"Such thanklessness," he said. "Perhaps I ought reconsider my verdict. No gratitude, have you shown. Not you, not the others. Perhaps I ought to reconsider about each of you."

"I'm going to kill you," Jacob said.

Justus grinned. "You've acquired the taste, I see."

He tried to sit up, but Justus pinned him with his knee, and Jacob howled in agony. Justus bent over him as might a ghastly incubus, knees upon Jacob's chest, their faces mere inches apart. Jacob struggled with every ounce of strength, but it was fruitless. He watched as Justus slipped a hand into his cloak and withdrew his dagger, the same, surely, with which he'd taken the life of the officer, and who knew how many others. Justus tapered the blade against Jacob's jugular, bore into his eyes with dark antiquity — lurid pools into which Jacob could not help but descend. He thought of Gabriel, of Anabel. If one's life flashed before his eyes, then they were surely his. And yet, in this most seminal moment, he could not bring himself to implore Justus to spare him. Not this man. Not again.

He groaned, as Justus dug his knees into his shoulders as he rose. Justus sheathed the dagger and looked down at his vanquished pawn. His expression and tone returned to their usual equanimity. "Your sentence is life. You will live with your failings, and with your fears." He turned once more to go, then paused, crooked his head ever slightly back. "The lives you spared were spared by me, their reprieve, and your own, by my hand. Never forget." His words hung there a moment like the lingering remnants of fog. And once more, he was gone.

"I won't," spat Jacob, groaning as he rolled to one side. He pushed off the cold pavement and lurched to his feet. "All or nothing!" he called again, reaching into his coat. He reached with his other hand into his pocket, loaded the jasper with an inscrutable fidelity, and pulled the payload back, taut. He stared into the abyss, beyond which lie their town, and where slumbered his wife and child. Everything seemed to have slowed. Soon cars would come trundling over the bridge, a barge or tugboat would churn down the river, and long ropes of smoke would rise from the industrial edge of town.

First, this, whatever *this* would be. He squinted across the bridge into the chiaroscuro of shadow and light. *All that concerns me,* said Emerson, *is what I must do.* He turned around, faced back the way he'd come, closed his eyes, and smiled. The river burbled below, accompanied by the shrill gossip of small birds. Any second now, the climax would arrive, then, one way or another, blissful denouement. One way or another, the end of this.

He'd come to know those footsteps, that telltale cadence of death. Justus had, he knew, burst from the shadows as an extension of them, birthed by them and set forth on their behalf. He came toward Jacob for what both understood was the final time. These last weeks had taught him the rhythm of things, of mountains and rivers and maybe more things than he knew, and so it was that he registered Justus's approach in his mind's eye, from the sound of it, from the feel.

Thirty feet now, twenty-five, now twenty.

Jacob whirled around, his hand and the sling curving up in flawless union, and when he released his shot, he'd known instantly it was true. He saw no blood, saw only the stone penetrate the temple and Justus flying backwards, disappearing once more into the brume. For a moment, nothing, but then came the percussion of something entering the water below. Jacob dragged himself over and stared down into the river. Nothing. Just the teeming current, which always swirled and coursed beneath the bridge. He bent down to retrieve the envelope, groaning as he did, and disjointedly stood back up. It was strange, or perhaps not in the slightest, that he harbored not the slightest doubt that all the money was there.

And then, after a moment's hesitation, he emptied the contents of the envelope into the teeming waters below. They fluttered about, most setting off into the current, but a few wayward bills caught updrafts off the river, and drifted momentarily skyward, before sticking to the white trunks of the sycamores that lined the river's banks. What a wonder it would be to anyone discovering it. Jacob hoped it would be a child, or perhaps the vagrant. Who said money didn't grow on trees?

He knew he'd killed Justus, knew this in his bones. He did not exult at this, for where in death lived exultation? Where was revelry in those things most primal? He stared a while longer into the waters, even glanced downriver, bracing for sight of a body, for the repercussions that would bring. He saw only the brackish waters, atop which rode the occasional bit of driftwood, and tendrils of green, fluttering bills. No body. It would wash up, surely, sooner than later, another bridge to cross, if cross he must. A pickup truck rattled onto the bridge, and Jacob faced the opposite direction until it passed. When it did, he peered a final time into the river, then cast his gaze about in hopes of locating the jasper.

A few minutes and a few more passing vehicles later, he abandoned the search.

He limped slowly back in the direction from whence he'd come, each step painful, but he smiled, for each step brought him closer to home. He peered about for the vagrant, but of him he saw no sign whatever.

CHAPTER 27 – HOPE

His hip was dislocated, and he'd no choice but to say he'd fallen. He'd have outpatient surgery in a couple of days.

He knocked on the door, his in-laws' door, wondering what words he'd use when she opened it.

Words. Spilled forth like so many footsteps of our journey, amassed like so many raw materials of the construction of our lives. In the case of scribes like him, coin of the realm for their profession and passion alike. How many he had uttered, received, written, revised? Which words had pressed in upon him even in—especially in—the throes of desperation these last weeks? While cold, ill winds beset him, the only things certain seemed despair and the death that might allay it. Words he endeavored mightily to find but futilely to ward. He searched for those words most simple, for they bespoke his most simple truth.

Make it back to her. Maybe she still loves you. Maybe there is hope.

He'd tried to parry these words, for hope, he feared, might prove deadly in its distraction. But now that he'd made it back, now that he stood again before her, he realized hope had been indispensable. Hope and duty. Hope for himself, that he might yet recapture the heart and hand of this woman, his wife, the mother of his child, the love of his life. Duty, as a father to Gabriel, that breathing embodiment of the redemption of Jacob's own listing soul.

Hope, Dickinson said, *is the thing with feathers, which perches in the soul.*

Jacob had not grown so cynical as to doubt it, but opposite each truth perched its countervailing twin, and as he inhaled, the frigid air rushed in and filled the empty places within him, places where things like hope had long ago lived. Somewhere in his blood ran memories of those things: hope, love. It was like walking around with the grandest of secrets. Unless, of course, it was lost, leaving in you empty places, which either remained empty or filled with cold, irredeemable things.

Anabel turned to regard him, and his heart raced as if seeing her for the first time. After all he'd been through—up on those mountains, out on those rivers, all those thousands of miles away—he'd remained tethered to her, hopeful, perhaps irrationally so, but was not that love? Hope, where no hope remained?

He was, if nothing else, a writer, and a decent hand at that, and from the moment he'd met her, he'd wanted to write her, to capture somehow her love and light upon the page. No one had made him want to write more, love more, be more. But quickly arose a paradox as beautiful and vexing as was she: as endless was his love for her, so too would prove the task at hand. The most gifted scribes in humankind, at the pinnacle of their powers, could scarcely hope to fare better—and probably knew better than to try—for the most learned in this world understood that the greatest gift of language—universal—rested not in any word spoken, but rather in every word not. In the spaces between, before and after. At our finest and most eloquent, the most we might hope to conjure was a fleeting sense of things, a beguiling note upon the page, a symphony that knows no end. Just as you should never look right at the sun, and just as you could never lasso a cloud... just as all of these things and none of these things, and just as sure as you ever were of anything, you knew to your bones you loved her, that the world did too, and you were glad for that. She was every word that was to him, and every word that wasn't. She was that score unfinished, that page unwritten, which could never be so, and to which its impossible completion he was nonetheless forsworn. She was that thrum and flutter of his heart—from the first time, and every time. He was, if nothing else, a writer, and just a man in love.

He wanted to pull her close, as was always his instinct, but something in him hesitated because of something he saw.

"I'm so sorry you got hurt," she said, and she looked it.

This exhilarated him, and he started again to reach for her, but saw something again, and once more demurred. He considered what words might arbitrate this most defining of moments, but after everything, could only summon the energy to cut right to the quick.

"I love you," he said, for so he did. "Will you please come home?"

"I love you too," she said, and his heart soared, but ever briefly. "But I cannot. I'm sorry. We will share custody, of course, but I'm not coming back."

When he'd first known she loved him, he felt he could fly; at these words, though, he was not in the least bit certain he could stand. He wanted to be strong, needed to be—in Gabriel's eyes, and in Anabel's. He clenched his teeth and fought back a great many things.

Breathe, he thought. *Start with that. Breathe and don't fall. Keep standing.*

He didn't know if he could, only that he must, though what pressed in upon him did so with a burden beyond anything he'd ever borne, including every affliction of the last few weeks. A sea change hit him, an abrupt twist of the kaleidoscope, a landscape altered in the blink of an eye. The world he'd known, his Anabel world, so beautiful and bright... everything had seemed so possible, but the one laid out before him now was barren and bereft.

He imagined a gray and mechanical existence, instructing himself in the methodical execution of everyday life.

One step in front of the other... this is how you walk, and you must walk. Inhale, exhale, in, out... this is how you breathe, and you must breathe. This pain you carry is phantom, for she you bleed for is forever gone.

Yes, he was dying. Not today, not tomorrow, but every day for the rest of his life.

"Dad?"

He closed his eyes, only for a moment, for he knew Gabriel was waiting, and that when he opened them, the boy must see no pretense that things would return to the way they were, but that they would, no matter what, turn out okay. His son must see reassurance, see love. He smiled. Sisyphus himself would smile beneath his boulder. Not that Jacob thought himself a martyr—far from it—just a man who loved his son. He'd push his rock the rest of his days, but if you thought about it right—and it was imperative that he did—there was as much blessing as burden there. For was there any grace more humbling than that of a child, whose love was so often more than we could fathom, whose forgiveness so often more than we deserved? Who endlessly reprieved us, for all our failings, to get up each day and try again, looking to us for all they needed, their heroes and protectors, when only if they knew the truth of things, that it was they who sustained us all along? No, he needn't worry what Gabe might see.

He opened his eyes.

CHAPTER 28 – PERFECT IN ITS WAY

He recovered quickly from surgery, though he walked with a slight limp, which the doctor said he might always do. And so it was, he hobbled through the gates of their town's cemetery not long after, and for the first time in years. On a lazy Saturday morning, foggy and cool, a few others moved about, heading to or from markers with that solemn posture unique to the bereaved.

No body had been found, not yet. Something within him knew it never would. Even if it did surface, it would probably be decomposed beyond recognition, and, unless there had been a witness that day upon the bridge, there would be nothing to tie him to it anyway, beyond the millstone of his own conscience.

Most of the money was found, and it caused quite the stir. The FBI was even called in, but they conjured no leads whatsoever and, in the end, the lucky discoverers got to keep their staggering finds. He knew it was irrational, but he became nervous when they were in town, since the cop's killing remained unsolved. For the time being, he kept the beard.

When he got to his mother's stone, a knot rose in his throat, and he folded his hands in front of himself and looked down.

"It's me, Mom," he said. "Jacob." He swallowed and dragged his shirtsleeve across his eyes. "I'm sorry it's been so long. I have so much to tell you."

And he did, starting with Anabel leaving him and including every detail of the ordeal that followed. It took quite a while, he wasn't sure how long, but at various points his hip hurt from the standing, and he resisted a temptation to lean upon the stone for support, instead shifting his weight every few minutes as he spoke.

"I don't blame you for not telling me," he said, glancing at her stone. "Perhaps years ago, I might have, before we had Gabe, but I would do anything to protect my child."

He caught a few visitors from the corner of his eye, gathering near a stone a few rows over, and lowered his voice.

"I guess not much was known about PTSD back then, when it happened. For me or Dad. He had to run away from it, from us. I buried it completely." He breathed in deeply, looked skyward as he exhaled. "Little things are starting to make sense now. Random things. Dreams I've had. The way things remind of something. *Deja vu.* Things I could never quite put my finger on, until now." He wiped his eyes once more. "I'm sorry I didn't handle it better, but I'll do better now. And I'll teach Gabriel. Hopefully, he'll never face anything like it, but everyone faces something, and I'll make sure he has what he needs to do so."

They conversed a while longer, reminiscing about a great many things, most of them happy, until at last Jacob told her he'd better go.

"I'm going to see Dad," he told her, glancing again at her stone. "I'm taking Gabriel. It'll be a nice little trip for the two of us." He turned and began to hobble off, but quickly stopped and cast a final glance back. "Did I do okay, Mom? There were so many, so many lives in my hands. I took life, Mom. God help me, I did. I'm sorry. All I could think of was one."

He regarded her a moment longer, deriving what comfort he could from her soft silence, then turned and headed home.

***

They drove all day, stopping only for food and bathroom trips, and found a hotel for the night. They ate breakfast the next morning and headed for the home.

"Why have you not taken me to see him?" Gabe asked, as they neared the entrance.

"We did," Jacob answered, "long ago, when you were very young."

"Why did you stop?"

"Your grandfather had problems, issues. Something really hard had happened to him. He loved us, all of us, but couldn't deal with all his problems. It's why he came here. It got to where he didn't want to see anybody. He was ashamed, confused, scared. Didn't want us to see him like that, and I guess I didn't want you to see him like that either."

"But why not?" said Gabriel, slipping inside past the door his father held for him. "It's my grandpa. He didn't have to be scared. I would love him no matter what he was like."

Jacob wiped his eyes with his shirtsleeve as they moved through the foyer toward the front desk.

"I know," he said. "It's why I'm bringing you now. Sometimes grown-ups don't see things as quickly as kids."

Gabriel smiled. "That's a little weird."

Jacob leaned down and kissed his son on the forehead. "Yeah, I reckon it is."

"Good evening, Mr. Fallon," said the desk attendant, looking up from a log in which she'd been jotting. "It's been a while."

"I know. I'm sorry. How is he?"

The attendant glanced briefly at Gabriel before answering. "About the same, I'd say. Good days and bad. Fades in and out. Physically fine, really quite good, but just so distant. Still has his quirks—still with the handwashing—but that's not terribly unusual. Many patients have them, for many reasons."

"Will he see us?"

She smiled wistfully. "I really don't know. You're welcome to see." Her eyes scanned quickly over the log. "Room 221 B."

The door was open, but with the lights in the room off and the shades to the east-facing window at the far end of the room drawn, the room was dark, save for the ambient light of the hallway and the illumination of an overhead TV. Jacob rapped lightly at the door and poked his head in, Gabriel peeking in around him.

"Dad? Hello?"

"He's in the bathroom. Come on in," said a gravelly, staccato voice.

"Hello, Mr. Hopper. I hope we're not disturbing you." Jacob motioned Gabe forward with him.

"If only there were something to be disturbed from," Mr. Hopper said. "This is the most exciting thing that's happened all day."

Jacob smiled and nudged Gabe from out behind him. "This is my son, Gabriel. Gabe. Say hello to Mr. Hopper."

"Hi," said Gabriel, proffering a small wave.

"Hello, young man," said Mr. Hopper from his bed. He inclined his very gray and wrinkled head toward the closed bathroom door, behind which running water and a strange sound like sandpaper could be heard. "Your grandpa's in there. As usual."

Gabe looked up at his father, but Jacob touched the boy's shoulder and said, "It's all right. I'll explain later." He knocked on the bathroom door, waited a moment, knocked again. The water ceased.

"What is it?"

"Dad, it's me. It's Jacob. I've brought Gabe with me to see you."

An uneasy silence followed, the room quiet except for the TV, upon which implausibly excited game show contestants and equally fervent audience members jabbered and cheered.

Jacob knocked again, softly. "Come on, Dad, Gabriel's here."

A click followed, and a narrow prism of amber light appeared.

Gabe placed a hand upon the doorknob. "It's okay, Grandpa, please come out."

A different click, and the slat of light evaporated, the door pulled back, and there stood blinking in the doorway, gaunt and of far more venerable appearance than his years, Jacob's father. Jacob winced. His dad was just thirty years his senior, not even seventy, but looked no younger than any of his elderly fellow residents. He began to shuffle out of the shadows, but his gait seemed uncertain, so Jacob stepped to him and steadied him by one arm.

Gabriel ambled around to his grandfather's other side and placed a small hand upon his elbow.

They helped him over to the easy chair by the window, into which he sank, his eyes wide now and roaming back and forth between his unexpected guests.

Jacob nodded toward a nearby wooden chair. "Sit," he told his son. "Mr. Hopper, would you mind terribly if we let a little light in?"

"Please do," came the gravelly response. "Your pa's the one who likes it dark."

"Thank you." Jacob turned back to his father. "Dad, we're going to let a little light in."

When Jacob tugged open the shades, a wash of chalky illumination spilled into the room and suffused it; his father winced and squinted but did not protest. Jacob eased over to the foot of his father's bed and sat. They regarded each other a moment, the three of them, and Jacob knew he must say something, but wasn't quite certain where to begin. He took a deep breath. There was time to figure it out. That's what was important.

His father settled his gaze on Gabriel and the boy smiled nervously, and so too now did his grandfather, ever slightly, but nonetheless. But a moment later, the old man looked down at his hands, which, Jacob now discerned in the morning light, were raw and chapped, his face awash in distress. He started to get up, looking nervously toward the bathroom, but Jacob reached out a gentle hand and stayed him.

"It's okay, Dad," he said. "They're clean. They're clean."

***

A few days after they returned, they decided on a walk along the river, like they'd done so many times before. Gabe wanted to find him another jasper. It took quite a while, the boy on numerous occasions sure he'd spotted one and rushing over to scoop up and examine the stone in question, only to let it slip through his fingers and look up with a disappointed look.

"Maybe there aren't anymore," he said at one point.

"It's okay if there aren't," Jacob told him. "But there's something to be said for looking. I've got time if you do."

Gabe grinned and nodded and skittered away along the bank, searching. Maybe an hour later, he looked up with wild eyes from his latest examination and came racing over to his father. The jasper wasn't quite the same as the original, but still beautiful, perfect in its way. It gleamed in the afternoon sunlight in which son and father stood. Gabe's eyes lit up much like the treasure he held, but now a trace of melancholy washed over them.

"Can we keep going?" he asked. "Can we walk a little while more?"

Jacob kissed Gabriel on the forehead and nodded to this soul so innocent, so precious, this living testament to the greatest thing he'd ever done. It occurred to him there was plenty to be melancholy about himself: his father's condition; Anabel, who wasn't coming back; Justus, whose body could still surface; and the poor officer, denied, along with his family, answers or peace. Maybe he would shave his beard and go to the authorities. Yes, that was what he must do. They wouldn't believe him, believe this tale beyond anything he might have conjured of his own volition, and that would be a problem. But right was right. Maybe at last, he had his story.

None of these considerations, consequential though each was, could deter him just now. He and Gabriel continued along the riverbank, the sun at their backs.

Onward.

The End

ACKNOWLEDGEMENTS

Big thanks to Dave Lane (AKA Lane Diamond) and the EP team for their patience and precision—writing is my passion, and I wouldn't entrust my work to just anyone. Their commitment to quality is the real deal, and I am the better for it.

Thanks also to my small but mighty cadre of beta readers—I am forever grateful for your incisiveness and support.

And all writers know countless others play a part, large or small, in letting us do what we do. Whether directly assisting in the creative process, helping us have the time to pursue our passion, or simply and wonderfully maintaining a kind and positive presence in our lives, from which all other things become possible.

About the Author

From childhood I kindled three dreams: to one day become a father, a writer, and a baseball player.

Two of three ain't bad. (I shall neither confirm nor deny holding out deluded hope for the third.) Most of what I write is fiction, but not all. I write the occasional article and guest post, and conduct some interviews. I'm an English major, have a masters in social work, and have been a nonprofit leader for many years. I am crazy for sports and animals, am helplessly in love with the written word, and am eternally grateful for my family, who make me luckier than I could ever deserve.

For more, please visit Daryl Rothman online at:
Website: www.DarylRothman.com
Goodreads: Daryl Rothman
Facebook: @AuthorDarylRothman

MORE FROM DARYL ROTHMAN

Be sure to check out Daryl Rothman's "David Rose" series of young adult fantasies.

Take an extraordinary adventure through time in an epic tale of hesitant heroism, and witness the timeless battle between good and evil.

www.EvolvedPub.com/DR

The Awakening of David Rose
Immortality isn't just about living forever; sometimes, it's about forever refusing to let things die.

David Rose and the Forbidden Tournament
It's one thing to discover a whole new world, but quite another to survive it. David Rose discovers that, on top of everything else, immortality can kill you.

David Rose and the Days of Awe
Marcel has returned from a mysterious excursion with possible news of David Rose's mother, in addition to a revelation that threatens to upend the course of human history.

More from Evolved Publishing

We offer great books across multiple genres, featuring high-quality editing (which we believe is second-to-none) and fantastic covers.

As a hybrid small press, your support as loyal readers is so important to us, and we have strived, with tireless dedication and sheer determination, to deliver on the promise of our motto: **QUALITY IS PRIORITY #1!**

Please check out all of our great books, which you can find at this link:
www.EvolvedPub.com/Catalog/

Thank you!